LIMBO

by
Eric Carlton Neperud

For Gary,
Brother, Friend and Warrior

By Eric Carlton Neperud

THE LIMBO CHRONICLES
      Trees And Weeds
      Limbo
      The Octagonal Knight
      Dragons And Golems
      The Brotherhood Of Giants
      Wizards And Druids

THE YELLOWSONE TRILOGY
      Wonders Of The Wilderness
      Fleas Upon Snow
      The Periphery Of Sorrow

ISBN: 0-9983838-1-3
ISBN-13: 978-0-9983838-1-1
Published by Valhalla Books

Cover Illustration by Eric Carlton Neperud
Map on back cover by Eric Carlton Neperud
Map on page 243 by Eric Carlton Neperud

Call me Dinga. I used to be known as Samantha Lyger, but that was when I was mortal. I long for the day I can die. It is better than the alternative. Without death there isn't life. As a woman I instinctively needed to bear and raise children. What kept me alive also kept me sterile. There were advantages: no longer worrying about becoming pregnant, or having periods. But I would gladly reclaim the complications of both if I could have my potential death back. Women are circular in biology, thought and action. I miss the reliability of my monthly bloodletting. I miss the certainty of my death and the rituals associated with it, my inevitable decline....

Chapter 1

ATTACKED

I stumbled as my right foot made contact, then my left. I had expected a hard, flat surface on the other side of the portal. Instead I met an irregular one that compacted under my weight. Being the type of person who hated being out of control I quickly recovered. In my determination I pulled a muscle. The injury was more uncomfortable than incapacitating.

Blue sky surrounded me, something I rarely noticed in the city I lived in. It wasn't that smoke concealed it---pollution was outlawed many years ago---I didn't notice it. Large cities over-stimulated one's senses: sights, sounds, smells. A sliver of sky between two skyscrapers couldn't compete with promises of good deals, inspired entertainment, and succulent food.

There was grass below me. I think it was grass. It wasn't green and lush like the grass found in parks. My feet felt like they were on the verge of tearing, the delicate flesh not accustomed to being unprotected.

There wasn't anyone within view. Most naked women prefer finding clothes before social interaction. There were disadvantages displaying the merchandise too soon---in my line of work marketing was half the battle---but it did make one more noticeable, and I was beginning to get hungry. Thirsty too, amplified by my arid surroundings.

A forest was in the distance, in the opposite direction as the sun. I thought of it as morning. I think because a person usually began the day in the morning, and the inauguration of a life sentence on a penitentiary world was like the start of a new day, a day that was never going to end. With it being morning the sun must be rising, not setting, which meant the forest was due west. Vegetation needed water, so there had to be a creek there or a lake---or a pond. I would even settle for a puddle. How low my expectations have already fallen. How low might they go before an equilibrium is reached, before I settle in? I was accustomed to a pampered lifestyle. My high-class life bestowed high-class business transactions. What transactions might occur in a backwoods penal colony?

Taxpayers were delighted when the Dartmoor Project was completed. One place to put all the lifers. After the initial construction costs, minimal funds were needed to maintain its operation, with the inmates living off the land. Without supervision what manner of society might such a group create? It fascinated me and concerned me.

My pace was steady, but unhurried. A relaxed gait creates a graceful dignity. When a woman rushes, her body has a propensity to go out of alignment. If swaying mounds become too chaotic untidiness supplants eroticism. Being an upscale woman I preferred my body to be well-groomed, and orderly. After gaining my sovereignty I had a full-body electrolysis, becoming completely hairless from head to toe---not that I ever had hair on my toes. If the procedure was done correctly it was expensive. In recent years the procedure had become very trendy, with numerous companies vying for the greatest share of the market. A woman using a cheaper alternative could be spotted kays away, her patchy stubble or splotchy skin revealing her indiscretion. An at-home version was even put on the market. Not only was the hair removal inconsistent, blisters sometimes developed in areas a woman shouldn't have blisters.

After ten minutes my chest began to hurt. The permanent stitch in my side affected my gait, generating more movement in my mounds than I was accustomed too. I was well-endowed, but not enough to become a burden, under normal conditions. They say you don't miss something until it's gone. On a world where men significantly outnumber women were bras even manufactured? Would I have to make one myself---which meant bartering for someone to do it for me? Maybe I could mass produce them. It could be more profitable than bartering.

I was becoming concerned about meeting someone in a timely manner. Even if the press release was true about the ten-millionth person being sent to Dartmoor, how many of those people were still alive? Even with heavy casualties, millions of them must still exist. But millions of people spread over an entire planet. One person per square kilometer perhaps. Less than that if it was a particularly large planet. I relied on certain skills to get the things I needed. Did I have any other skills, skills that would permit me to survive on my own? There was food in a forest: nuts, berries. Animals too, but I was a strict vegetarian. A moral epiphany, but also a means to avert weight gain. A trim figure increased the quality of bartering transactions, but I did it more for myself. A svelte person was tidier than someone with rolls and bulges. I wasn't sure what food looked like in its natural form, but I was confident it would be found in the forest, maybe on the ground, after falling off trees. The forest would also provide shelter. I just had to find that species that produced those two by three meter sheets. I didn't have nails, but I could prop them, against one another, like when I built card houses as a girl. I knew my limitations. I could never build a real house. But an adult-size house of cards would keep the rain out and protect me from wild animals. Eventually someone would find me. Men noticed me. If one was within a few kays of me I was confident he would instinctively be aware of my prescience.

My reverie was broken when I heard something I thought I would never hear again: dogs. Kids generally reacted one of two ways when they were abused. They either abused, often younger siblings or animals. Or they befriended them. Being an only child I took care of animals, the more needy the better. Sometimes my mothering backfired. I once put a baby bird back in its nest after it had fallen out. After I touched it its mother no longer wanted it. It was pushed back out of the nest and abandoned. I attempted to raise it myself, going so far as feeding it with an eye dropper. The chick survived just a couple of days. It probably died from complications of falling, but I blamed myself.

Many women self-medicated, the majority by shopping or eating. When I got depressed I went to the zoo. All it took was seeing that first sign announcing the zoo to cheer me up. Hearing the animals from the parking lot made the ends of my mouth raise. I didn't realize I was depressed until that barking returned pep to my steps.

The dogs were excited about something. They were in the general direction I was heading, so I didn't have to decide between them and the forest. Memories of my childhood, the fonder moments, filled my head. Feeling like a girl again I ran towards them. I stepped onto a ledge, overlooking a shallow ravine. Below was a handful of the scrawniest, mangiest mutts I have ever seen

LIMBO

ripping apart two human bodies. They looked---and smelled---like they had been dead for some time, but it was still unnerving, enough to force bile halfway up my throat.

I must have still been in a state of regression, because I slid down the scree to befriend the beasts. Cognizant the men hadn't been killed by the dogs, at least not on this day, clouded my judgment. Maybe I was too trusting, or just naïve, like when I returned the chick to its nest. Whatever the excuse, I paid for my error. The dogs, upon hearing me scramble towards them, turned. Startled initially, it took them a moment to realize their good fortune and attack. Not being accustomed to animals assailing me I was unprepared for the onslaught. As I went down I thought I saw a man watching me from atop the bluff. Was I was hallucinating from the shock? Maybe it was just a dream....

Chapter 2

BARTERING

I was sentenced to Dartmoor Penal Colony after being convicted of killing my father. I did it, but he had it coming. That should have counted for something. It didn't. Justice wasn't subtle. Nuances weren't considered. No blurring around the edges. Shadows are created when light penetrates darkness. Murderers were imprisoned for life, which meant forever on Limbo.

When I was arrested I attempted to use my feminine wiles to resolve the misunderstanding. I was a bit put out when my invitation of putting out was denied. Sure, releasing me risked losing government benefits, but in exchange for a memorable experience, guaranteed, or your payment fully refunded. It sounds like I was a prostitute, but money never was directly exchanged for services. Gifts were given, some very expensive. Rent was paid, and utilities. I was taken to exclusive restaurants, when courting occurred. Given take-out when my business associates wanted more immediate exchange of goods.

There was a time bartering excluded the middle-man, a.k.a., the government, but after too many people discovered this loophole and abused it the I HAVE TO PAY TAXES SO YOU DO TOO ACT was enacted. Every exchange was now taxed, with every transaction assigned a nine-digit code. Hundreds of people were hired to match codes to products and services. For their profession to sustain, code technicians had to become increasing creative.

A CHILDLESS TAX CREDIT was created to discourage overpopulation. Supplemental to---not replacing---the CHILD TAX CREDIT, to appease the fundamentalists in Parliament who believed it was God's will to have as many kids as possible, even if they couldn't be provided for. Pregnant women received both credits. The exchange that enabled the birth of the child was deemed a windfall for the mother: Barter Code 173,438,001. The potential financial gains from viruses and diseases were debated. It was determined that benefits received due to death or absences from work could be measured. It was more difficult to monitor the mass dispersion of contagions. Further research on unintentional dispersions was temporarily shelved to discuss staff reductions.

I was relieved when I was asked to remove my clothes. My flirtations hadn't been completely futile. "Place your clothes in the opening in the floor." Nudity didn't bother me, but losing my clothes....

"When will I get them back?"

"When you leave Dartmoor."

It wasn't a complete loss. Nudity had a tendency to expedite transactions. Not always. Some men preferred a partially disrobed woman. Hints were more enticing than a thorough reveal. But unlikely in the gray jumpsuit I was wearing. I was looking forward to bartering on Dartmoor. Considering the supply, I'll be in great demand. It wasn't just the scarcity of woman incarcerated, but also their appearance and demeanor. These weren't the types of women men put on pedestals. The first thing I would barter for would be clothes: elegant dresses---and shoes. The only accessories a woman needs are shoes. A woman may want jewelry, or a belt or hat, but she needs shoes. I had an epiphany, one that made me shiver, and not with exhilaration. The penal colony might be too primitive to produce luxury clothing. I didn't mind wearing a bear skin---as a coat. Women prefer something silkier next to their skin, and more flattering to their figure.

I removed my clothes as scandalously as I could. Did I hear a yawn? Have the jailors become that conditioned to nudity? Professionally indifferent, like surgeons? Or did I hear a sigh? Did not being with me make them melancholy?

Gas flooded the featureless room I was in. How many people panicked during this stage of their incarceration? There was no escape. The doorway that had been carved into the electromagnetic wall filled in after I passed through it. I shared the room with a transport portal. A harbinger or an affront? My transportation to the penal colony, no doubt, but not yet. It was dormant. I can handle most situations. Those I can't, I run from. But a person can run only so long before her past catches up with her.

Why did my father have to beat my mother? My mother wasn't completely without fault. Her unconditional love for my father gave him permission to continue his treatment of her. Eventually it became too much for me. Some might say I snapped. My father abused me too, but it hurt me more when my mother was beaten. The one thing I can thank my father for is desensitizing me to intimate relationships. What he did to me was payment for me living in his house. I enjoyed living there most of the time. My large bedroom was filled with things adolescent girls coveted.

I didn't leave immediately after solving my mother's problem. The worst part was all that digging. My hands had become raw and blistered by the time I finished. Adolescents were susceptible to blemishes, their formation and the emotional trauma that follows. Oozing wounds were harder to conceal than pimples. I stayed home after the incident. My hands needed to heal, and it was a personal holiday, like my birthday, but better. It was a significant landmark in my life, more so than having my first period or developing mounds. I was emancipated from the sorrow of my mother's pain.

When people began to ask about my father, most of them his superiors from the transport company he worked for, it was time for me to leave. I was protecting my mother, but murder was still murder. The legal system was more concerned with who did it than why. In exchange for the room and board I would lose upon my departure I extracted travel funds from my father's bank account. My mother was still in shock from her abrupt freedom. She silently retrieved the funds for me as I gave her instructions. I would miss my mother, but in the state she was in she wasn't too fun to be around.

I subsisted on the severance pay for many years. Before the money ran out---I was mature enough to plan for my future---I developed my bartering skills, perfecting them in a very short time.

The one drawback to fleeing my home was leaving my mother alone to defend herself. In the catatonic state she was in she wasn't very effective at it. She was blamed for the murder. She actually confessed to it, not mentioning me at all. Even if I was charged she would still have had to pay for her role as parent to a murderer. People didn't just start killing other people. It was either the environment or genetics. Both were the parents fault. People choose to have children. If their genes were going to create criminals it was their duty to not procreate. Mother actually enjoyed prison. People took care of her in a manner her husband never did. I felt guilty she was sentenced for something I did, but I got over it. She chose to confess didn't she, to protect me, or maybe she felt she deserved it because she allowed my father to do those things to her. Before she was sentenced certain details had to be confirmed, like if she was the person who actually killed my father. When her memories were probed her innocence was discovered---and my guilt. It took awhile before I was found. There was a biological database, but on the fringes of civilization, records were inconsistent, as was the diligence of local law enforcement.

The gas smelled like a combination of disinfectant and metal polish. It reminded me of the glue I used to sniff. When I became emancipated I no longer took drugs, in any form. I had to look after myself now, and I couldn't do that if I was drunk, stoned, or passed out. Diminished intellect created a disadvantage when bartering---which I encouraged in others. Sometimes drinking, snorting, and injecting got messy, but it was a sacrifice I was willing to make to improve my business leverage.

When the gas had dissipated enough for me to see again I became fixated on the portal: a black and white circular frame enveloping a color wheel spinning slowly counterclockwise. "Enter the portal. May your crimes be fully compensated."

"BORE YOU!" No response. The jailors had to have heard worse. The pleading of innocents wrongly accused. Newlyweds. Parents of small children. What was I going to gain by delaying the inevitable? Thirst? Hunger? Weariness? I mooned them. Juvenile, yes, but also a mixed message from an attractive woman. It will be as much your loss as mine.

Here goes. I didn't instantaneously appear at my destination. My body was held in stasis until all of it passed through the portal. The slight delay was unnerving....

Chapter 3

ATTACKED, AGAIN

I woke hours later. The sun had set. I jerked up and around to assess my surroundings.   The dogs were gone. Light shined down at me from a full moon. I must have been dragged off. The bluff was no longer above me. I was still in the prairie, but in a part of it that was more level, a scattering of boulders preventing the landscape from becoming completely desolate. The forest was closer, maybe half the distance it was before I was moved.

Could I have been dragged that far? Three or four kays? I should have become a bloody pulp. Could they have carried me? But how? And why? Guilt for attacking me? I had startled them. They never intended to attack me. It was a reflex, which they stopped after I became unconscious.

I glanced at my arms and legs. The skin was smooth and unbroken. I remember being bit. Even if their teeth didn't break the skin there should have been indentations or scratches. I couldn't have healed that quickly. Being thrown to the ground as violently as I was there should have been bruising. I was blemish free. No discoloring. No raised skin. Reminding myself of my imperfections I felt my face. Prior to the start of my cycle, and under stress, I broke out. Both coincided on the eve of my arrival. What the….? My face was as smooth as my arms and legs. Could I have slept a full three hours? I must have. I felt lethargic, but in a good way---waking up, not exhausted. My feet were no longer killing me. That was going to be one of my biggest adjustments--- having to spend so much time on my feet. Without mechanized transportation I was going to have to walk more.

Back to heading towards the forest. It would be more dangerous in the dark, but better than remaining exposed in the prairie. Those boulders provided partial cover, but not only to me. After a kay my female intuition kicked in. Something felt wrong. Not bad, just different. Movement had been uncomfortable since I stepped through the portal. My civilized feet weren't the only part of me that ached. My unbound mounds pounded into me, stretching painfully, and pummeling. Or did. Since I woke the assault was less severe. Noticeable, but not painful. I looked down. My mounds were more firm, less pendulous---and smaller. How...? It wasn't a complaint. There were rumors about prison: hard labor during the day, and entertaining Big Bertha at night. But modifying my appearance? Experiments were performed on convicts, by their approval, in exchange for a reduced sentence. For a life sentence to be reduced, the convict had to die early. Did it happen to me when I passed through the portal? Chemicals in the environment? Radiation?

A large lizard reclined, on a boulder. If I had a projectile it would provide food, for weeks---if I could preserve the meat. I had changed, and not just physically, if I was already contemplating abandoning vegetarianism. I picked up a two-kilo stone. I heaved it with all my might. It landed closer to me than to the lizard.

The commotion caused the lizard to turn towards me. Its interaction with me made it appear larger than it had been, now four meters from snout to tail instead of one. Maybe I was hasty in determining who was to be the chef. It stared at me. Being a woman, especially one whose physical attributes enhanced her business opportunities, I was used to such attention, but usually from two-legged beasts. I became uncomfortable, feeling more like a commodity than I had during any of my bartering transactions. I struggled to turn away. I became transfixed---a rodent facing a snake---psychologically restrained. But also physically? I wasn't even able to wiggle a finger or a toe. My muscles clenched tightly, and continued to tighten. I believed I might pop. My heart was also a muscle. It also contracted. Before it imploded my brain must have been affected, because my thoughts slowed as my surroundings faded....

Chapter 4

INDENTURED

I regained consciousness in a bedroom. I lay on a wooden floor. To my left was a straw mattress, covered with a red blanket, supported by a rope frame. Beyond the bed was a closed door. At my feet was a wooden wardrobe and a chest-of-drawers. Behind me, a porcelain wash basin and a kerosene lamp on a wooden table. To my right was a window, the drapes covering it glowing.

A shadow fell over me. A man wearing a flowery shirt and white pants stepped in front of the window. He looked down at me. The bored look on his face indicated he had been waiting awhile for me to wake. I was still naked, but enough people had seen me in that state that I wasn't embarrassed by it. Free publicity was as valuable an asset as machinery or real estate. There was little doubt my bartering skills would be required before the day was over. I would have preferred to partially conceal the assets, mystery being rewarded with a greater return, but one must play the cards she is dealt. I had miraculously survived another near-death. Death limited a woman's business opportunities. I leaned up, concealing what I could without appearing to do so. Even an unclothed woman could create a state of obscurity if she was gifted.

"I paid a substantial amount to revive you," spoke the man. "It's time for you to begin repaying me."

I shuddered. In my line of work the greatest fear was being forced to perform transactions without pay. Being my choice what and when I bartered, I never felt defiled.

"No, not that, at least not yet. In exchange for me becoming your benefactor, you're required to work for me. It will take considerable time to repay the debt considering the low wages I pay my employees. Of course there are ways a beautiful woman could earn a little on the side, or even an ugly one, on a planet that's predominantly male."

My indentured employer looked me up and down one more time. For the first time in my adult life I had an overwhelming inclination to conceal. I yanked the red blanket from the bed and wrapped it around me. I stood up, not wanting him to be in a position of power above me.

"You can replace that blanket with some real clothes. You'll find them in the wardrobe and the dresser. Be downstairs in five minutes. We're a girl short and men don't come in here anymore unless there's curves to view, not with competition across the street."

My employer/slave master thankfully departed, allowing me to dress without an audience---something I rarely did, even after being offered substantial compensatory incentive. Disrobing was enticing, but some of the movements required to put clothes back on were...embarrassing. I found white cotton panties in the chest-of-drawers, but no bra. Being fully supported didn't enhance revenue. I debated whether to wear something flattering, to be able to pay off my debt more quickly, or something frumpy, because my employment was not of my choosing.

Why didn't I just run away? Loyalty. My benefactor clearly saved me from that lizard. I preferred to be part of the negotiating process, but I did owe him. I also needed a place to sleep and something to eat. Until I was able to manipulate my surroundings I had to do something to provide.

The attire issue became moot. All the clothing was a bit revealing. Tops consisted of cotton blouses that were cut low enough that even the least endowed showed cleavage. Bottoms were skirts, also so skimpy they didn't completely conceal unless the person wearing them remained erect, with perfect posture. Being more aware than most women what enticed men, I wore the largest, least thread-bare white blouse I could find. A hint of my mounds was exposed, but just a hint. I looked for footwear, but couldn't find any. To discourage women from running away? Aesthetics? Women barefoot in the kitchen. And hopefully not pregnant.

FEEK! The greatest contribution to reducing birthrates was a contraceptive added to the water supply. It was unlikely the penal colony had a similar program. How long would it take for the contraceptive in my system to dilute enough for me to be able to become pregnant?

Most girls wished to become mothers one day. They had their momma dolls that gave birth to baby dolls. Most of the momma dolls drank milk, their mound reservoirs enlarging as they filled. Minutes after the babies suckled, the milk was discharged into their diapers---if the mothers-in-training remembered to put diapers on the babies. One brand of baby turned the milk yellow before it was released. The eating version of the baby wasn't as popular. The most controversial doll mimicked how babies were made. Most of them were returned after complaints the connecting parts didn't always work.

I opened the door confidently, smiling. A friendly, but assertive interaction maximized transactions. It was much darker in the hallway than in my room. I turned left, towards a window, which I presumed not only illuminated the hallway, but also the stairs.

One of the doors I passed was open. A man stripped down to his underwear looked out at me. He shouted, "How about a bore? I'll pay you a silver now. Maybe more if you're good." It was rude for a man to shout out a price like that like he was buying produce at a market. A barter could be negotiated but I was always the one who initiated it. I ignored the man, appearing oblivious to his offer as I passed his room. Without being obvious about it I sized him up. Not wishing to barter with him now didn't dismiss future transactions. Sometimes men who were bold had limited gratuitous options. If I chose to barter with him he could become a repeat customer, accumulating dozens of transactions. I shuddered. The thought of boring someone, someone I would never consider spending time with outside of business, nauseated me. Shame? I had never felt embarrassed before, not for the profession I chose to immerse myself in. Prisons were supposed to rehabilitate a person, but this quickly? I've been here just a day. I still intended to barter, but I now felt guilty about it. I paused in the middle of the hallway. I pulled down at my skirt where it had ridden up, then continued towards the stairs, which I could now discern a couple of rooms further down.

A single flight brought me down to a pub. Drinks and food were being served to a dozen patrons, all men, and none too clean or well-mannered. Three-quarters of the room was empty, but with any pub, it probably picked up at night. The server was a woman dressed similarly to me except she wore a skimpier, more transparent blouse. The tips of her mounds were prominent, the men probably thinking it was their prescience that caused their state instead of her exertion. Her skirt was tight on her in a manner that wasn't attractive, but that didn't deter the patrons from fixating on that region of her. When she leaned over to place a round of mugs on a table a greasy hand print was revealed on one of her cotton cheeks. If someone did that to me it would be the last thing he would do with that hand.

"You must be the new girl," spoke the server. A redundant comment, considering how I was attired. "You'll take that side of the room." A swift scan of the tables she was referring to indicated

17

I wasn't going to be eased into the job. The tables she allotted me had the rowdiest, nastiest looking men in the pub sitting at them. It was easier for me to make friends with guys than with girls. I understood how they thought. I appreciated their direct thoughts, and interactions. Guys were more active than girls---doing instead of discussing. I hated the other server instantly. To put another woman through what she did to me that first night in the pub.... I called her certain names under my breath that shouldn't be repeated in polite company. I would have said them to her face if I didn't like mixing business with pleasure.

"What do I do?"

"Just give them what they want. Beer's behind the bar. Food's in the kitchen. Nickel will even dish it up for you if you give him a hint you might have some interest in him."

"He's the owner?"

"GAEA, NO! I'm not that much of an actress. Flotsam's a bastard. He's so hard up for a woman he sometimes spies on them in the toilet. I was in the middle of emptying my bowels when I look up and see his eye peering through a hole in the wall."

"That perverted pile of...."

"Don't call him that to his face. It gets him off. Just make sure you plug any holes before you drop your drawers. Nickel's the cook. He's barely out of puberty. He's shy. I don't think he's ever been with a girl. It might be interesting to educate the young man. Not sure I would enjoy it, not with him adverting his eyes while we're doing it. And never having done it he's probably not very good at it. With demand being greater than the supply a girl can be selective. I'm Loam."

"That's an odd name. Were your parents eccentric?"

"It wasn't my parents who tagged me." Loam paused, then smiled. "So you haven't been named yet, have you?"

"I'm Samantha Lyger."

"No you aren't. Not anymore. I've never named an infant. Tell me about your first day on Limbo." Limbo? Is that what the

18

inmates call this planet? Many days later I learned the ramifications of that name. "Your name has to represent you."

"It wasn't a particularly good day for me."

"The first day never is."

"I found myself in that prairie outside of town. Wild dogs attacked me a couple of hours after that, then I woke...."

"Wild dogs? Dingos? But you're a woman. How about Dinga?"

"A female dog? I've been called that before, but I don't want it to be made official."

"Dinga it is then." Loam chuckled as she walked away. Great, so from now until eternity I was going to be known as THE BITCH. We'll if I was going to be called Dinga I was determined to act the part, at least when it came to Loam. Why can't women get along with one another as easily as men got along with other men? Was it that they all wanted to be queen bee? At least I got along with men. On a planet with a larger percentage of men than women there was no reason I had to make friends with any of them.

Loam and I never became friends, but sometimes we looked after one another if it wasn't too inconvenient. I still silently called her impolite names, but less often than I intended.

The first time Loam stepped onto the platform at the back of the room it pissed me off: doubling my tables to allow her to take a break. She began to sing. The reaction from the audience was mixed. Considering the mediocrity of her voice---and looks---it was understandable. When she was finished three members of the audience left a coin in the wooden bowl placed at the edge of the platform. All were copper. It might take years to pay off the debt to my benefactor.

Loam may be a mediocre singer, and even less of a human being, but she was an experienced waitress. Serving was a balancing act. After serving drinks to one table, Loam would take a food order from the table next to it, and clear dishes from a third.

As long as a server kept it organized she didn't have to take as many trips to the kitchen.

Nickel wasn't just taciturn. He was painfully shy. As were many of my favorite trading partners. Just being with a girl was enough to rile them up, in a good way. They were very appreciative of the service I offered them. They thought of me as some exotic creature, to be awed and cherished. Once we became familiar with one another---verbal intercourse always preceded physical contact---they would become less inhibited. Most matured enough to no longer need my services. I felt good about that. Although my liaisons were primarily sexual, what I offered emotionally was more substantial, in the long run. When I was in a particularly selfish mood I would wish for one of my once shy clients to return to me. Such a renewal of business usually meant difficulties in their current relationship. Most of my long-term clients were men confident about themselves on the outside, extreme enough in many cases to come off as being rude. But hidden within was crippling insecurities. Such deficiencies couldn't be concealed indefinitely, which resulted in a series of failed relationships. It bothered me that someone's sorrow contributed to my solvency.

"Here's your stew, Ma'am." Nickel handed me two wooden bowls full of potatoes, carrots, onions and whatever scrap of meat Flotsam found the day before. Sometimes I attempted to attach a name to the token protein, but learned that didn't always encourage sales. I returned to just calling it STEW. What the customers didn't know wouldn't hurt them. With the care that Nickel cooked the meat, and the seasonings he added it to it, it tasted as good as the choicest cut of farm-raised beef, pork, or poultry. With Briarwood---the name of the town Flotsam dragged me to---being just half-a-day from the sea, fish was a perpetual fall-back. Being so accustomed to eating fish Briarwoodians paid more for meat. Even snake and turtle sold for a premium. After numerous complaints about fish in the stew Flotsam was forced to modify his pricing. Instead of lowering the price of fish stew he raised the price of meat stew. The customers didn't notice. As long as they didn't have to pay as much for fish they were content.

"Please don't call me Ma'am, Nickel. I'm young enough to be your sister. Older sister perhaps, but still your sister."

"My sisters never looked like you, Ma'am." Nickel glanced briefly in my direction, then turned away. His face was crimson.

"And I bet they never did this either." I intended to peck him on his lips, but as soon as I came towards him he turned away. I was able to reach a cheek, the contact being substantial enough to him to drop the ladle he held. I wasn't trying to flirt with him, not consciously. He was just so cute, a boy barely out of school that looked too innocent to be sentenced to life. What could he have done to earn a trip to prison? Did he defend a damsel in distress? Maybe he stole something he was too embarrassed to buy.

I picked up the ladle, washed it, then left. It took Nickel awhile to recover from my interaction, and the pub was packed. Nickel was the type of person I would give a discount to, initially, writing it off as a marketing expense. Earlier in my life I might have been able to separate business from pleasure, before I became so inundated with work that I was no longer capable of a having a personal life. If I hoped to ever have a real relationship it would be after I gave up bartering. But bartering was my life, my career, my passion. Maybe I could continue it as a hobby. No, I had to leave it cold turkey when I decided to retire. It was too addictive. How long would it take after I weaned myself to be able to have a relationship with someone? Months? Years? I lived a third of my life already. Would I ever have kids? Did I even want to have kids? What was I thinking? I was in prison, and I was going to stay there until I died. Why was I having such maternal thoughts, now?

My days at the Musky Foot were full. The more hours I worked, the more money I earned. Folsom wasn't exaggerating when he said he didn't pay much. In fact, he didn't pay anything, after room and board were deducted. The only way I was going to leave his service was to die, either by old age or by working myself to death. The only way I was going to earn supplemental income was to perform on stage. I couldn't sing, but I was able to move provocatively. Some might call it dancing.

Servers weren't the only entertainers. Dozens of singers, dancers, and musicians preformed for the few coins they collected after every performance. Some of them eventually moved to Sunset City or to Rhinopolis to assess their true talent, but most subsisted on the hope that one day they would be discovered.

Nothing was given freely in a medieval society. What was earned was really EARNED. Being on the fringe of the Beetlewoods, Briarwood had a thriving lumber industry, harvesting and milling locally, then hauling to Rhinopolis for immediate transformation into furniture and housing, or to Sunset City to be shipped to distant ports.

It was eerie not seeing any motorized vehicles. Or horses. Oxen did most of the heavy hauling, with men themselves doing the light work.

The few women I came into contact with did traditional woman's work: cooking, cleaning, laundry...and prostitution. A population that was four-fifths male guaranteed a market. You might think I would have leaped into that profession, considering the similarities between it and bartering. There were similarities, but they weren't the same. Prostitutes provided a sandwich and water. I provided a full-course meal with wine. No, there wasn't a market for what I did---what I used to do---when those LADIES charged a tenth of what I bartered for. I don't know if it was the length of time I was away from bartering or I had just grown out of it, but my passion for it was waning.

The one thing I had enthusiasm for was Nickel. A fondness for him was growing. I was almost ready to pursue a non-business relationship with him---almost. Something was still holding me back. It felt like I was waiting for something to happen, but what?

As the days passed, my sentence lengthening---every day lived extended my life-sentence---I discovered some oddities about this planet. The most blatant was the stationery sun. Either the planet didn't rotate or...it was artificial. But why? The universe had so many naturally habitable planets. Another thing that disturbed me was the penal colony not occupying the entire planet. Was the rest of it reserved for future expansion, or for something else? Perhaps only the portion the penal colony was built on was habitable, most of the planet being too hot or too cold, too wet or too dry.

It wasn't just the physical aspects of Limbo that shocked me. Some of the people living here weren't human---anymore. Scientists were upset that sentient life hadn't yet been discovered. The mathematical probability of it existing was high. The universe wasn't always logical, increasing the likelihood, if a supreme being did exist, it being female. Bore the sexist swine that believed divinity was patriarchal. Millennia of self-image supplanted by the inconsistencies it was conceived and sustained.

Chapter 5

LIMBO

It took me three days to meet my first mutant. There were two of them, both about 20 sims shorter than me---and I am petite. Being small was an advantage in acquiring new clients. Some may have associated my size with youth, possible younger than what was legally permitted. Others believed there was a correlation between the disparity in height and a snug coupling. Not always true, particularly on their end. They were bald and pale. Their heads and extremities were disproportionate relative to their torsos---like infants. Instead of wearing cotton---Briarwood's standard attire---they wore metal. They moved slowly, but that was to be expected considering the rigidity of their apparel. Each carried a hammer, nearly as large as they were tall. One side was blunt, the other jagged and sharp.

"What are they?" I asked Loam.

"Trogs. They live in the Platinum Mountains, beyond the Western Sea."

"What happened to them? Radiation? I've heard of people not being properly shielded mutating."

"Something like that, but not before coming to Limbo."

"Why do the locals call this place Limbo? Purgatory, perhaps, but why Limbo? Being sentenced here is a termination, not some perpetual steady-state."

"You sure about that? What are your plans for the future? There is no possibility of escape, but we still exist, day after day, all the same."

"But there is a foreseeable end to all of this, likely not very pleasant."

"Is there? How many elders do you see?"

"How often are elders sent to prison? How many of us will survive long enough to wrinkle and gray?"

"Few...some. Cultures that were decimated by war and disease produced elders. Not many, but enough to provide wisdom, and expectation."

"Feek. Something was put in the water to kill us slowly, like that contraceptive added to prevent unauthorized pregnancy."

"I don't think so. I've met people who have lived here more than twenty years. One for over thirty."

"That's impossible. No one lives that long. Not many. Not under these conditions. They must be lying, but why?"

"I don't think so. When someone ages they change, not just physically, but psychologically. They acted...old."

"But they didn't look old. They weren't gray or bald, or as wrinkly as a raisin?"

"They didn't look much older than you or I. The one over thirty looked to be beginning his second decade."

Sweat began to bead on my forehead. "Are you saying that transport portal, or this planet, has made us immortal? We will live forever on this desolate, feek-covered, dreary.... Bore me if it's true."

"Limbo. The same thing that caused those trogs to look the way they do prevents us from dying."

My clothing became soaked. My skin was so saturated perspiration began to cascade beneath my top, then my shorts. "There are still accidents...murders...and suicides. Not the most welcomed consolation, but...."

"There have been rumors of people dying and coming back to life. Exaggerations possibly, of people being critically injured and recovering."

My clothes had become so drenched they now stuck to me, and not in a flattering manner. Could I have really died, temporarily, or partially, when the dogs attacked me? "How quickly do these people heal? And after they are healed are they sometimes healthier than they were before they were injured? Like a surgery that not only corrects vision, but extends it."

"Why do you ask? Have you had a near-death experience? Folsom said he found you petrified in the prairie. But he gave you the antidote in time."

"Remember me telling you about those dogs that attacked me? Before I passed out they were ripping me to shreds. When I awoke I didn't have a scratch on me."

Loam backed away from me. She had talked to people who went through a similar experience, but she didn't have daily contact with them. "I better take those trogs' order. They look sedate now, but when they get riled up they sometimes go into a berserk frenzy, and end up breaking things, including people."

Loam continued to be cordial to me, to the degree she was capable of, and even confided in me when she wished to discuss, or share, female specific issues, but there was definitely more of a wall between us than there had been before I mentioned my near-death experience.

Other mutants passed through Briarwood. Arbols were taller and lankier than standard men and woman, and hairier. They resembled monkeys---what the offspring of a man and a gibbon might look like. Wilson, two days west of Briarwood, beyond the boundaries of civilization---what people referred to as the FRONTIER---had mutants as permanent residents. Most mutants lived in the Frontier. Arbols were less stoic than trogs, having a keen sense of humor. They were impetuous, most noticeably in sexual matters, viewing intimate liaisons on par with cordial handshakes. There were laws forbidding such behavior in public, but if a person was curious he or she or it could walk a few meters beyond the city limit.

Partials, from a distance, might be mistaken for locals. Their clothing was more colorful, and their manners more polite, but up close the differences became obvious. The tallest were about half the height as standard men and women, with the smallest being half that height.

The mer, mutants that had adapted to living in the sea, didn't come as far inland as Briarwood, but many travelers passing through spoke of them. There were two varieties. The blue-skinned ones hid their mutations. Boots concealed their webbed feet. High collars, their gills. Those with green skin were bolder. The only part of them that was covered was their loins, and just barely. The females pierced their chests, embellishing them with colorful ribbons. I never pierced anything for the same reason I defoliated. The more perfect a woman's natural curves the less they needed to be embellished. Most men wanted a woman that was all woman. Jewelry distracted. Both species and genders were bald---not surprising considering how much time they spent in the water.

As the days since my last intimate contact increased my craving for it increased. The building of desire was usually associated with males, the physical release eventually resulting in a nocturnal emission if not taking care of in other ways. Bartering for physical intimacy still nauseated me. I assumed with the whorification of my prior profession that if I ever moved to a city that had a market for a more sophisticated product my enthusiasm might return. Might. I wasn't confident. Limbo had changed me, more than the lifting of my mounds. Psychologically I was different. Would the changes progress? Or would they settle into an equilibrium? If they did, was I in that equilibrium now or would it take years for me to bottom out, or rise above, depending on how one perceived the changes?

After the pub closed I intended to release what had been building since my arrest. Nickel bathed after spending most of the day cooking and cleaning. Another plus for him. Few men in Briarwood were so fastidious in their personal hygiene.

I knocked on the tub room door. "Can I come in?"

A startled splashing was heard. "I'm....ah....still washing."

"I need to bathe too. I'm very sleepy. Can I come in and wash before I fall asleep?"

"I'll be done in a couple of minutes."

"There's two tubs in there. I'll try not to bother you."

"But I'm naked."

"I won't look."

"But you'll have to get naked to take a bath."

"You don't have to look either if you don't want to."

"But you'll still be naked."

"Your room is next to mine, isn't it? You've been naked in it, haven't you? And I've been naked in mine. The tubs are far enough apart we'll be as far from one another as we were in our two rooms. I'm very sleepy, Nickel. Please unlock the door."

It was quiet for half-a-minute, then I heard someone get out

27

of the water, step on the wooden floor with a splat, unhinge the door, then rush back into the tub with a kaplunk. "You can come in now. I'm not facing the door and my eyes are closed."

Not wanting to startle the boy even more than I had I slowly opened the door. Nickel was huddled stiffly in the far tub. All I could see of him was the back of his head, with his matted-down hair, and his shoulders, much broader looking bare than in his cooking uniform. I closed the door, latching it afterwards. The scraping of metal against metal echoed through the room. It felt like I was trapping the boy, and in some ways I was. Given enough time I could seduce anyone, as long as they couldn't escape before they were snared.

Some people might think I took advantage of the boy. He was younger than I and didn't possess the social skills to adequately defend my advances. Don't get me wrong, he enjoyed the activities as much as I, he just didn't have much say when, or if, they occurred. Being young and inexperienced Nickel was a hasty in some areas, but enduring in others. It came as a surprise to me---quite a surprise---when I discovered I was a born-again virgin. I knew it had to be connected with my body healing so quickly and my mounds firming, but it was still shocking to feel that unexpected pain and see those drops of blood. Some feminists associated the male anatomy with a dagger, and for a moment the analogy seemed all too real.

When the fires of passion finally distinguished, responsibility replaced impulse. I was not only embarrassed that I took advantage of someone just days removed from being a minor, but that I did so without any consideration for prevention of pregnancy or sexually transmitted diseases. I was confident---fairly confident---I still had enough of the pregnancy prevention drug in my system, but the other? He couldn't transmit something to me that he didn't have. That required him having been with another woman. It was extremely unlikely there would be complications, but I was still ashamed for creating the possibility, after being so careful for so many years.

Nickel had other thoughts. "When should we get married?" He had been so shy at first, not even looking at me in the beginning, but after his first release he had loosened up. It was an ordeal for that to happen after I shrieked when I learned my virginity had returned. Nickel had thought he had done something wrong. After reassuring him that the outburst was due to he being more endowed than what I was accustomed to he was finally able to complete the task. Now that what had been building up in him all his life had finally been allowed to be released---multiple times---he thought of my body more as a new toy than the embodiment of a lover. Why were men so fascinated with mounds? Not having any themselves, I understood the novelty of it, but women didn't play with the part of their anatomy that was different to pass the time.

I'm not bashful---that's an understatement---but when Nickel asked that question, I hastily covered myself with one of the towels of dubious cleanliness that could be found in the tub room. My indiscretion had complications I never foresaw. Not wanting to shatter the fragile, newly modified world Nickel lived in I was cautious with my response. For someone who never intended to get married, to be tied down to a single man, one---ah four--- intimate encounters with a boy, a BOY, wasn't going to persuade me. My father's treatment of my mother jaded me. Marriage wasn't something to look forward to, or dream about. It was a curse. "Wouldn't you rather marry a girl more your age?"

"But it will take a couple of years before she becomes as pretty as you." Nickel's double complement had weakened my resolve. If I was his age and hadn't experienced what I did maybe someone like him wouldn't be too bad to spend some time with, maybe not indefinitely, but for a year or two.

"Once you got to know me more I don't think you would still want to marry me. There must be hundreds of girls your age that will be lucky to have someone as kind, polite---and virile---as you."

Nickel grimaced. "There aren't as many girls here as guys. The girls that are either ignore me or make fun of me. They would rather be with guys that hurt them. That's one of the things I like about you. You won't let anyone to treat you like that."

I almost had second thoughts about making my relationship with Nickel of a more permanent nature, then that maternal instinct that started me thinking about having children took over. I needed to look after this boy, to protect him, not make him my lover. "I'm flattered by your marriage proposal, Nickel, but I must decline---for your own good. There are girls out there younger and more innocent than me. It would be a mistake to settle." Nickel became sullen. "I'll help you find someone more your age, with similar experiences."

It wasn't easy. Few girls Nickel's age were ready for someone like him, maybe in a year---or two or three---definitely not girls with the curves of a woman, but the desires of a child. Inmates preferred adventure over settling down. My greatest failure in Briarwood was not finding a good match for Nickel. I tried, going so far as setting him up a couple of times, but the imbalance of their aggressive nature and his reserve didn't work. After the initial excitement of breaking a young buck waned, they got bored with him and returned to more sullied pastures.

Being past due on having a period I began to worry. The one---ah four---interactions with Nickel were the only ones I had since I was sentenced to Dartmoor, but it took just one to drastically change a woman's life forever. Loam reassured me. "Do you see any babies anywhere? Any children? We're sterile. I don't know if we were made so before, during, or after our arrival, but it worked whatever they did. I don't think they intended for us to be quasi-immortal, but they definitely didn't want a self-propagating society. Not only would our numbers increase, so would our technology if we wished to make the world better for our children."

"Sterility doesn't prevent a woman from ovulating. Our bodies would still prepare for the possibility of incubating a child."

"You haven't bled yet have you? It's been three years for me---since I've had the pleasure. If it wasn't for the medieval food and lodging, and the fear of being attacked by a monster if you wander too far from town, this wouldn't be too bad a place to spend the remainder of your days: never having to deal with your drips, and being able to bore whomever you like without worrying about becoming pregnant. With so few of us here women have attained a prominence. I can turn away four guys in five or take the whole lot of them." You would think with the bartering I have done in the past such thoughts wouldn't bother me. When I began my line of work I did allow certain combinations, but I felt guilty afterward for the decreased individual attention. Quality was more important than quantity, so my services became exclusively one-on-one. I also took breaks from bartering when I felt I was on the verge of burning out. After a week or so away from the job I became rejuvenated, anxious to resume work---before I came to Limbo. I had many fond memories, but still no desire to add to them.

As my dancing improved I began to draw a group of regulars. Many became aroused, but just as many thought of me as living art. I was entertainer and visual artist. My body was my canvas. Some of the more experienced performers became jealous. I was not only receiving more applause than they, but significantly more coin, even the occasional silver. I didn't fear for my safety--- since the day I killed my father I was able to take care of myself--- but that didn't dissuade me from being more cautious. Folsom and Nickel also looked out for me, for different reasons. Although we had been intimate just once---one night---Nickel and I were still friends. I looked after him in my way and he looked after me in his. Folsom didn't want his cash cow to go off to pasture.

Whenever my performance was particular good, inciting the crowd into a near-frenzy, transients---travelers, not vagrants---were drawn to the Musky Foot. On such occasions the pub filled beyond capacity, with people standing between tables, and occasionally overflowing into the street. Sometimes the excitement of the crowd carried over to my performance. My past profession and my prior merged. Entertaining one become entertaining many. There were ways an experienced woman could give the illusion of disrobing without actually doing it. Men were quite capable of filling in the missing parts when given hints. As the crowds became larger and more exuberant I became more bold. I almost had no control over what I was doing, the crowd's energy and adoration nourishing my rapture. I began to show more skin. It felt insincere concluding a business transaction without an exclamation. The only comparable climax was a full reveal. It would be brief, and I intended to leave the stage immediately after, but there would be that instant when the fulfillment of expectations would be met.

What stopped me was seeing a familiar face. It felt like someone I respected catching me doing something I shouldn't have been doing. Who was he? He was obviously a traveler, so I must have seen him the last time he passed through Briarwood.

After my performance I rushed outside. The pub was full of sweat, lust, and kerosene. I needed some fresh air and not so many bodies around me. The crowd sensed there was to be more, an encore that was rudely dismissed. Some of the patrons followed me, two men in particular. Both propositioned me. I ignored them, distracted by my curiosity for the familiar traveler. Should I return to the pub to speak to him?

The two potential suitors no longer spoke to me, but to each other. Both claimed ownership of me, and neither wanted to give in. A knife was drawn. I remembered where I saw that man. He was on the bluff when the wild dogs attacked. So seeing him wasn't a hallucination. The man without the knife grabbed me. The other struck, his blade clutched tightly in his fist. Somehow I got in the way---unintentionally. I couldn't care less if they killed one another. I was more surprised than hurt, not yet realizing the severity of the situation. The knife was pulled out of my chest. Blood gushed. The pain was brief. I passed out as I saw the two men run off....

Chapter 6

HAIR

It didn't---completely---surprise me that I woke. I should have been dead, but Limbo has a way of preventing that. I was in that prairie again, but a part of it that was lusher, without boulders. I was naked. One of those guys who propositioned me must have dragged me out here. And violated my near-corpse? It didn't feel like I had forced penetration, but with how quickly bodies heal on Limbo would there be any evidence of something that happened hours before? Considering my astounding discovery during my seduction of Nickel I was confident I was now a twice born-again virgin. For some women such a re-growth of tissue may have been a relief. It made me sad. It was like that one wonderful night with Nickel didn't exist. How long would I remain a virgin this time? Probably longer than last time, considering the quality of men here. Nickel set a high standard. Maybe someone older next time---who retained most of his innocence. How likely was that here?

It bothered me what that man did to me, but not enough to scar my psyche. If someone doesn't remember a tragic event, did it happen? Now, being stabbed with a knife, that was something that will take a while to recover from. No more crowds for me, or men gawking, or rude innuendos. My days as a barterer were definitely over. Thinking about my prior profession no longer made me nauseous. It no longer occurred: shelved memories of a prior life.

Well, what now? I attempted to orient myself. The sun was always to the northeast---what a strange thing to say---but in which direction relative to Briarwood? The same? The opposite? Right?

Left? I'm just as likely to walk away from town as I am towards it. The Beetlewoods were a landmark, but no forest could be seen. The few trees I could see were scattered. Most were single specimens with the largest copse consisting of less than a dozen. The unfamiliar terrain suggested I must be north of Briarwood. I arrived from the west, and the Beetlewoods were to the south and east. With the sun askew I had to frequently redirect.

Something was wrong. I had first thought the sun looked the way it did because of the time of day, but if it was stationery why would its appearance change? It was slightly larger than I remembered and much higher in the sky. It was possible the sun finally moved, but it was far more likely I had. How far had I been dragged? The guy who did the dragging wasn't going to be too happy with me walking away. Not only did I have to focus on the direction I was traveling, but also on the man that might be following me.

I shuddered to think of what he might do when he caught up with me. I could take care of myself, but both of those guys who propositioned me looked like they could overpower me. Considering my profession you might think I was familiar with such treatment. Prostitutes, but not barterers. I always had the power. I did what I wanted when I wanted. The men may have suggested certain things, verbally or non, but it was always I who determined what was to transpire. I had never participated in intimate contact against my will.

The possibility of assault brought on a bout of vulnerability. I suddenly had the urge to cover myself. Not having any clothes to wear or vegetation to hide behind I instinctively used my hands. Being a voluptuous woman since the latter stages of development the one arm technique wasn't sufficient---my other arm being used to conceal my lower anatomy---until today. I was temporarily saddened by the loss, until recognizing the advantages of having smaller mounds in such a mobile society.

My virginity wasn't the only thing that had returned. The

removal of hair was supposed to be permanent. By the time I nearly died a second time a sim had grown back on my head. I considered shaving it, declining due to the rudimentary nature of Limboan razors. Fortunately what little body hair that grew did so at a much slower rate. It was as short and downy as peach fuzz. It tickled, but wasn't noticeable unless someone got extremely close to me, and the only person who has since I was incarcerated was Nickel. In the state he was in I'm confident he hadn't notice.

My body hair was more pronounced, in length and hue. The hair on my head was also darker and longer, but that was emotionally immaterial compared to the changes my body was going through. After I permanently removed my hair I became content---with my body. The clean, smooth lines made me feel beautiful. But now.... I covered myself to reduce the threat of being violently taken against my will, but also to reduce my shame. I was becoming as hairy as a cave woman, with highlights in an area that in this period of my life I preferred not to be highlighted.

The unsettling of my nerves extended to my digestive track. The last thing I wanted to happen, a close second to being reacquainted with that man that had abducted me, was to squat in the middle of that prairie. Implementing intense concentration I attempted to calm myself, to ease the turbulence in my bowels.

As I sat in a near Zen state a small insect buzzed around me. I swatted at it, my futile attempts becoming frantic after a minute of token resistance. I was in no mood for additional anguish. It disappeared, likely withering on the ground, after being struck inadvertently. I wanted it to die, but not carelessly. A firsthand experience was more enjoyable than a recap.

The distraction eased the burden on my stomach. The evil within it and below began to dissipate. Physically and emotionally restored, I was momentarily healthy enough to resume what I hoped was my journey back to Briarwood.

A cluster of trees was spotted on the horizon. I had been walking for at least half-an-hour, 50 minutes of looking over my shoulder to retain my bearings and prevent a clandestine attack. A finite cluster of trees. Not large enough to be the Beetlewoods, but they might provide some protection. Evening was approaching. Being healed by this planet altered me. I began to perceive things differently. My senses became more acute, including those that weren't easy to define. The sun was less than an hour away from...dimming? Suns don't normally do that either. They set, they didn't transform into full moons. There was no one within kays of me. Once I was concealed in the grove I would be safe.

My right ear began to tickle, not consistently, but frequently enough that it was noticeable. I poked a finger in as far as it would go. Not far enough. Before I reached the grove I lost hearing in that ear. The irritation stopped. The brief moment of relief was replaced by concern for permanent damage. The desire to return to Briarwood intensified. It had a healer, possibly a quack, but the only hope I had to recover my hearing short of dying. And I wasn't yet willing to force the issue, not with its complications---and no guarantee of recovery. I wasn't going to bet my life on rumors and coincidences.

I reached the grove about the time the sun dimmed, confirming my prediction. I don't think I'll ever become content seeing the sun dim instead of set. There were no colors associated with dimming, and it happened so quickly. Women liked to ease into things, to contemplate, to gradually intensify.

I anticipated finding something to eat or drink in the grove. It was unlikely so many trees clustered together by chance. I was out of luck. If there had ever been a spring or a pool there it had long ago dried out. Placing a pebble in your mouth was supposed to relieve thirst. Saliva was created, but the volume disappointing.

I climbed a deciduous tree, believing wild animals were less likely to injure me five meters above the ground. I know, looking back on it sleeping in a tree didn't sound that safe to me either. With hopelessness setting in---or a mutational diminishing of reasoning---it appeared to be the most reasonable alternative at the time.

Chapter 7

FLESHY CRAVINGS

When I woke my muscles were stiff and sore, they not being accustomed to straddling a tree limb for such an extended period. My bladder also needed to be drained. It was still dark, exaggerated by the leaves and branches above me blocking the lunar nightlight. I had no idea what might be below me. I could wait until it got light. No, I couldn't. I did what had to be done. Better now than what felt like minutes away from happening on its own. Climbing down wasn't a viable option. Even if it was safe on the ground, I still had to reach it. The consequences of dying were too dire. I made a mess on myself and my bed. If I was more of a tomboy I may have traveled to another branch. Lounging in urine was healthier than a crippling fall or being eaten by a wild animal.

I had never been so relieved in my life when the moon began to brighten. I wasn't able to fall back to sleep, my allocation of discomfort exceeding my tolerance.

About the time I was able to see the ground beneath me enough to judge it safe, a bird, but not quite, flew up to me. It was a hybrid, of a butterfly and a lizard. Its scaly hide, and tail, were green. Together they were half a meter long. Its yellow wings were shaped like elephant ears, each nearly the size of its body. Its head was out of proportion to its body, being considerably larger than it should have been. Its eyes were even more exaggeratingly out of proportion. They expressed a mixture of wonder and sorrow.

"I wonder what it tastes like," I thought.

The complex eyes doubled in size. It was remarkable they could do so considering how large a portion of its head they already occupied. The bird backed away from me.

I didn't really intend to eat it. I was just curious. Would it taste more like chicken or turtle soup? Even if I wanted to, I didn't have a weapon. I was much too weak to throttle it with my bare hands.

"I think I would concern myself more with preventing my own demise." I wasn't talking to myself. And it wasn't the bird. But it had to be. There was no one within kays of me. Was I imagining it? How long must a person be without food or water for them to go mad? Maybe the bird was of a species that could mimic human speech. But what an odd statement for it to repeat.

"Not a parrot, and not odd. And I wouldn't be too quick to criticize others, MISS SOILED HERSELF BECAUSE SHE WAS TOO SCARED AND TOO LAZY. We flyers may be liberal in the manner of our excretions, but we don't do so on ourselves. There's a pond two kays that way." The bird bent its beak to the left. "I suggest you throw yourself into it to take your yearly bath."

"HOW RUDE!" I lost my balance. I put out my arms to break my fall---breaking both wrists. "AHH!"

"On the positive side, you won't live much longer, so they'll only bother you a few more minutes."

I backed away.

"Heaven forbid. I'm a vegetarian, by choice. Sometimes I do get that fleshy craving, but it passes. Just a nibble of flesh, or a drop of blood, and I'm off the wagon again. Cold turkey---and mouse and frog---is the only way to go. Sometimes when the craving becomes unbearable I talk to one of my friends who has also quit. That helps. No, I'm not going to eat you. That insect in your head has claim to that. Once the coordination goes its just minutes before the end."

It was chilly that morning, but I suddenly became dripping wet. I violently jammed a finger into my deaf ear---not the easiest maneuver considering the state my wrist was in. I still couldn't get at that itch. I looked for a stick. Rushing towards the tree I had been in, I tripped over my own feet.

"Yes, just a few minutes more."

I lay where I had fallen and sobbed. Cognizant of the passage of time---very precious to me now---I stopped. I had squandered my life, hadn't I? What had given me pleasure, more professionally fulfilling than sensually, I had recently discarded, so I didn't even have that. No sense of calling. No purpose. Maybe it was all for the best. I didn't have any plans---not really. Trying to survive day to day wasn't an ambition. My mind and body began to numb. My broken wrists no longer hurt. That was something. The last thing I heard was, "I'll find you after you return."

Chapter 8

RE-CREATED

I woke beside water, not the clean, cool, crisp cascades of a mountain stream, but the barely translucent, brownish-green, warm, stagnant pool found in the middle of a prairie. I must be beside that pond that bird mentioned, or what my delirious mind told me it said. Three willows, shivering in the light breeze, encompassed the backyard pool size puddle. My wrists no longer hurt, even when I moved them, and I could hear in BOTH of my ears.

I felt rejuvenated but weak. I sat to scan my body. Yep, just what I feared. My hair was longer and was spread over a greater portion of my body. It didn't get any darker. That was something. How many more rejuvenations would it take for me to no longer need to wear clothes? I had two options: to begin shaving---risking lacerations and tetanus---or find people as hairy as I. Was that how the first mutants were created? They just became more this or more that over a series of near-death experiences? In many ways I looked like an arbol now, without the lankiness, or exaggerated limbs. There had to be a community of people as hairy as I but normal in other aspects. Not entirely normal, relative to how I used to look. My mounds continued to shrink. I still looked like a woman, but for how long? Did mutating males also have their sexual traits minimized? In time would the two genders merge into one? Some people may have been attracted to people that looked like them, but I was more attracted to the differences. Being with someone with the same equipment felt redundant.

I looked at the water. Post near-death healing always made me thirsty, adding to the thirst I already had from not drinking anything the day before. Still I hesitated. Murky water didn't always harm. Even if it did, Limbo's regenerative properties would prevent it from being fatal. I cupped my hands, filled them, and drank. It tasted as bad as it looked. I needed to re-hydrate before I resumed my---what was becoming a perpetual---journey, so I forced myself to take another sip, then another. That was enough for now. I nearly gagged on the last sip. If I spit up as much as I drank I would be just spinning my wheels.

Didn't that bird mention something about finding me? I didn't entirely rule out the bird communicating with me. If people could mutate, why couldn't birds? Or maybe someone had mutated into that bird. How many near-death experiences and accompanying healings would that take? I didn't believe the bird intended to harm me, but I was going to be prepared if it did. Willow branches weren't rigid enough to be used as spears, but maybe a long enough one could be made into a crude whip. I may not be able to pierce the little bugger, but I could at least slap it senseless.

"If you continue having thoughts like that, you'll be bedmates with ogres before you've spent a year on Limbo."

So it did find me, but where was it? I looked at the pond, then the brush side it.

"Higher. I'm a flyer, dammit, not a fish."

A spec in the air became an object, which became a.... "What exactly are you?" It was the first time I spoke out loud to it. Was there some way I could block my thoughts? It was creepy having someone penetrate my mind. My greatest fear was having my body violated, but having my mind pried open would be much worse. There are some thoughts you don't want to share. Not only might they be embarrassing, they are the only things that are truly yours. When they no longer become exclusive you lose a substantial part of yourself, possibly the only part that matters.

The bird landed on the ground beside me. It may have preferred a branch to perch, but the only trees nearby were willows, which lacked turgidity. "My name is Fred. There is no other like me, so classifying me as this or that isn't relevant. I am Fred. I should have been an albatross, but one can't choose his re-creations. I entered Limbo in the water. I was a life guard in college. It's ironic that I drowned. I was too far from shore. The nearest land, the Rainbow Isles, was about 20 kays away. Or maybe I was eaten by sharks. I forget. That was a long time ago, when Limbo was still young, unsure, not fully developed."

"Dartmoor was constructed over a hundred years ago. Are you saying you're that old? Aging is slowed, but not circumvented. Accidents happen, more often in a place with such a harsh environment."

"Like drowning?"

"But you're here, substantially mutated, but still living and breathing. After losing consciousness, you're body repaired itself.

41

It adapted to the environment. Instead of growing gills, you grew wings."

"The...Fred you see in front of you is very alive. The man that drowned, decomposed, or was eaten, died many decades ago."

"I'm confused. That insect must have damaged more than my hearing. Are you saying you actually died? That you didn't have a near-death experience?"

The bird chuckled. "Did you think you spent the last ten hours as a comatose convalescent?"

"I was unconscious that long?"

"Wounds are as fatal on Limbo as they are off world. The difference is that after we die here we are re-created?"

"Reincarnated?"

"Not quite. We are still who we were after Gaea re-creates us, just slightly mutated. Sometimes when you pass along information to a person some of it isn't received. If that information is passed along to a third person there is a compounded opportunity for errors."

"Then why aren't the people who have been here longer than me more muted?"

"It's not just the number of times someone dies, but how they're clustered. Those who hide in cities die infrequently, or not at all. You're too death prone. Gaea curses as many as She favors."

"Gaea?"

"The earth mother. A world god. A symbiotic or parasitic relationship, depending on the sect. Praising and fearing. Most view the concept of Gaea as local folklore, but others.... Let's just say when people truly believe in something, they can be quite fervent."

"Are there Gaea churches? I didn't see one in Briarwood."

"Not in the sense that large groups of people congregate and formally worship her. There are temples, but most are small, open-air structures, looking more like gazebos than cathedrals. Most people who praise Gaea do so in private. Whenever a small group gathers it's usually a family."

"I didn't think we could bear children."

"We can't, but for some people there is a need to bond communally. Small groups of people sometimes choose to form a union. An outsider may view the relationship as a formal orgy, but most of these unions are platonic."

"I don't think I could ever commit myself to so many people. I can't even commit myself to a single person. Sometimes things happen in our lives that prevent us from living a normal life."

"We all have things that happen in our lives. On Limbo there is a greater opportunity to overcome them, or sink deeper into them."

"Greater opportunity?"

"We don't just change physically when we mutate. Intellect and morality can also be altered. The monsters that inhabit Limbo weren't always as horrid, or the angels as pleasant."

"So someone living here can truly change? Not just how they appear, but who they are?" Could the change in how I now feel about bartering be a mutation instead of a moral epiphany?

"Compounding has created moral extremes, with the less effected clustered in the center of Limbo, the deviations at its perimeter. Morality doesn't just consist of good versus evil, or what we Limboans like to call positive versus negative. There are also individuals who are exceptionally ordered or extremely chaotic. With the blending of the two moral axes eight combinations are formed, nine if you include neutrality"

"And we might progress from one morality to another over time? If Gaea wills?"

"Or digress. We do have some say in the matter. If we chose to live a more moral life, a life more representative of the morality we are striving to possess, Gaea is more likely to mutate us in that direction. Conversely, if you are content with who you are the best way not to mutate is not to die."

"I'll try to work on that. I haven't had much luck so far."

"Cheer up. Some mutations are beneficial. Look at me. I enjoy being able to fly, but hearing people's thoughts can be a bummer. I can chose not to probe a person's thoughts, but sometimes it becomes too tempting. I've been on the wagon when it comes to eating others, but I haven't completely lost my appetite for mental eavesdropping."

I had forgotten about that. I wonder if there was some way to block my thoughts from that bird. The easiest way was to increase the distance between us.

"Ah. Thanks for the information. I got to be going. I'm starving, and Briarwood is still hours away." I began walking towards the forest. I heard laughter behind me. Not the playful, shared glee of friends, but the laughter of someone laughing at another, the laughter that a creature that defecates on your car was born to make. I had to concentrate on the task at hand: finding food. Don't stop. Don't turn around. No more delays. I couldn't help myself. It wasn't that I was curious what the bird was laughing about. I was angry. How dare the bird delay my supper. Maybe I WILL find out how good it tastes. With steps laden with purpose I turned around and walked back to the mini-oasis. My third step didn't happen. I was glued to the ground. My legs couldn't move. They weren't paralyzed. I could feel them. They just wouldn't budge. I tried to lift them with my arms. Still nothing. I became angrier. The bird did this to me, but how? "RELEASE ME!"

Fred flew towards me. There was a twinkle in his eyes, but also pity. "Not until you calm down."

I rolled my eyes, then took a deep breath. "Okay, I'm calm. RELEASE ME!"

Fred flew closer, almost close enough for me to grab him. I lunged towards him with my arms. He backed away, but just a couple of meters. He knew the limit of my reach. "I believe you need some more time to calm down. Maybe if I sang something soothing."

"Please don't," I sighed. I surrendered without further

aggression. Why waste the effort. If the bird could read my mind, it knew what I was going to do, seeing past my mock submission. "So how did you do it, freezing my legs?"

"The same thing that re-creates us bestows to us certain ABILITIES. Terra-forming continues to create." Some people gestured while talking. Fred flew. You could tell how he felt about something by how rapid his movement was. When he was pensive he was nearly stationary. Most of the time his velocity was somewhere in the middle. "Dinga, wouldn't you be more comfortable if I released you, but before I can you have to calm down."

"How did you know my name? Oh, I forgot, you have that rude habit of listening in on my thoughts." If the animosity I felt for him this moment persisted it might be days before he released me.

"Memory isn't usually one of those things that mutates, but you might want to get it checked, just to be sure. Preventing the muscles in your legs from contracting and expanding is no more remarkable than mixing two clear liquids together and them turning blue. Or an eel producing an electric current. Or clouds producing rain. The more this planet fuses with my soul, the more I'm tuned in to how it works."

"You said your name was Fred. Who would name you that? I thought we were named for something unique about us, something that happened our first day?"

"That was not always so. It took many years for that custom to develop, millions of arrivals after mine." Sometime during our conversation my legs broke free. A loss of concentration, or a time limitation? It didn't matter. I was free. I could have attacked Fred, maybe even successfully, because he was distracted, but I had become interested in what he was saying. Maybe there was something good to come out of me being death prone and mutating. Perhaps enough of Limbo will enter me to give ME special abilities.

"Will you teach me some of things you can do?"

This question must have taken Fred by surprise, because he came to a complete stop. "I don't think I can. My abilities are innate. Every time I was re-created a larger percent of me became the planet. I don't think you have enough of the planet in you yet. And what you do eventually receive probably will be different than what I received. We've talked about our abilities in my support group. Very few of them overlapped."

"I would enjoy talking about them. There has to be similarities in how they are accessed."

Fred paused for a long moment. He landed, becoming completely immobile. "I've never had an apprentice before," he said. "This might be amusing. I'll do it. But only if you do exactly what I say. I don't want you killing yourself, or me, accidentally. Although we are re-created, death is still painful, and re-creations can have unexpected consequences, some of them unpleasant." The hair on my body stood up. I don't know if it was the UNEXPECTED CONSEQUENCES part or just that he might teach me to do some of these miraculous things. After giving up bartering I felt lost. It had been such a part of my life for so long. It was more than a job. Being a barterer was who I was. Now I might have another opportunity to be more than someone who worked a certain numbers of hours then went home. "Do you agree to do what I say?" Fred's tone was normally jovial, but there was no frivolity in these words.

"What if you say something stupid?"

"Then you smile politely at me and suggest an alternative. But if we are in immediate danger, don't take the time to weigh the ramifications. I've lived on Limbo a lot longer than you, so I know the dangers."

"I'll do what you say," I said humbly, "as long as you teach me your abilities."

"It may take years before you can do something you couldn't do before coming to Limbo."

"I have all the time in the world. It's not like I'm going to die before I accomplish what I want."

"Some days you may wish you could die. We call this planet Limbo for a reason. After we first die we're never completely alive or dead again. Hopelessness is taken to the infinite degree."

"I'll need to return to Briarwood before becoming your apprentice. There are certain affairs I need to attend to, including repaying a couple of travel agents. I also could use a few provisions. I'm no longer starving---I think my stomach went numb from non-use---but my strength won't completely return until I begin eating regularly. Wearing something would be nice too. Someone who has mutated into a bird may no longer be affected by my non-attire, but there are others that are. Adoration is fine, as long as it's from afar. Inmates have a tendency to cross boundaries."

From the beginning of my oration Fred chuckled. What now? I thought if I continued speaking he would eventually lose grip of the juvenile amusement, but the snickering persisted. "I'm sorry," he said. "I shouldn't go off on an emotional tangent in the prescience of a neurotic. I'm laughing because we are nowhere near Briarwood. It would take more than a week to reach Briarwood, and that's assuming passage on a ship is immediately available, and the weather, affable."

"We're not in that prairie north of Briarwood?"

"Technically we are north of Briarwood, but just as far east. Your estimate was only off by a 1000 kays."

"I thought the center of Limbo was just over 600 kays away."

"It is, relative to Briarwood."

"And the sun is directly above the center of Limbo, isn't it? That means we're on the other side of Limbo. So when I thought I was heading south I was really heading north."

"Not exactly. You're not directly across from where you were. You're more to the south."

"So that first time I died I may have also been re-created hundreds of kays from that first version of me? I thought the differences in terrain was because someone---or thing---moved me a few kays. If I moved the last time I was re-created how were you able to find me? And so quickly."

"The last time you were re-created, you moved just ten kays. Sometimes we are re-created near where we died. Other times from one end of Limbo to the other. It's partially random, and partially how much we've changed morally since our last re-creation. Not too farfetched considering we're living in a penal facility."

"Which way to the nearest city then?" I asked with little enthusiasm. Suddenly learning that you have been transported hundreds of kays does that to a person, especially when she still has many kays to go.

"Capetown is 80 kays northwest of us. I could reach it in an hour, flying. It will take you two days, that's if you can push through your starvation for that long. I'm willing to share what I eat, but those who are less mutated are usually picky eaters."

"I've eaten some unusual things in order to keep my weight within professional parameters. How much longer can we walk today?"

"We? My plan is to fly a couple of kays ahead, do some reconnaissance while I'm airborne, land, eat and rest while waiting for you to catch up. Rinse, repeat, until we reach Capetown."

"How long until it gets dark?"

"One hour, 16 minutes."

"That precise?"

"Once we've lived on Limbo for awhile we become more attuned to its cycles. Modern man lost this innate ability when the clock was invented. It's like what happens when a flashlight is turned on in the dark. We may have limited vision, but become completely blind when the switch is flipped."

"Should we spend the night here, then? It has water."

"Only if you enjoy company. You had the right idea about sleeping in a tree. If we hurry we can make it to the Eight-Leg Woods in two hours."

"Eight-Leg Woods?"

"Think about it." The memory of a spider egg sack breaking open and the babies scuttling in every direction, including up a little girl's legs flooded back to me. I shivered. I slid my hands down my legs in a sweeping motion. The fine hair felt like velvet. Would it deter the spiders or encourage them? Would it give them something to hide in? I shuddered again.

We reached the Leg-Eight Woods a few minutes short of an hour, seven to be precise according to Fred, my unease agitating me enough to push me along. The exertion tapped what remained of my energy reserves. I fell to the ground beneath one of the pines on the perimeter of the forest.

Fred looked concerned. "I can bring you some food."

"I'm not hungry." My eyes remained open, continuing to stare into oblivion. I didn't have enough energy to shut them.

"I'll return in a few minutes."

He returned, but with my mind functioning at such a low level I had no concept after how long. It could have been three minutes, or three hours, or three days. He dropped a cluster of nuts beside me. If I was capable of expressing any emotion I would have. I envisioned astringent vegetation, or insects. Maybe not the latter, Fred being a vegetarian. Without turning my head I looked down at the nuts. I think they were filberts. I told my hand to pick one up, but nothing happened. Fred, sensing my inability, cracked open a nut and flew it up to my mouth. Hovering like a hummingbird, the maneuver wasn't a great feat for him. He forced it into my mouth. The contact was enough to stimulate that part of my body, enabling me to chew and swallow. After being fed a second nut, enough energy returned to me that I was able to feed myself. Fred flew off again. He returned a few minutes later with some huckleberries. They were too tart for my liking, but the sugar content in them was significantly higher than the nuts, giving me a stronger burst of immediate energy.

Having now the strength to move about, I stood up. I felt

almost human again. I stretched, which not only wrung out my muscles, but increased circulation. Feek. Did all of my body have to be that active? I began walking deeper into the forest. Fred followed me. I stopped, then turned towards him. "Ah...I'm going to need some privacy for a couple of minutes."

"It can be dangerous in the woods at dusk. That's when most of the animals---and monsters---come out."

"I think I'll be okay for a couple of minutes. I'll shout if I get into any trouble." I turned back around and resumed my push to privacy.

"There is nothing you're going to do I haven't seen before. Flyers aren't bashful when they eliminate waste. I don't mind keeping a closer look out for you."

Continuing to move away I shouted back, "BUT I DO!"

After returning to Fred I climbed into a tree and reclined in the manner I did the night before. Two more days until I returned to a city---and a bed. I hoped I was able to sleep in a bed. Before I changed my view on bartering it would have been easy to find some place to sleep. And when I really wanted to sleep there were certain techniques to encourage my clients to nod off. I was determined not to return to my prior profession, even for one night. There were other things I could do. I was a good server---and dancer. I would probably have to shave at least my legs, but I was willing to make the sacrifice if it meant a warm, soft bed and a full belly.

Fred perched on a branch of the tree beside me. We were eye to eye about three meters apart. "Thank you for feeding me."

"You're welcome. I wasn't being completely altruistic. If you died your body would have begun to stink. I might be tempted to go off the wagon and dig in. I would also feel obligated to find you again. I enjoy flying, but not for hundreds of kays."

"Fred, you said morality often determines were we are re-created. What kind of mutants live in the direction I was sent after I died, in Briarwood?"

"We're still close enough to the center of Limbo to be surrounded by neutrals. But if you continue to head in that direction, once you reach the Frontier you'll be met by mutes that believe in strictly enforcing the laws they have created, a majority of them brutally. But the last time you were re-created, you moved slightly away from them. And the randomness of re-creation is at least as great a factor as morality."

As I drifted off to sleep I pondered where I would wake, and in what form, many of the permutations revisited in my dreams.

Chapter 9

AIR SHIELD

I woke up happy. Sometimes a good sleep does that. I felt stiff, but not as much as I did the night before. Maybe the hair on my body meant I was turning into a monkey. Was sleeping in a tree going to be my preferred method of slumber? The thought didn't make me sad. Was I getting used to the idea of mutating? Dappled light fell upon me, a natural mosaic formed by sunrays and a forest canopy. If possible, I was even in a better mood. Just two more days of walking to reach Capetown. But then what? I was no longer as happy. Did this once gregarious city girl really rather spend time alone in the wilderness?

What finally broke me out of my despair was seeing Fred. He flew up from the forest floor. "I brought you a gift." He flew back down to the base of the tree. My eyes followed his descent. He landed beside a heaping pile of berries. They were the size and texture of grapes, but orange.

I climbed down with an agility I didn't possess before I was incarcerated. I may no longer be beautiful, but it wasn't taken from me without compensation.

The berries were fleshy, like olives, but tasted like tangerines. In the center of each was something larger than a citrus seed, but smaller than an olive pit.

After breakfast we resumed our journey to Capetown. A majority of the two days would be spent in the Eight-Leg Woods. No spiders, or webs---yet. Relief, but only temporary. We were still much closer to the perimeter of the forest than its heart.

It concerned me the first couple of times Fred wandered off. What would I do if I wasn't able to find him? I had a terrible sense of direction. I used the sun when I could, which became increasingly obscured the further we plunged into progressively denser forest. Fred flew back to me more often, sensing my unease. With my confidence in him not leaving me building, I began to worry less. I no longer contemplated my steps. I fearlessly walked in the direction I last saw him fly.

As the day warmed, I began to perspire. The water droplets clung to the tiny hairs on my body. I had to shake like a dog for them to detach. Before I had time to catch my breath, mosquitoes appeared. Clothing did more than maintain modesty. Without a layer of armor, my arms got as much exercise as my legs.

"I think I can do something about that," said Fred, recently returned from one of his mini-excursions. He appeared to go into a trance. A moment later my surroundings appeared slightly distorted, like looking through an impure sheet of glass. The mosquitoes continued to buzz around me, but they no longer made contact.

"HOW DID YOU DO THAT?!" Mutations, I could wrap my mind around, but this---it was the closest thing to magic I ever saw. But magicians created illusions: sleight of hand and misdirection. Fred looked quite pleased with himself. He wanted me to approve of him. His confidence wasn't entirely intrinsic. "Could that be one of the first things you teach me?"

"No."

"No?"

"Just because I can create an air shield doesn't mean you can? It has nothing to do with desire or hard work. It's an innate ability. It can be developed or not. An animal can't fly unless it has wings."

"But I MIGHT be able to create an air shield. I MIGHT have the ability, but haven't developed it yet."

"True."

"So let's try." In addition to being the type of person that didn't waste her time doing something unless she intended to do it well---putting all her effort into doing it---I leapt at tasks, not putting off until next week something that I could do today, or this hour.

"You agreed, in exchange for being my apprentice, to do whatever I said." I nodded enthusiastically. "Then I say you're not ready to attempt what I just did." The emotion dropped from my face, like wet clay that had become a casualty of gravity, or a wax dummy that was left out in the sun. "Oh, don't be that way. I'll explain what I did to create the air shield, but the next few days should be spent observing and listening, not doing. Think of all the people who shot themselves in the foot when they bought their first gun, or blew themselves up the first time they ignited dynamite. An air shield is not a toy. I say this from experience. I've been on Limbo longer than you---a lot longer. There weren't that many people here when I arrived, and none of them had been here long enough to have the experience to mentor me. When I discovered my ability to manipulate air I expelled so much of it--- from the area I was in---that I nearly suffocated. A tornado is essentially air. Think of the destruction something like that could do unleashed. It's not only yourself you must think about. And sometimes not even the people near you. You've probably have

53

heard of the butterfly effect. A single butterfly flapping its wings causing an unforeseen chain of events: someone being struck by lightning, or a farm hundreds of kays away becoming destitute from draught."

"Go ahead then, tell me what you did to make that air shield." Confident that Fred wasn't going to change his mind I didn't waste my time attempting to convince him.

"It helps to think of my abilities as science instead of magic. Nothing happens miraculously. Being re-created connects us to our environment in a manner never experienced before. When we're re-created we are remade, from the surrounding elements. Our essence---our soul---is retained, but nothing else. It happens to everyone, everything---everywhere---eventually---when cells are replaced."

"What does this have to do with making an air shield?"

"Before you learned Algebra you learned Arithmetic, didn't you? To fully grasp what you are doing, so you don't develop bad habits---like killing yourself---you need to learn the basics, the foundations of elemental manipulation, before you cluster air molecules and move them."

"Okay. Got it. Continue." If you've been wondering if we plopped down on a sofa---or a log---to have this conversation, we didn't. Being advanced organisms we were able to speak and move at the same time.

"Just because something looks inert doesn't mean it must remain so. A puddle of water looks harmless, but what if it freezes and someone breaks it into shards. Wouldn't one of these ice daggers make a formidable weapon? Air can be as easily modified. Gas molecules aren't as tightly packed as those in liquids and solids, but what if they were? Or they moved. Think about how much damage a tornado can cause. Air can destroy, but the same forces that make it so deadly can also protect. A person can easily tear one piece of paper, but has trouble tearing fifty, and it's almost impossible to tear five-hundred. The same concept can be applied to air. An object can easily pass through a few air molecules, but how about a thousand? A million?"

"Yes, I understand the concept, but how do you get the air to pack like that? It's easy to grab some paper, but if I did the same to air my hand would pass through it."

"That's where us being connected to our environment comes in. I view the interaction I have as a sixth sense. It's like I'm seeing or hearing or smelling, but instead of observing I'm interacting. I'm not being bombarded by stimuli. I am the one doing the bombarding. It's like I have these ethereal fingers that can ensnare the air around me, moving it, pressing it upon itself."

"It must be invigorating to have that much control over your environment." One of the reasons I became a barterer was to control my environment. I determined who I did business with, what that business consisted of, when it occurred, and where.

"As frightening as it's stimulating. I never have complete control. It's like trying to row a boat across a river. If I concentrate on what I'm doing and the conditions are right I have no trouble reaching the other side, but if the current is strong, or I must pass through the wake of a larger boat, I have my hands full. Sometimes I'm fortunate not to tip over."

"Can you make another air shield? So I can analyze what you do."

"Not right now. Let's wait until we stop for the night. THINK about what I told you. Sometimes thinking is as beneficial as doing. My basketball coach taught me to imagine shooting free throws, and making them. The mental repetition paid off. I became a much better shooter."

"It's just that the quicker I learn to do something, like making an air shield, the safer I will be. Under normal circumstances I do a pretty good job of taking care of myself, but here...."

"Review what I said, and think about it. Really think about it. It will help. Until you feel like you can adequately protect yourself I'll be here to protect you."

A moment later that statement was tested. Something large and rubbery dropped from a tree. The weight of it knocked me over. It was able to coil around my body in the time it took for the shock of the encounter to wear off. I was trapped. Every squirm from me brought a reciprocal squeeze from it. I panicked. I attempted to flail my arms madly. My muscles expanded and contracted, but my limbs couldn't be pried from their prison. A serpent head twisted, looking directly at me. The inhuman, satanic eyes twinkled, then spun, or was it my head spinning? It needed to consume me for its survival. I existed so it could feed. I felt warm and loved in its embrace. If only it could hug me tighter. It did. JOY! Then suddenly.... HEY! It no longer loved me. Its embrace was weakening. It no longer loved me. NO, DON'T GO!

"Pull yourself away, Dinga. I can't hold it back much longer."

But Fred loved me too. I pushed against the rubbery scales. I rolled onto the forest floor. The fresh air cleared my head. I looked up at my captor. It was ten meters long, 20 sims in diameter, its scales---IT HAD SCALES---were a mottled green. "FLEE!" shouted Fred.

I ran away as fast as my legs and the forest terrain allowed. The dense canopy prevented a majority of the sunlight from reaching the forest floor, resulting in near non-existent brush, but there were enough fallen trees to retard my progress. The terrain became muddy as I spotted a lake in the distance. A marsh surrounded it. If I was clothed I would have made a detour. The water began to creep up on me, reaching mid thigh. Where was Fred? I better head for dry land, but in which direction? Where did that lake go? It was on my right before I got twisted around.

Something moved ahead of me. Something red, no blue...yellow? It was a person---two of them. What were they doing? Digging? Looking for mushrooms perhaps. I would do about anything for a mushroom? No I wouldn't. Not anymore. The men looked like they were on dry land. That was the direction I needed to head, but should I? Can a woman alone trust men in the middle of the woods? Did I have a choice? Where was Fred?

My options were rapidly becoming more limited. The men looked my way. Their mouths dropped. Hadn't they seen a muddy, naked woman before? I continued to look at them. They continued to look at me. Being a woman not wanting to be outdone by men, I made the first move: I fainted.

Chapter 10

TWELVE STALKS

I awoke beside a campfire. A lake, possibly the lake I had seen from a distance, was just 20 meters away. A grassy bank led down to the water. "FEEK! So I died again. I'm another step closer to damnation."

"Hardly," spoke a deep voice from behind me. A man in green trousers and boots, and a red shirt, pulled on a rope tied to a bag. The rope draped over a branch five meters above the ground, forming a simple, but effective pulley. Once the bag reached a certain height, the man tied the rope to a neighboring tree. "But if we didn't see you when we did, you probably would have died. Those were stuck to your legs." The rugged, veering towards homely, man pointed to four crinkled brown clumps that looked like prunes. He was one of the largest men I have ever seen, so large that even those insecure men who were always looking to start a fight to prove their toughness would think twice about challenging him. Men like that exuded calmness. Fear, insecurity, wasn't in them. I was instantly attracted to him. What was I thinking? Were my hormones so mutated that I became enamored with someone after saving me?

"They were bloated with your blood when we removed them. Salt does more than season."

"I didn't even feel them," I said as I sat up. I was wearing a yellow shirt and green trousers.

"I hope you're not too distressed about wearing clothes. You were distracting the way we found you."

"I prefer wearing clothes, when they're available. Lately I haven't lived long enough to finish the stitching."

"Everyone has a week or two like that. The leeches use an anesthetic secretion to deaden the area they plan to drink from. The first time you realize something is wrong is when you are too weak to be able to do something about it."

"So I'll recover?"

"Fully, but you need to rest for a few days. The bloodletting has weakened your body."

"Thank you for saving my life and for letting me borrow these clothes." Where was Fred? "I need to find someone." I attempted to push myself up with my legs. My legs buckled. I collapsed, then fell soundly asleep.

The next day I felt refreshed. I was ready---more than ready----to walk the rest of the way to Capetown, and to find Fred. The other man I saw before I passed out was beside the fire with the large man. He wore green boots and breeches, like his friend, but topped with a blue shirt. He was much smaller that his companion, nearly my size. He was also considerably more hansom, in a sly way. He was the type of man I would have fallen for before I was incarcerated.

"So, Sleeping Beauty has finally decided to grace us," spoke the smaller man in a sultry baritone. "My name is Thumbringer Northern Spine." Being drawn to his hands, I noticed a platinum ring on his left thumb. The ring had markings on it, but I couldn't distinguish them from the distance I was away from him. "You can call my Thumbringer. I feel we got to know each other as I dressed you."

"Don't worry," spoke the bass voice of his companion. "I made sure all Thumbringer did was dress you. My name is Claw Raspberry Mountains, or just Claw Raspberry, or just Claw. I assume you had a revitalizing day and a half."

"Thank you, I did. By the way, my name is Dinga. Did you say a day-and-a-half?"

"Sometimes one's body has more common sense than the head it's attached to."

What was that smell? Now I remembered---meat cooking. I breathed in deeply. What had I been thinking when I became a vegetarian?

"Help yourself," said Thumbringer. "Be careful. It's hot." Not only hot, but juicy. It was good whatever it was, and I didn't dare ask the particulars, not risking to ruin the satisfaction I was feeling.

The one bad thing about eating such a good meal was how messy is made you. I walked down to the lake to wash up, initially just to wash my hands and face. But it had been awhile since I bathed. I took off my shirt, then my trousers. By now you've probably learned I'm not bashful.

"I wouldn't do that," said Thumbringer. He grinned mischievously, quite pleased with the view. Claw had his back me to.

"Because you can't control yourself seeing me like this?"

"Now that you mention it.... No, there are things in the lake even more unpleasant than leeches."

"I'll just take a quick dip. I'll be out in five minutes, ten minutes tops." The lake bed was a bit gunky, but 10 meters from shore the water was well over my head, so it no longer mattered.

After washing the best I could without soap and a

washcloth, I did some exploring. No, I wasn't very bright as an infant. The temperature of the air and water was perfect. What could hurt me? The far side of the lake, probably the marshy side I arrived from, was about a kay away. That was my goal. I haven't been mobile for a day-and-a-half? About time I did something about that. I loved to swim as a child. As an adult I spent more time beside the pool. The best barterer goes hungry unless people were aware of her.

Something nudged me from below, about a third of the way across the lake. Then a second nudge slightly to my right, and a third to my left. They were probably fish being playful, but why risk it. I began to swim back to camp. Claw and Thumbringer were preparing to retrieve me with their log raft, but upon seeing me return, they ceased their preparations and just watched.

Abruptly they rushed to untie the rope connecting the raft to shore. After pushing off with a paddle they frantically struck the water, propelling them towards me. Aware that I should focus on swimming faster, I looked back---I couldn't help myself. Four stalks were sticking out of the water and two more were rising. They twisted around awkwardly, like freshly dug up worms. At the end of each stalk were two eyes and a mouth. Incisors were revealed as the six stalks simultaneously smiled at me. More stalks broke the surface of the water.

I resumed my swim. Panic set in, my thrashing strokes slowing me down. Claw and Thumbringer were about halfway to me now. Maybe the stalks were just curious? Something bumped my legs, followed by a rush of water away from me. I was pulled into the jet stream. I was released seconds later, after the flow subsided. I bobbed to the surface. Twelve stalks appeared in front of me. They were attached to the torso of a creature resembling a manatee.

The stalks leaned backwards, like a snake preparing to strike. Before they lunged, two of them were hit from behind, the entire creature convulsing from the shock. "SWIM TO THE RAFT!"

Claw insisted. All twelve stalks and their accompanying rows of teeth turned towards the raft. My revulsion of temporarily getting closer to the monster was outweighed by the potential safely on the far side of the raft. I no longer worried about the creature striking me. It was too transfixed on my benefactors. What had I gotten these two into? I had been with them just over a day, and I was already causing them problems. Being death prone didn't give me permission to infect others.

I reached the raft before the monster attacked. Normally I would have been offended for not being helped up, but Claw and Thumbringer were preoccupied, with a weapon in one hand and a shield in the other. Claw's weapon was a mace with sharp knobs embedded in it. Thumbringer used a sword. Their silver shields were round, 75 sims in diameter, and most importantly, slightly convex, encouraging most blows to slide off.

The monster's heads pulled back. I pulled myself onto the raft, then crawled to the far end of it. It wasn't that I was afraid. I didn't have anything to protect myself with. My defenders apparently knew what they were doing. It would have been rude to get in their way.

The heads flung themselves towards my benefactors. Four of them missed badly, slamming into the water. Another four struck one another. The last four were intercepted by Claw and Thumbringer. Even they appeared to be discombobulated, possibly in consternation to what happened to their brothers. Claw easily dispatched one of his opponents with a bash between the eyes. Thumbringer was even more efficient, decapitating one of his. The remaining two antagonists backed off. The four heads that accidentally struck one another did so intentionally the second time. When the drenched heads re-emerged they also began attacking one another. A civil war had erupted.

Claw and Thumbringer threw down their weapons and shields, and began paddling. The two heads that had attacked, but survived, lunged at the departing craft. One head splashed into the

61

water. The other broke a tooth on the edge of the wooden raft. They recovered quickly enough that they that had time for one more strike, but being miffed at the other heads for not helping they struck at their two closest companions.

"Thank you," I said, sprawled out on the raft, feeling neither embarrassed nor sexy. Anyone who saved your life, be it a doctor or a soldier, viewed you impartially, didn't they? Not as a woman. Of course, it was ridiculous to think such a thing---doctor-patient relationships did happen, and women were brutalized in wars, including being raped---but it was something I needed to be true, so it was, to me. I had been through so much since my arrival on Limbo that my safety, tenuous as it may be, was more important than retaining absolute sovereignty. I had looked after myself because no one else did. If I continued with that philosophy SLEEPING WITH OGRES, as Fred put it, would come to fruition. Failure was severe on Limbo, and almost guaranteed. Having Claw and Thumbringer save me in the manner they did convinced me it was in my best interest to no longer shun assistance.

"How could two gentlemen not be compelled to save such a fine damsel in distress?" Thumbringer commented. Claw said nothing as he adverted his eyes.

After the raft came to shore I quickly redressed. Afterwards Claw came up to me and asked, "You weren't harmed were you, Miss Dinga?"

"Just my ego. As you have seen I have a short supply of common sense."

"Don't be so hard on yourself," said Thumbringer. "How long have you been on Limbo?"

"Two weeks."

"If a baby two weeks old got into trouble, would you blame it? You're an infant, Dinga. That's not an insult. It's fact. A year from now, maybe two, when you're a toddler, you won't get into so much trouble."

"You'll be surprised how much trouble I'll probably still get into."

"That's what makes life interesting. Living in a city, working in a cubicle, you'd be bored to death. It's better to die contributing to an adventure."

"But the more I die, the more I mutate. You've probably noticed I'm a bit hairy."

"I've known woman as hairy as you who haven't been re-created. I think it's kind of sexy."

I did something I haven't done since I was a child: I blushed.

"Thumbringer and I also don't fall in the middle of some bell curve," said Claw. "We're aware we're a bit odd, but we like it that way."

"And we like other people like that," Thumbringer added. "Especially those more extreme than us. They're more interesting. Some of our best friends are demons."

"Demons?"

Claw answered. "I apologize on Thumbringer's behalf. The name is considered to be derogatory."

"So you two haven't mutated?" I asked.

"I wouldn't say that," said Claw. "As YOU have probably noticed I'm a taller than the average person and more...feral."

"Thumbringer?"

"Believe it or not I'm still a virgin." My stunned disbelief forced an explanation. "This ring I was named for has been my chastity belt. It's not flawless in protecting me, but I have rarely reached third base. If you don't believe I haven't been mutated, feel free to examine me, Darling."

I could have been offended. Instead, I just laughed. Thumbringer was probably one of those guys if a girl called one of his bluffs he would run away so quickly he would trip, pick himself up, and run some more until he was far enough way to not find his way back.

I just thought of something. "If someone mutates enough to be called a demon are they forced to move to the perimeter of

Limbo?"

"Are you just curious, or have you already packed your bags?"

"I must again apologize for Thumbringer," said Claw. "He can be blunt at times. Most of the time he doesn't even realize he is being offensive."

"No offense taken." And I meant it. I've never been ashamed of who I was, as a barterer, or now as someone on the fast track to becoming a demon.

Thumbringer continued. "There are more mutants living in what we call the FRONTIERS than in central Limbo. Not only are they re-created there more often, once they are re-created they are psychologically compelled to live there. Having others of their kind there must also have some influence."

"Is this compulsion part of their mutation?"

"Indirectly perhaps. For some reason mutants of similar morals are clustered together. It might just be because they have things in common, but there's more to it."

"Gaea's will," Claw added.

"So Limbo's version of God has segregated the mutants?"

"How much less bloodshed would there be if the Almighty did something like for the entire galaxy?"

"You have almost made me a believer. Gaea doesn't have something like the Ten Commandments does She? I've never been good at following rules."

"Not that I'm aware of. Remember, Gaea is aligned more with nature than with man. She tends to go more with the flow, unless there is an extreme need to muddle."

"Time to break camp," stated Thumbringer, abruptly.

"To Capetown?" Claw was already on the move. If his pace continued, the tent, bedrolls, clothes, and cooking equipment will all be packed within minutes.

"Appropriate and prudent." Thumbringer was just as hasty and efficient.

My head spun from the activity surrounding me. "Ah, may I....I mean...." How could a person like me, with my experiences, be hesitant about anything? "May I travel with you to Capetown?"

"It's the reason we're heading to Capetown, Darling," Thumbringer replied.

"The main reason anyway," added Claw.

"You're willing to leave this wonderful place just to help me?"

"Even if the hydra doesn't survive," said Claw, "the commotion it made, and is still making, will bring every monster within 10 kays. There are other places to prospect."

"There is gold by this lake?"

"Something more valuable than that," said Thumbringer. "Elem."

"Elem?"

"Particles of elemental energy," Claw enlightened, "like those that exist in Thumbringer's ring."

Suddenly I was very excited. These elem sounded like those innate abilities Fred spoke of. But if they could be found instead of being mutational residue, I might be able to do anything I wanted: fly, make an air shield, walk on water, create food. For elem to fit in Thumbringer's ring they had to be small, microscopically so. Panning for gold would have been child's play compared to finding elem in its natural state.

I studied Thumbringer's ring without being obvious about it. What post-pubescent girl wasn't able to check out a cute guy without him being aware of it? The same couldn't be said when it came to guys. In many circumstances their boldness deterred what may have been a very pleasurable experience for them. Most guys were oblivious to subtle observation. Thumbringer, apparently, wasn't one of them.

"You like it?" I was so taken off guard that I wasn't able to respond. "I haven't known a girl that didn't covet jewelry? Or maybe I'm wrong, and you just can't keep your eyes off me."

"Leave the girl alone. Such comments are what got you here."

"I don't see her husband or boyfriend around."

"That doesn't mean she doesn't have one."

"Maybe off world, but considering how often someone leaves this place all prior relationships become annulled."

"I don't by the way," I interjected.

"Don't what?" asked Thumbringer.

"Don't have a husband or boyfriend." Maybe I wasn't too subtle, but a girl has to do what a girl has to do. Guys were sometimes dense when it came to being aware of girls attracted to them. The problem was getting the right guy to fall for me. When a dart is thrown sometimes it hits the wrong balloon. My eyes returned to the ring. That's not to say I really wanted to form a relationship with either man, but it didn't prevent a girl from keeping her options open.

"Would you like to see it?"

"If that's all I have to see."

Claw laughed. Thumbringer frowned, but within seconds turned it into a grin. He also laughed. He handed it to me, but after a warning. "Place it on your palm or hold it between your thumb and index finger. Don't actually place it on a finger. The ring shouldn't harm you, but why risk it."

I expected the ring to do something when Thumbringer dropped it in my hand: vibrate, glow, explode. Nothing. It was slightly larger than the typical metal band. Refinement was one of the requirements of being a good barterer. I was an expert in fine wine, works of art, and expensive jewelry. To most people the ring would have appeared to be made of silver. I knew it to be platinum. Five symbols were engraved in the metal---three asterisks separated by two swooshes. I was tempted to place the ring on my finger. The longer I held the ring the more tempting it became. The temptation become almost overpowering, like when I'm dozens of meters above the ground and the voice inside my head tells me to jump. I pressed the ring into Thumbringer's palm and closed his fingers around it.

"It wants to be possessed, doesn't it?" he said. "It's almost like it has a will of its own. I believe the pull is more than psychological. The cluster of elem creates a magnetic field. The attraction between two bodies is inversely proportional to the distance between them, so the closer the ring is to you the more you want it." Thumbringer slid the ring back over his left thumb. He sighed, relief flooding his features. "I used to smoke before I was incarcerated. The relaxation I achieve when I return the ring is even better than that first drag in the morning. Sometimes I remove the ring just so I can put it back on."

It had been a century since smoking was legal, but there were always people who broke the laws just to say that they did. Because smoking was illegal, when the government discovered someone doing it they rejected all medical procedures. Having some trouble with the law in the past I preferred not to associate with anyone the authorities might have an issue with. Some clients wanted to do business with me so badly they concealed their criminal activities. Occasionally their addiction overpowered them. Once such occurrence happened prior to completing a business exchange. The gentleman fled the venue, urgently. After covering myself in appropriate attire I sought him out. He was outside puffing away. After being relieved in one manner he was ready to be relieved in another. No longer smelling clean I sent him away, without refunding his deposit.

"So what does the ring do?" I asked. By the time my reverie had concluded Thumbringer's relief had leveled off into a refreshing calm. "Is it some kind of shield? Most of those heads missed you."

"I guess you could call it that, but it's more a psychological shield than a physical one. It protects the wearer, and by proximity his companions, by disrupting the psyche of those attacking him. A mild disruption is all it takes for a leg to slip or a talon to strike a meter to the left. A stone wall seems like it would do a better job, but stone can be broken. When someone's discombobulated they're moderately impotent until they recover. Well, time to go."

The packs Claw and Thumbringer wore were large, but not large enough. Each pack had numerous items tied to its exterior. Once they began to move those loose items began to oscillate. I expected some of them to detach and be left behind. None did. It was unlikely the first time they had packed in this manner. They were nearly out of sight before I sprinted to catch up to them.

Chapter 11

EARTH, WIND, FIRE AND WATER

The forest thinned once we left the lake. There wasn't a trail, but Claw and Thumbringer seemed to know where they were going.

Thumbringer's oration was too succinct. He described his ring's abilities---what it did---but not how it worked. How could a particle of energy disrupt a person's thoughts? Or cause air to cluster in specific patterns? I pestered Thumbringer until he relented.

"Elem are the building blocks of elemental energy manipulation. The table of elements you learned from chemistry class is just one way of organizing and describing matter. The ancients viewed the universe as consisting of four elements: earth, wind, fire and water. Did the two theories conflict? Not necessarily. They were just different points of view. The manner in which Limbo was formed has made it hypersensitive to change.

Mutations occur more frequently and more severely. Cell development is so accelerated that a person's body is able to regenerate itself before its essence is completely, and permanently, released."

"So we never die, not permanently?" I interjected.

"Our soul doesn't have time to reach heaven," Claw clarified.

"Murderers, thieves and rapists weren't the only people sentenced to Limbo," Thumbringer continued. "All walks of life, including physicians and scientists were sent here, some for diverging too extremely from standard practices, others for a brief immoral outburst. A few years after Dartmoor opened, a group of scientists began to study the planet's unique properties. They discovered the terra-forming process, still ongoing, produced a residue, the energy-enriched matter we now call elem. Four varieties were discovered, each pairing with one of the ancient elements. Through trial and error, some temporarily fatal, these scientists were able to isolate and retrieve elemental energies. Through additional experimentation, also causing temporary fatalities, they discovered they could be combined, like molecules, with each unique combination having a unique property. Matter was transformed, air moved, temperatures rose---when five elem bonded. If fewer than five elem were clustered nothing happened. If more, only five elem combined, but which five? It was unwise to allow certain groupings to occur randomly. An active elem grouping is called a penta. The scientists, calling themselves WIZARDS---half of them finding great power in the name, the other half, great humor---learned how to group the five elem in isolation. A trigger released their separation bonds, providing an almost instantaneous activation."

"It sounds like these user-friendly clusters of elem are Limbo's version of electricity, but portable, like batteries. More than that. Batteries and the devices they power wrapped into one. Why haven't I seen any?"

"Penta are very expensive. With a monopoly the Wizards can charge whatever they want."

"Wouldn't they make more money if they dropped the price? There can't be that many people that can afford to buy them."

"True," said Claw. "But that's how they like it. You see, the more penta that's out there the less powerful the Wizards become. They must be hording a stockpile, but for what?"

"Weren't there a couple of groups on Earth that stockpiled weapons like that?" I asked.

"Nuclear weapons. They each had their horde, in case the other side attacked."

"The difference is there's not another group to balance their power," said Thumbringer. "You think it's too late to become a scientist?"

"There have been a few groups that attempted to counter the Wizards' power. Amazons developed an extensive herbalism. Elem is not only found in isolation, but in the soil, in rocks, and in certain plants."

"So I might be able to use telekinesis if I ate a carrot, but not if I ate a tomato?" I conjectured.

"Maybe if you ate a lot of carrots, and lettuce, and celery, within a brief amount of time," Thumbringer responded. "Remember, it takes five elem to create a penta. The odds of randomly eating the right combination of plants to form a specific penta must be astronomical."

"But not impossible," said Claw. "Instantaneous combustion being the most obvious example."

"Tell me more about the types of elem." Now what where they again? "Earth. Wind. Fire." What was the other one? Sometimes when I thought really hard I perspired. A person sweated when they did physical labor. It was logical for mental labor to cause a similar reaction. Then why did everyone make fun of me in school when my forehead began to bead? "And water."

"Why don't we break for lunch instead." Did Thumbringer intentionally delay my gratification?

Claw and Thumbringer dropped their packs. They detached a water flask and a food bag from each pack. They had the common sense, and experience, to not bury them within their packs. Thumbringer ferociously gnawed on a piece of dried fish. Claw was polite enough to offer me a piece from his stash before he began eating. "Thanks. I'm sorry, but I don't have any way to pay for this." I did, but once I decided I no longer wished to be a barterer it no longer became a via option.

"Don't worry, miss. We got enough to share." A barterer never shared. Nothing was given away for free. Even my old clothes I sold instead of giving them away. When I ate at a restaurant I always took the leftovers home with me. My clients insisted I didn't have to do that, that they would send fresh food to my home. I couldn't allow the food to go to waste. There was one client who bought my uneaten food---from me---to humor me. I don't think he ever ate the food, but he was at least gentleman enough to take the food with him.

The best thing that could be said for the dried fish: it was palatable. Someone who sleeps on the ground, and in trees, isn't too picky. I had been a vegetarian, but that changed when I came to Limbo. There weren't many viable vegetarian options. I didn't eat meat for moral reasons so the transition wasn't THAT difficult. In a modern society everything was specialized, including food. Not so on Limbo. Convicts tended to be meat and potatoes kind of people. They rarely ate something that didn't once walk, fly, or swim. For desert I was given a handful of dried berries. Before living on Limbo I never imagined how good a bed the ground made.

Claw and Thumbringer put their packs back on. "Time to get up." Thumbringer made a swooping motion with his hand as he walked past me. Claw leaned down and extended a hand. I was concerned he might tip over, so laden was his pack, particularly the top of it. I reached up to take his hand. Before coming to Limbo I

71

wouldn't have allowed a man to help me like that. I was the type of woman who frowned when someone held the door open for her. If the man didn't follow the cue, I was content to wait him out until he went in first. I wasn't going to be in debt to anyone. Services provided were to be settled on the spot. In exchange for someone's apparent goodwill I would momentarily become subservient, someone taken care of because I couldn't take care of myself. In exchange for that extra second I gained from not exerting myself pivoting a door, I lost minutes fretting about my helplessness. But coming to Limbo changed that. A kindness didn't have to be a cloaked attempt to control. No one was in complete control here, where a monster could jump out at you any minute, sending you to a painful death, to be reborn as a grotesquely mutated version of your prior self.

"So what were you saying about the types of elem?" Thumbringer may have delayed my gratification, but I wasn't the type of person who let someone off the hook until I was completely satisfied. I bugged the hell out of my teachers by questioning them incessantly until I understood what they were trying to teach me. I didn't like going to school, but if I had to be there I sure wasn't going to waste my time not learning anything. I must have gotten a bit of a reputation. As I got older I was assigned to mostly new teachers. My zest for knowledge didn't wear them out like it did the older teachers who taught the same thing year after year. The new teachers believed my demands were commendable, instead of an attempt to waste valuable class time.

"All elem in its natural state glows slightly. Elem aqus has a slight blue tint. It's prevalent in liquid, but can be found in anything with a significant water content. The Amazons found it to be abundant in fruit."

"You think the Amazons would be willing to take in a runt as an apprentice?" In addition to learning elemental manipulation from them, I wouldn't have to worry about being molested. Not guaranteed, but less likely. They might be a pack of butch women primed to pounce on someone cute and naïve. The downside of being in an all-woman group was the lack of men. Those hormonal urges weren't going to go away. And I just liked being around men more than I did women. I was more a doer than a discusser.

Claw answered. "The Amazons no longer exist."

I was shocked. What could wipe out a group of giants? How was that even possible, with re-creation? "What happened?"

"There was a schism within the Amazons. To prevent the inevitable conflict with the Wizards some of them chose to join them. It would also fulfill other needs that had been growing in some of the women. The Amazons intimidated most men. Confident women did that, especially confident women who rewarded poor behavior with a group rebuttal. Scientists didn't have the reputation of being charmers, so they were as desperate for companionship as the women."

"Are you telling me the Wizards and Amazons merged to bore?"

My language shocked Claw. Thumbringer was amused. "I think the relationships they ended up having were more substantial, but you are essentially correct. We believe most of the things that occur in history are either noble or horrendous, but a majority are mundane. Sex, companionship, raising children, those types of things happen more often than the writing of constitutions, the construction of magnificent wonders, or the fighting of deadly wars. Those Amazons joining the Wizards became too powerful, forcing their sisters to flee. The conflicts between the two groups were getting nasty. It was only a matter of time before the battle would become physical. Those that fled eventually settled in the Honey Mountains. Being part of the Frontier, it was one of those areas of Limbo that was inhabited by the morally extreme. Being a large group of woman they couldn't help but be drawn to chaos."

"What's that suppose to mean?"

"Their humanity was eventually re-created out of them. The larger, more refined version that exists today call themselves Titans, to distinguish themselves from the gents, those brutish monstrosities that pillage the lands around them. Those joining the Wizards now consider themselves to be Wizards."

"Neither group is likely to welcome someone new into their fold, are they?"

"You could establish your own tribe of Amazons," Claw encouraged.

"No thanks. I have enough trouble looking after myself. Now, how about fire elem?"

"Elem fiero has a red tint to it," Thumbringer continued. "It is commonly found in hot areas, in deserts or volcanoes, or in spicy food. Elem aero remains airborne until it collides with an object. The most likely place for this to occur is on mountains, or in trees. It is prevalent in leaves and needles, but primarily in fresh ones, ones that have been plucked or freshly fallen. Elem terra is dark green, verging on brown. It's found in soil, or things that grow in the soil."

"And you can just look under a rock or sift through some water to find elem?"

"Find them, yes. Collecting them? That takes some skill. Using a collection rod helps. It's a magnetized device that attracts elem like a magnet collecting metal shavings. It's also a reservoir that holds up to ten elem. The proper storage of elem is crucial. Five elem without proper separation will cluster, forming a penta."

"Is it possible to collect elem without one of these collection rods?"

"It's possible, but more difficult. Have you noticed whenever you swat at a flying insect it tends to no longer be in the place it was a fraction of a second ago? Elem has similar properties. Magnetism attracts them, but almost everything else has the opposite effect. Picture yourself trying to swim towards an object in water. Every sim closer seems to push that object that much farther away. You must not only concern yourself with fluid dynamics, but thermal dynamics, and earth displacement."

74

"Isn't there some class I can take?"

"Darling, why fish with a pole when you got a net. That's why they make collection rods."

"So you have one?"

"Four actually, each of us," said Claw. "One for each variety of elem. You can't safely mix different kinds of elem, even with them retaining some separation in the rod. The worst thing that could happen if the same elem form a penta is a big puddle, or a strong wind."

"Or a fire."

"That might be dangerous. But worst things happen when different varieties of elem mix. That's when truly powerful effects occur."

"Can I see one of the rods?"

"No," said Thumbringer bluntly.

"He means not right now," Claw specified.

"We'll see."

Talk about your delayed gratification. Handing me a present, then taking it away before I can open it.

Chapter 12

VIRGIN

We---meaning Claw and Thumbringer---set up camp in a clearing a hundred meters from a creek. "Wouldn't it be more pleasant if we were closer to the water?" I asked.

"Pleasant for the predators that hunt this time of day,"

Thumbringer replied.

After the tent was erected a fire was built. "An additional precaution to limit our re-creations," Claw enlightened.

Thumbringer handed me a pot. "Here, fill it with water from the creek."

"I thought it wasn't safe this time of day."

"Yell if something begins to attack you."

Let's just say I was quicker returning from the creek than walking towards it.

I handed the pot to Thumbringer, who set it directly into the fire. Within minutes it was boiling. Thumbringer dropped dried meat and vegetables into the water. It didn't take long for the clearing to be permeated with succulent odors. "Won't this attract animals?" I asked.

"How many animals do you see cooking their food? The animals in the area already know we are here. Most are afraid of people. The others are afraid of this fire."

"And I assume we intend to keep the fire going all night?"

"I don't intend to stay up, but you're welcome to."

Claw came to my rescue again. "Smoke from the fire is nearly as beneficial as the flames. There'll still be some lofting up from it when we wake."

The soup was delicious. It was starting to get chilly. The warmth it brought I needed as much as the nourishment. "Can I see an elem collector now?"

"You're persistent, aren't you, Darling," said Thumbringer. "And I imagine you'll continue to pester us about it until we show you." My response was a focused glare. Thumbringer rumbled through his pack, pulling out a 30 sim long cylinder seconds later. It looked like a flute, but with just one hole at its base, and a knob, near its opposite end.

Thumbringer handed it to me. After all the buildup I became hesitant taking it. "Do you have any elem in it...right now?"

"Do you see those faint blue dots?" There were five of

them, evenly spaced, stretching a third of the rod's length.

"I'm not going to release them accidentally am I?"

"Not unless you twist that knob. The rod is in collecting mode. The worst you could do is collect additional water elem."

"What if I collect a fire, air, or earth elem? Will the rod explode?"

"There's a failsafe built into the rod. If there's water elem in it---already---that's all it will collect until the rod is emptied."

I snatched the rod out of Thumbringer's hand. I examined it, including looking down its barrel. Why do people always do that with loaded firearms? I was careful to keep my hand off that knob. For the elem to be discharged I would have to accidentally twist it. The experience was underwhelming. I handed the rod back to Thumbringer, who immediately placed it in his pack.

"Maybe we could do some prospecting before we leave tomorrow," I suggested.

"We still have a ways to go before we reach Capetown," said Thumbringer.

In my sweetest voice I responded, "I'm sure we don't have that far to go. Just a few minutes tomorrow morning. Half-an-hour tops."

Thumbringer loudly tightened the ties on his backpack. Well, that didn't sound like he was agreeing with me. I don't remember the last time I didn't get my way when I used that voice. Not since puberty. First I turn into to this hairy cave woman, now my feminine wiles misfire.

The sleeping arrangements, although not what I preferred, were adequate. The tent was large enough for the three of us, but just barely. Each of the men had bedrolls. Thumbringer was eager to share his with me. "If you are afraid something might happen because of your attraction to me we can sleep head to toe."

"But won't certain parts of our body still be aligned?"

"Technically, but they'll be facing the wrong direction."

"If you think that matters, you've been living a sheltered

77

life." Thumbringer's mischievous grin suggested he hadn't.

"You can use my bedroll if you wish," Claw hesitantly volunteered. "You would have it all to yourself, of course."

"What would you sleep in?"

"The ground isn't that hard."

"But it's starting to get cold. I accept your offer if you agree to share it with me. I promise the most I'll do is snug up to you."

"I don't require any promises," pleaded Thumbringer.

"You must lead a lonely life," I told him.

"But not from the lack of trying."

Thumbringer was not completely left out. I agreed to sleep in the middle. For my own protection, he insisted. If there wasn't some truth to that statement I would have insisted I sleep on the outside.

"So, Dinga, what did you do before you were incarcerated?" asked Thumbringer. It wasn't exactly a lullaby, but I appreciated the attempt. "I'm guessing you were a librarian, probably with your hair in a bun, a constant look of disdain on your face."

"So you made the assumption I am both reserved and uptight? Do any of the reserved women you know defoliate?"

"I thought it was one of your re-creation mutations."

"Let's just say I was well respected in what I did. I acted professionally, and in doing so was more than adequately compensated."

"Now I'm really curious. Real estate agent, perhaps. I'm guessing you aimed to please, not stopping until your clients were completely satisfied." He got at least part of that right.

The conversation we were having was beginning to make me uncomfortable. It wasn't that I was ashamed at what I used to do. It was no longer part of my life. It was like leaving high school. You may have had some good times, but your new life was going to be even better.

"What do you do with elem after you collect it? Do you just save it until you need it? To strike a predator with a lightning bolt?

Or drown pestilent insects in a torrential downpour?"

"Neither Thumbringer or I is a Wizard," Claw declared. "We don't know what every combination of elem will do. We have created a few penta on our own. They can be a life saver if they're properly mixed and manipulated."

"If we aren't careful, we could get ourselves killed," Thumbringer added.

"Elemental energy isn't a toy."

"What do you do with it then, if you don't plan to use it?" I asked. "All of it."

"Every month or so we take our accumulated stockpile of elem to the Wizard's Keep," said Thumbringer.

"It's near Gulag, Limbo's pseudo-capital. There is no centralized government here, self-preservation being more important than empire building," Claw explained. "Gulag is more of a trade center. City-states like Capetown administer day to day existence."

"I imagine there's a lot of money to be made from selling elem."

"Oh, there is," said Thumbringer. "If one is willing to risk their humanity in the wilderness, they can make hundreds of gold a year."

"We're paid a gold per elem if we deliver it directly to the Wizard's Keep. Substantially less if we go through a middle-man."

"How many elem do you typically harvest each month?"

"Between the two of us, thirty or forty," Thumbringer answered. "Sometimes, much more. Sometimes, just a handful."

"So these Wizards buy elem from prospectors, then re-sell them to the public? Is the average person able to manipulate elem properly to get the desired effect? They must come with an instruction manual or something, but who can figure those things out?"

"Oh, the Wizards do more than provide retail outlets," said Claw. "They package the elem as penta."

79

"Isn't that dangerous? I thought when five elem mix they become active."

"They do, but the same thing that prevents elem from mixing in a collection rod keeps them from mixing in the packaging the Wizards provide. The most common is a capsule, which is swallowed. Once the digestive juices breaks down the barriers between the elem, the elem bond, forming a penta. Being constructed of the same matter as the elem we act as natural conductors."

"What if we haven't been re-created, our bodies haven't been rebuilt with indigenous materials?"

"It's unlikely those people can harness elemental energy," said Thumbringer. "But how many people on Limbo haven't been re-created once or twice?"

"The apprehension swallowing one of those penta capsules must be unbearable. I have trepidation taking an extra-strength pain reliever."

"If you survive the rush, it's worth it. Imagine combining being electrocuted with having an orgasm."

It was amazing some of the freakish things my clients wanted to do. You would think after thousands of transactions you would see it all. Many of their suggestions I had to decline, if not for my safety, for theirs. There was a certain professionalism I had to retain, that included my clients not receiving permanent damage or dying. "Addiction must be rampant."

"For a select few. Capsules---stones, as they're more commonly called---are expensive: ten gold if sold from a Wizard-certified vendor, much more on the black market. There is also the discomfort a person feels with so much energy flowing through them. It feels like a combination of painful urination and insects crawling over you. Some people feel the rush more than compensates for the negative aspects. There are elem addicts, but their numbers are small."

"Most addicts bypass capsules," added Claw. "There's a

discount if they buy in bulk. A device similar to a collection rod is used. Up to ten penta can be stored. Like collection rods there is a safeguard built in to prevent mixing. If ten charges aren't enough there's a third device that's supposed to never run out."

Thumbringer held up his right hand. The ring on it was barely visible against the flickering silhouette of the campfire on the tent's canvas wall. "Rings cost 1000 gold. How many addicts you know have that much money? They'll have to be either independently wealthy or constantly stealing. These rings are perpetually charged, but within certain parameters. I've heard of addicts so consumed by their lust for elemental surge---those that discharge three or four penta a day---to have actually drained their ring."

"Or burnt it out."

"Once a cluster of elem obtains a critical mass the elem become regenerating. I don't know if they are actually created, or those in the area are simply attracted to the mass. Either way, as long as the ring isn't abused, it can be discharged indefinitely."

"And you just found this ring?" I asked Thumbringer. "Or did you take it from someone, or thing?"

"Providence. Or blind luck. I found it my first hour on Limbo. It's the reason I haven't died yet in my five years here."

"So you really are a virgin?"

"Are you interested in de-flowering me?"

"I thought someone who wasn't re-created couldn't use penta?"

"Not actively. This ring is passive. It does all the work. It protects me without direction."

"So if you were being attacked by something and you had penta that could strike back you wouldn't be able to do anything?"

"Oh, I would do something about it. Living in the Limboan wilderness for many years I've learned to take care of myself. If my fighting skills appeared to be inadequate I wouldn't think twice about running. Sometimes a good defense can trump a good offense. Our large friend here on the other hand would rather tussle."

"It invigorates me."

"Sometimes Claw plays too rough."

"Bones aren't as hard as they used to be."

"It's not the bones getting weaker, it's you getting stronger. You see, Dinga, Claw's re-creations have caused certain ogre tendencies. He even found himself in the Frontier once."

"Until I repented."

"His next re-creation returned him to Neutrality."

"So Miss Dinga, I can relate to your jet-lag---both of us being members of the thousand kay re-creation club."

"You're larger than normal, but you look less mutated than I."

"Why, thank you. I try to take care of myself."

"Claw is one of the lucky ones. He's mutating gracefully."

"Do you have penta other than that ring, in case we're attacked in the middle of the night or something?" I asked.

"Three stones," Thumbringer answered. "The one we found we have no idea what it might do."

"Are there people that careless, who drop penta and not look for them?"

"Sometimes when they drop them they are a bit distracted, Darling."

"Their biggest distraction is dying," Claw clarified. "As you have experienced, it happens quite often on Limbo. The only thing a person takes with them when they die is their soul. Their decaying body, and possessions, stay behind. If you want to become a scavenger watch for vultures circling. You're more than likely to find something valuable beneath them."

"What do the two stones you're familiar with do?"

"You're full of questions, aren't you? I like a woman who does more in bed than sleep, but...."

"I'm an infant remember. Aren't children supposed to ask a

lot of questions?"

"We need to leave something for tomorrow, don't we? Now go to sleep, Dinga." Like that was going to happen. There were some things a person shouldn't do before going to bed: exercise, drink caffeine, watch scary holographs, and...get riled up about something. To remedy the excitement I felt Christmas Eve, I opened my presents as soon as my parents went to bed. I wasn't able to re-wrap the presents very well, but my parents never said anything. I couldn't do the same here. I could, but I wasn't willing to pay the price if caught. Claw and Thumbringer may seem like good guys, but inmates have a tendency to favor their less-savory attributes when riled.

Come on, sleep. As a young girl I used to snug up to a large teddy bear. One day my father decided I was too big to have a stuffed animal. To make a statement, he didn't just throw it away, he burned it. Until my mother's beatings got worst it was my most disturbing memory. Claw snored softly, almost sounding like a purr. I tentatively snuggled up to him. It didn't wake him. I hugged him tighter. I don't remember crying during the night, but when I woke the next morning there was a salty rind around my eyes.

Chapter 13

GLITTER

I woke to the smell---and sound---of bacon frying. The one fond memory of my father was him making breakfast for my mother and me every first-day. He even placed the food on a tray and took it to my mother. He would have also given me breakfast in bed, but I was always too excited to wait. It also was the one time each week I had my father to myself when he wasn't in a bad mood. Every girl loved their father---even those who eventually killed theirs---but I loved him a little more the first couple of hours every week.

I had the tent to myself. I was tempted to stretch out and extend my sleep, but the wafting odors were too tempting. Did I also smell bread and coffee? One of the advantages of not having hair was not looking like a wreck when you woke. I didn't have a mirror, but from the feel of my mane, it had to be matted in the worse manner. I attempted to pat it down, going so far as applying saliva, but it persisted to stick out, like it was wire. Adhering to the adage MISERY LOVES COMPANY I stroked my hairy arms and legs. Well, I no longer have to worry about unwanted advances.

I undid the tent ties and walked out. "Good morning, Darling," said Thumbringer as he removed a snake from a spit with makeshift tongs: sticks held like chopsticks. On a flat rock at the perimeter of the fire a gooey paste was beginning to turn golden brown. A dark liquid, with darker specs floating in it, boiled in a kettle in the center of the fire.

"I never imagined a snake smelling like this."

"And it tastes as good as it smells, Miss Dinga." Using a cloth to protect himself, Claw grabbed the kettle by its handle. Before pouring the liquid into the three wooden mugs beside him he covered them with a threadbare cloth. As he poured, coffee grounds were left on top of the cloth. Once all three mugs were full he flung the coffee grounds behind him. He handed me a mug, then Thumbringer.

Before tasting it I brought it up to my nose. "It sure smells like coffee."

"Oh, it is. One of those genetic engineers who designed this planet must have been a connoisseur. We were permitted a few horticultural luxuries."

84

I cautiously sipped it. After getting past being scalded I was able to enjoy the thick, rich flavor. It tasted very organic, almost gamey, like how a person might compare eating duck to chicken.

"I should have warned you, Miss Dinga. The coffee is hot."

"I should have known better. It just came out of the fire. If the blisters on my tongue don't go away soon I'm sure my next re-creation will remedy them."

"There you go. I like positive people. Here, try some bread. I prefer mine wrapped around snake, but it's also good on its own." Thumbringer tore off a chunk of bread, placed it on a wooden plate, then handed it to me. The outside of it was burnt, and the inside, doughy, but that thin layer between was perfect.

"What's in it?"

"A little bit of this, a little bit of that. Things I collected along the way."

After taking a bite of the chunk of bread Thumbringer had given him, Claw grimaced. "It tastes like feek. Pardon my language, Miss Dinga."

"Some of the healthiest grain grows in that stuff. Highly nutritious."

Claw spit out what was left in his mouth.

"The fire killed anything harmful in it."

Thumbringer stretched the crispy snake out on a flat stone. He struck it multiple times with a long dagger.

"It's definitely dead now," I commented.

Thumbringer placed a 10 sim segment on my plate, then Claw's, then finally his own. True to his word, he wrapped a scrap of bread around it, like it was a hot dog. After the first bite he raised an eyebrow. "A bit tough, but still tasty. Next time I'll try to slow cook it, maybe bury it in coals."

It was chewy, but good, a cross between calamari and bacon.

After breakfast I collected the dirty dishes and headed to the creek. "IF SOMEONE ATTACKS YOU, JUST YELL!" Thumbringer bellowed. Nothing did. Before I met Claw and Thumbringer it wouldn't have mattered too much if I died. Death was just a temporary condition on Limbo, a break in someone's routine. Leaving now would be devastating. Claw and Thumbringer may not be family, but they were the closest thing I've had so far on Limbo. How long would it take before they became irritated with me?

Before heading back to camp I took care of some business that didn't need to be discussed, then made myself more presentable. In a relatively calm portion of the creek I was able to view a distorted image of myself. Well, you'll never be considered a looker again, will you? That does take some of the pressure off me. Not having the capacity to be beautiful gave me permission not to try.

When I returned to camp the tent was taken down. I handed the washed dishes to Thumbringer. He placed them in his pack. Claw hauled the lodging.

"Can you show me the three stones you have before we leave?" Without argument Claw did what I requested. Considering our conversation the night before, and my tenacity, he was probably expecting it. He detached a pouch from his belt. On a cloth he poured its contents: four gold coins, eleven silver, eight copper, and two dark gray stones.

Thumbringer emptied his pouch on a similar cloth: four gold coins, eleven silver, five copper, and one stone.   Dark stains streaked the material.

"What made those?"

"You don't want to know, Miss Dinga," Claw responded.

"It's a cleaning rag," Thumbringer declared.

"What do you clean with it?"

"You don't want to know."

"Whatever is clinging to it after a battle."

"So that's...." Breakfast---and possibly dinner---began to work its way back up.

"I warned you, Miss Dinga."

"Not all of it's from blood. There are some vile things in the wilderness, some acidic enough to eat a hole through my sword if I'm not diligent in its grooming. Blood takes weeks to rust a well-made blade."

Claw handed me one of his stones. "Please don't lose it Miss Dinga. And make sure you don't put it in your mouth." Like I would ever do that.

Calling them STONES wasn't a stretch. They looked like oblong pebbles, but with markings on them. The markings were similar to the ones on Thumbringer's ring. Three swooshes separated two pairs of chevrons, stacked with a vertical bar under each. Trees? It was unlikely trees represented fire. Possibly air, because air elem sometimes gets trapped in a forest's canopy. More likely earth. Trees grew in the ground. What might happen if earth is mixed with water? "This stone creates mud?" I conjectured.

"Clever, she is," said Thumbringer. "It's a transmutation stone. It transforms a hard substance, usually stone, into a soft substance: mud. How about the stone beside it?"

With my arm extended and holding my breath, I returned the transmutation stone to the cloth. I was scared that just touching it would detonate it. Women's perspiration was supposed to be more acidic than a man's. Considering how few women there were on Limbo did the Wizards even consider how these stones might react being in a woman's prescience? I forgot about the Amazons merging with the Wizards. No, touch alone wouldn't dissolve the barriers between the elem.

I examined the second stone. It had two tree runes like the first stone, but instead of swooshes it had dots. Air? What does one get by mixing earth and wind? A storm? A tornado? "This stone creates a tornado?"

Thumbringer smiled. "Not as close as last time. It's a transportation stone. So many kilos can be transported so many kays."

87

"How many kilos, and how many kays?"

"That depends," said Claw. "The more that is transported the less far it can travel, and vice-versa. It also depends on the user, how well he or she manipulates the penta. The consumer version is less elastic, but there is still some flexibility."

"Consumer version?"

"The ones the Wizards sell. Safeguards are added to reduce risk."

"And the potency," added Thumbringer.

"To retain their power the Wizards prevent others from gaining it. Alchemists, those that mix their own elem, create much stronger versions of the penta than is peddled to the public."

"So if one wanted to compete with the Wizards they would have to make their own penta?"

"If one was foolish enough to attempt it," Thumbringer countered.

"How far could a person travel using the stone?"

"Fifty kays, I believe," Claw replied.

"So the three of us could travel more than fifteen kays, almost instantaneous, if we needed to?"

"More or less. But I don't think I could be counted on to place us where we wanted to go."

"We could end up inside a tree?"

"Not that," said Thumbringer. "We are prevented from being transported into solids, or hundreds of meters into the air. I believe it's our subconscious that saves us."

"May I look at the unknown stone?" I asked.

"By all means, Darling. Infants have been known to do wondrous things, but someone still needs to change their diapers." There was one thing I could say about Thumbringer, he wasn't trying to win me over with false praises.

Concern rippled Claw's features. "Careful, Miss Dinga. We must be particularly cautious when handling penta of an unknown nature. That's why we kept this one separated from the others. I shudder to think what would happen if we accidentally activated it. Instead of the rock wall in front of us melting, a terrible wind might blow us into it."

The third stone had an earth rune and three wind runes, plus a rune I hadn't seen so far: a cross. "This stone has a fire component?" I conjectured.

"No," Claw replied hesitantly.

"I thought there were just four elements."

Claw and Thumbringer shuddered. "Maybe we shouldn't have shown her the stone," Claw declared.

"She was going to find out eventually," said Thumbringer. "It's better she's aware of the fifth element, so she can be properly fearful of it."

"Some people call it the death rune."

"Or the soul rune. Black elem is created when someone dies, that moment between death and re-creation."

My mouth dropped. "Are you saying black elem are stolen souls?"

"It's just a rumor," Claw emphasized.

"Black elem has to come from somewhere. A fifth element has been associated with spirit---historically."

"What happens when black elem bonds with four other elem?" I asked.

"No one knows, for sure," said Thumbringer. "Again, there are rumors. This is the first black stone we've possessed. We bought the other two stones from the penta shop in Capetown. This one we found."

"Life is destroyed, or instantaneously transformed," Claw conjectured.

"Or possibly created," said Thumbringer.

"Have you thought to ask the Wizards?" I asked. "Or sell it back to them?"

Thumbringer shuddered.

"Black elem isn't supposed to exist," said Claw. "If we even mention it in the prescience of a Wizard we'll be denied access to their keep. We'll be blacklisted. Elem prospecting is our livelihood."

I verbally hypothesized as I examined the stone more closely. "Wind is prominent, so motion must be involved, possibly the air itself. Earth is also involved. Maybe transportation again, but it's less significant in this penta, so movement is just a secondary characteristic. Life has to be involved, with air and earth moving. A sentient tornado?"

"AN AIR ELEMENTAL!" Thumbringer exclaimed. "Why didn't I see that? This stone creates an air elemental."

"Why would anyone want to create such a creature?" asked Claw.

"As a weapon I imagine," I stated.

"But if we released it could we control it?" asked Claw. "I fear it would just as likely attack us?"

"Of course we would be able to control it," said Thumbringer, "to some degree. Why would it have been created if it was harmful to its user?"

"It wouldn't, but what if it had a built in safeguard in case someone unauthorized obtained it? If I was trying to keep a secret, I wouldn't want the person discovering it to live long enough to share it with others."

"But why go through the trouble of killing someone if they're going to be re-created in a few hours?" I asked.

"Those newly re-created have what we commonly refer to as re-creation fever," Thumbringer responded. "They're confused for hours, sometimes days." I definitely felt disoriented. "People have learned to not believe the ravings of the recently reborn--- likely the origin of most of the rumors of black elem---that's why they are viewed more as legend than fact."

"How about we do some prospecting before we head out?" suggested Claw.

"We still have a ways to travel today," Thumbringer insisted.

"Not that far. We traveled extra yesterday, JUST IN CASE. I'd rather our JUST IN CASE be prospecting instead of being attacked by something."

"You make a good point. Prospecting is definitely more fun than fighting."

"I wouldn't say that."

"That birthday party didn't go over very well, did it? When we jumped out at you and shouted SURPRISE we didn't expect you to decapitate two of us."

"I apologized afterwards."

"Now we know. Come along, Darling. It's time to teach you prospecting." Thumbringer didn't have to tell me twice. The men left their packs at the campsite and headed into the woods.

I couldn't help myself. I smiled from ear to ear. I floated on air as I ran with abandon after them. I expected to see colorful sparkly bits everywhere, like someone had spilled glitter. Nothing. "Do we just look at the ground, like we're hunting dropped coins at a carnival?"

"More like fishing. Find a strong, forked stick like this." Thumbringer picked up a stick 125 sims long. It was completely stripped of bark. It split three ways about two-thirds down its length. I found a four-pronged stick, longer and wider than Thumbringer's. If Thumbringer's stick was satisfactory, mine was even better. The bark was dark in a couple of spots and damp to the touch. It definitely had more character. Thumbringer smiled at my choice. I glowed. It was like my father approved of me.

"Now, rake the leaves and pine needles. You don't have to dig down. Just stir up the loose material on top. If you see something glowing, it's probably elem."

"Prospecting should be peaceful, Miss Dinga," said Claw, a ways away, but still visible. "It's not very exciting, but it can be relaxing." It was exhilarating: a scavenger hunt, an Easter egg hunt, and gambling, all rolled up into one. "Imagine you're fishing, wiggling your line to get the fish's attention. Yell if you think you found something."

"Like we really had to tell her that," said Thumbringer as his route gradually diverged from mine. He was much more animated than Claw. His large companion may have viewed prospecting as peaceful bliss, but Thumbringer was all business. "They'll probably hear you in Capetown when you find your first elem. Virgins are so loud. Oh, a final thought. Stay close, within sight of one of us. Yell if you're being attacked, emphasizing the lack of pleasure you're having."

Like all novices, I thought I would be successful the first time. On the first scrape, my stick broke. I heard something that sounded suspiciously like a giggle. I looked towards Thumbringer. He had his back to me. The second stick I found worked much better. It didn't break until the fourth scrape. Another giggle. I took my time finding my third stick. This one looked just like Thumbringer's except it was split just two ways at the end. I settled for it. I was just learning today anyway.

"DINGA, OVER HERE!" shouted Thumbringer with reserved excitement. He had experienced the discovery hundreds of times, but it was to be my first. I rushed towards him, dropping my stick. DAMN, I thought halfway to my destination. I hoped I could find it again. Thumbringer moved out of the way when I arrived. The forest floor had been stripped bare to the earth. In the center of the patch, a green spec as small as a grain of sand glowed faintly. "That's about all the time we can spend gawking. We don't want to lose it. We can live a week comfortably in a city off just a couple of these." He unsnapped a metal cylinder from his belt. He brought it near the elem, then depressed the knob on its side. The elem was sucked into the cylinder. "Twenty minutes more until we go. Make the most of them."

I found my stick and began digging frantically. The stick caught in the ground and broke. FEEK! "You're much too impatient," spoke a voice I hadn't heard in two days. I looked around. "Over here, to your left, 50 meters away."

There he was, on a branch, about eye level. I was compelled to run up to him and embrace him, until halted by the perceived inappropriateness of doing so to a reptilian bird. "You could stroke my back ridges instead." I forgot he could read my mind.

"Where have you been? I thought you had been killed, or worse, that you no longer liked me." I rubbed his back. He cooed in response, his eyes half closed.

"Never think that."

"Then why haven't I seen you for two days?"

"The humans. They don't like people like me."

"Demons?"

"I don't like that word."

"But it's not a bad word. It's just a label. Claw and Thumbringer like demons. They find them interesting. They even have demon friends."

"Humans just say that to sound hip. Meeting a mutant isn't the same as being their friend."

"They aren't critical of me. They just tell me what I need to hear. They're generous. They share their food and shelter."

"Maybe you should go back to them then."

"And they're showing me how to find elem."

"That stuff that glows in the dark? So much of it is near my burrow it keeps me up at night."

"Can you take me there?"

"It's 10 kays away. Won't your HUMAN friends miss you?"

"Couldn't you show them too?" No response. Still no response. I attempted to rub Fred's back ridges again, but he flew off before I could reach him. I guess that meant no. IF YOU CAN STILL HEAR MY THOUGHTS, I WOULD STILL LIKE TO BE YOUR FRIEND, EVEN IF YOU DON'T SHOW ME THE ELEM.

With Fred's departure squelching the excitement from the hunt, I sought Claw and Thumbringer. Neither had found an additional elem.

"That's how it goes, sometimes," said Claw. "I enjoy the

process as much as the product: walking through the woods, being one with nature. But Thumbringer, he views failure as an affront to his manhood."

"I wouldn't say that. It does really piss me off, though."

"You did find ONE."

"That's true, and under these unfavorable conditions."

"Thumb, what's that over there?" In addition to using a double-headed hammer, one side jagged and sharp, Claw carried a sling shot. Wasn't a bow more effective? Sure, but they reminded him of a harp, and real men don't pluck harps. He loaded the sling with pebbles---relative to his size. To me they were miniature boulders.

Hey, that's Fred. "Don't shoot," I pleaded. "He's a friend of mine."

"He looks more like a pet," said Thumbringer.

"I thought you've known a lot of demons."

"Mutated humans, but this thing...."

"I like him," said Claw. "He's kind of pretty."

"Thank you?" Fred replied hesitantly, still keeping his distance. "I don't think I have ever been called pretty before. Someone so pretty would look less so if he was splattered by those stones you have in that sling."

"A precaution," spoke Thumbringer. Not having the same prejudices as Claw, he carried a bow, cocked.

"I told you they wouldn't respect me," Fred whined to me.

"Of course we respect you," Thumbringer countered. "Do you think we cock a bow for everyone?"

"Put down your weapons," I insisted. "I told you, Fred here is my friend. And Fred, don't take their rude dispositions as a denial. It's their way of selling hello."

"Bore your mother."

"See. This is how they speak to me and we're good friends."

My argument was good enough for Claw. He was a loyal chap. It was logical that a friend of a friend would automatically become his friend. Thumbringer wasn't as trusting. He didn't put his bow away, but he did lower it.

A flash of comprehension flooded Claw's features. "You wouldn't happen to know Beaver Haunt Woods, would you?"

Fred flew closer to us, landing on a branch a meter above us. "Why do you ask?"

"She gave us refuge after losing a battle with a retch plant."

Fred made the most awful sound. It sounded like he was gagging, but he was smiling. "So two humans really were to blame for stinking up her cave. We mocked her choice of food and the odiferous fallout. We believed she had fabricated the befriending of two unfortunate souls."

"How could you make fun of such a kind person?"

Fred's shoulders slumped. He looked down at the ground. "We were only having fun. I need to apologize the next time I see her. I took advantage of her, because she was an easy target. She's a member of my carnivores anonymous group. I wasn't being very supportive. I should have applauded her choice of eating beans instead of foxes."

"If you stunk that bad," I asked, "how was Beaver able to tolerate you living with her?"

"She doesn't have scent glands," said Thumbringer.

"I never knew that," said Fred.

"People perceived her as having low intelligence because she couldn't distinguish one odor from another," said Claw. "Without being able to smell her prey she failed as a hunter. To conceal her shame she became a vegetarian."

Fred was speechless, which was a first for him. But our break didn't last. "I'll take you to the elem now, if you're ready."

"Elem?" Thumbringer was somehow able to appear simultaneously dumbfounded and ecstatic.

"Fred lives in an area practically drowning in the stuff," I explained.

"Claw might find you pretty, but I think you're the most

95

gorgeous thing I've ever seen."

"How about you Dinga, do you think I'm more pretty or more gorgeous?"

"I'm thinking if your head becomes any larger you might have trouble flying. Fred, this is Thumbringer---."

"Northern Spine."

"And Claw---."

"Raspberry Mountains."

"Why don't I have a last name like everyone else?"

"Where did you enter Limbo?" Thumbringer asked.

"I don't know."

"Well, that's the problem. A Limboan's last name matches the place they were reborn."

"If I never learn that?"

"Then you'll just be known as Dinga." Not having a surname, a family name, was like losing my family all over again. For me to feel like I belonged I HAD to have a last name. How was I going to learn what that first prairie was called? No one was there to ask? Actually, there was. A man watching as the dogs attacked, who I saw again at the Musky Foot in Briarwood. People say things come in threes. I needed to see him again. Not only see him, but actually talk to him this time.

Chapter 14

DISCHARGE

It took two hours to reach Fred's borrow---one of his burrows. Apparently, a...whatever Fred was...had as many homes as sailors had girlfriends. We weren't going to reach Capetown today. But if what Fred said was true---about the piles of elem---it was worth a day's delay. A girl could give up a warm bed and bath one more day if she was showered in riches.

We had to squeeze through a hole at the base of a large tree with waxy leaves. By large I mean large enough for a decent size room to be whittled out of its interior. Fred's borrow was snug enough to feel cozy, but roomy enough to move around in. "It looks comfortable," I told him, "but doesn't seem very safe. The entrance is too accessible." The opening shrank until it was too small to stick an arm through. "Can you show me how you did that, one day?" I asked.

"Only if it becomes available to you," said Fred.

"I wonder what combination of elem will make that happen," I thought aloud.

"Remember, it's not just the penta, but how it's manipulated," said Claw. "I've spoken to a few Wizards---outside their keep. Transients are more open. There is as much an art to manipulating penta as there is a science. The intensities of each elem in a penta can be manipulated, as can their arrangement within the penta. In its most basic form a penta has 50,000 concentration-position permutations. Each creates a slightly different effect. A Wizard can isolate these permutations mentally, the most gifted and trained Wizards being the most successful at it. Allegedly, all permutations of every penta have been cataloged. Millions of permutations if elem essence is included."

"I knew penta manipulation was complicated, but...it's too much. How can anyone learn all that?" More than a college degree. Also a masters---and a doctorate.

"Dinga has agreed to be my apprentice," stated Fred.

"Good luck." Thumbringer smiled widely at me. Did he insinuate my incompetence, or Fred's? "So where are these piles of elem you...?" Before the words were completely out of his mouth, a score of glowing specs beneath a bank of caves, 50 meters from the entrance to Fred's home, caught his eye. Some of them glowed green, others blue, red, and yellow. I let out a deep breath. None of them were black. How eerie would that be to harvest someone's soul? We would have become grave robbers.

After the entrance was enlarged, Thumbringer dashed towards the elem, a collection rod in his hand. After a minute of frantic vacuuming he suddenly stopped, staring dumbfounded at the rod. "I've actually filled it up. That's never happened before."

Claw's rod also became full. "I don't believe it. There's too much to collect. I'm going to have to abandon some of it."

"It sounds like elem has been here for quite awhile," I said. "Maybe it'll still be here when you return."

Thumbringer smiled, a continuous arc from one ear to the other. "And maybe with more elem arriving all the time. There must be a vein running through here."

"I've never heard of elem behaving like that," stated Claw.

"Once elem is collected, it isn't lost?" I asked.

"When elem is consumed it changes form, no longer existing...as elem. But more appears, like Gaea is radiating the stuff. We have an unlimited, but slowly produced supply."

Something black and hairy leapt at Claw from one of the caves. It was as large as the prospector, but with twice as many appendages. Claw screamed as it nibbled on his shoulder.

Thumbringer charged, a sword replacing his collecting rod. A spindly black leg was cut in two. Hobbled on seven legs, it returned to its hole. Claw convulsed, then vomited.

A second spider leapt from a hole, this time at me. Pebbles showered the ground in front of me, pummeling the creature, first knocking it down, then crushing its exoskeleton. Fred dove from an elevation I wasn't aware he obtained, stopping three meters short of me, then hovered in a defensive stance.

More spiders leapt from the holes, but hesitant to move past the carcass of their fallen comrade. Thumbringer's ring glowed. Maybe that's what was keeping them away.

"Why didn't that thing work earlier?" I asked while watching Claw vomit a second time.

Thumbringer stood beside him protectively. "He probably wasn't close enough to me. Sometimes it doesn't work at all. It doesn't offer immunity to danger, just protection, a reduced likelihood of harm."

"Will it keep the spiders away?"

"Not permanently, but it may lessen the effectiveness of their attack. It's time I cashed in an investment." Thumbringer reached into Claw's wallet and retrieved a stone, but which one? More spiders were arriving, seven now between the caves and their fallen brethren. The tension was building. Their agitated pacing was a precursor to an all-out attack. "You're going to have to swallow it."

"What? Feek, no. This is something I've been wanting to do ever since I learned about elem, but...I'm not ready."

"Claw's in no shape to swallow it, and it won't work for me. You're our only option."

What he said was true, but all I wanted to do was run away. It was like the first time I bartered---but I eventually did it, because I had to. The second time wasn't as bad as the first. Eventually I became numb to the experience.

I held out my hand. Thumbringer placed the stone on my

palm. I looked at it for a moment, something I didn't do during my first bartering transaction. It was over in less than five minutes. I opened my eyes a moment before, then I had to close them again. The face that looked down at me was frightening. I opened my eyes for good after the man got off me. He apparently was as anxious to leave afterwards as I was for him to leave. I just laid there, unmoving. A quarter passed, then another. I didn't break out of the trance I was in when until my stomach rumbled. I took a shower first, then a bath. I put on loose slacks and a turtleneck sweater. I snatched the buffet certificate the man had left me on the night stand. I stripped off my clothes and replaced them with a sheer tank top and a short skirt. After dinner I had to provide for my next meal.

I popped the stone into my mouth. It sat there as I contemplated if I really wanted to go through with it. Then I became concerned that it might dissolve in my mouth. The consequences were unfathomable. Here I go. Nothing happened. My mouth had become too dry. I created saliva. There, that should be enough. It almost wasn't. It got caught about halfway down. I cleared my throat. The phlegm that was released had just enough bulk to dislodge the stone.

Once it reached my stomach the protective barriers between the individual elem dissolved simultaneously. The initial sensation was similar to having butterflies. It transformed as it oozed down my body. So intense was the stimulation I had difficult standing. It was a wonder everyone didn't become addicted to penta. Instead of the body tremors that usually followed such intensity, energy flowed from my abdomen to my extremities. It felt like it did that day I probed an electrical outlet with a fork. Some of the things yearlings came up with were worse than what filled their diapers. I was concerned, no, scared to death, of what I might discharge, and who it might be directed towards. I spun away from my companions. To emphasize my trepidation I bent over and stretched my arms. The release was even more intense than I imagined. It felt like a combination of urinating after holding it in all day and having an orgasm, not one sensation added to the other, but multiplied. Women often lose control of their bodily functions during childbirth. My concern was overwhelmed by the anticipation of the relief of built-up pressure finally being expelled.

I was so consumed with the experience I was having that I was oblivious to my surroundings. The spiders must have sensed what was building within me because they rushed back towards their hidey-holes. There was a dull illumination associated with my discharge. The dusty hillside before me began to darken. The overhang above one of the spider holes melted. It dropped into the hole as one gooey glob. Other openings were sealed in a similar manner. Then almost simultaneously the entire hillside melted. It flowed into one great heap, like a candle at the end of the evening. The substance began to spread, its solidity not great enough to support its current thickness. Someone pulled me away. I shirked. The extreme sensations and their release had made me hyper-sensitive. Even a light touch was enough to give me the heebie-jeebies. The arm returned. I pushed it away and stepped back on my own. The thick, wet concrete-like substance consumed half the spider carcasses before it finally came to rest.

"Well, that worked out well," commented Thumbringer. "I knew you could do it, Dinga."

The afterglow gradually dissipated. After a couple of minutes I was able to speak again. "Well, that was interesting. I'm not sure if I want to swallow another of those stones immediately, or never again."

"I've heard the sensation is more intense for women, something to do with them being inconsistently aroused. Men on the other hand, being continuously aroused, a little extra stimulation isn't as big of a deal."

"I'm not sure I'm comfortable talking about it."

"You're more a doer than a talker, huh? One of these days I might get rid of this ring just to see what the fuss is all about. Then again I've enjoyed my humanity."

Claw forced a smile. His face had a green hue to it. Now it was just pale. "You would think with how many times I've been re-created I would have developed an immunity to poison. Sorry about not helping out much. A bad belly is my Achilles heel."

"Not completely unhelpful. I believe you vomited on a couple of those spiders. From the stench it couldn't have been too healthy for them."

Thumbringer scanned the area. It was possible some of the spiders might have escaped and held a grudge. "I became concerned after you swallowed it. What if you hardened their lair instead of melting it? One aspect of intensity is intention. Cold or hot. Up or down. Hard or soft."

"I guess it's about time to be going." The remaining elem were buried under hardening molten rock. Claw pressed his hands against the ground, using them like pistons to elevate himself. He wobbled to his feet, then fell back down.

"WHAT'S WRONG WITH HIM?!" I shrieked. "He's not going to die again, is he?" What was it with my emotions since coming to Limbo? I had been so stoic since I fled my home.

Fred brushed up against my legs. It startled me at first, then it became comforting. I stroked the bony ridge on his head. "He'll be okay," he spoke to me after he stopped cooing. "If it had been either of you," he looked at me and Thumbringer, "you would be dead by now." Well, that was comforting. "Venom can do more than irritate a stomach. It can weaken, effect coordination, force muscles to contract or spasm."

"I think we've heard enough," Thumbringer interrupted. "Dinga here doesn't need to hear such things." It was sweet of Thumbringer to protect me like this. Even sweeter to think that I haven't heard worse in my, shall we say, worldly, past.

Fred pouted, then inspiration ignited his features. He half-leaped, half-flew to Claw. He swept a wing over him, then repeated the movement, again and again. Claw's pained, delusional

102

expression changed to one of relief. He closed his eyes. "I wasn't able to completely expel the poison, but I was able to dilute it. The strain on his body was severe. When he wakes he'll be better, but weak."

"Are we going to camp here?" I asked.

"I for one prefer a more hospitable location," Thumbringer replied.

"Are we going to be able to move Claw? He isn't exactly PETITE." I looked down at Fred.

"I can't do everything. One of the abilities I don't have is telekinesis."

"The stone. We could use the transportation stone."

"No," murmured Claw softly. "We're not going to waste it because I'm lazy." Claw opened his eyes and pushed himself into a sitting position. The action consumed what little energy he had remaining. "Some days it feels like dying and being re-created would be a lot easier than recovering."

"Don't even think about it," Thumbringer warned. "Considering your luck with mutations you probably won't turn into more of a monster than you already are, but I don't want to spend the next month looking for you."

"That's quite selfish of you."

"Dinga, you get that side. I'll take this one. If Claw is determined to travel we need to help support him." Claw was definitely a big boy. If he had been completely immobile there was no way we could have been able to move him, short of putting him on a stretcher and both Thumbringer and I dragging it behind us. "How about your gear?"

"We'll come back for it. I don't think we'll be able to get very far. The first even marginal campsite we come to will have to suffice." Thumbringer paused a moment to catch his breath. We had traveled maybe 20 meters. He looked back at the hardened mudslide. "In a couple of months I may be ready to return to collect those remaining elem, but right now you couldn't pay me a handful of diamonds to chip around those spiders."

It took us a quarter to reach our campsite, about 10 times as long as it would have taken us if we weren't so heavily burdened. I estimated us being just 500 meters from the spider holes.

I snuggled up to Claw again, this time more for his comfort than for my own. Fred slept in his burrow. I apologized for ruining the view. He shrugged it off. "I wanted a change of scenery. I no longer have to move to experience it."

Chapter 15

DEMONS AND PERVERTS

Claw looked much better in the morning. Even his fatigue had abated. Before we left for Capetown the boys wanted to view the mud heap one more time. It had hardened considerably over night. The upper torso of a spider stuck out of it, reminding us what we went through the day before.

"We couldn't just take the elem and leave, could we?" I commented.

"Life is a balancing act," said Claw. "For every good deed, there is a bad one. For every fortune, there is misfortune. For every great view, there is a mountain to climb in order to see it. It would have bothered me if we had taken the elem without a fight. If good is balanced with bad, then bad isn't balanced with good."

The trek to Capetown was uneventful. We intersected a road 10 kays from the city. We followed it. Our speed more than doubled, with us no longer stumbling over logs and weaving around trees and brush.

In returning to civilization we lost Fred. Associating with three humans was manageable---made easier with two of them no longer being entirely human---but accommodating an entire city.... "I'll see you again," he promised me. "I've never been to the Southern Spine. There has to be hundreds of carnivores there I can convert to vegetarianism. I can't fly there on my own with these wings." He lifted them for emphasis. "But a friend might be able to give me a lift."

Capetown had 40,000 inhabitants---middling for a city-state. A great wall surrounded it, with watch towers spaced every hundred meters. Three gates provided access to it, a small one at both ends of the highway, a larger one at the waterfront. The Liver Peninsula, with Capetown at its tip, was adjacent to the Frontier, the part of it populated by negative mutants. The only people traveling by foot into Capetown were farmers, or merchants from satellite communities. The city was a more desirable destination by sea, perhaps the most desirable in Limbo. It certainly had the busiest port. Capetown was adjacent to the Crosshairs, a convergence of four straits, each strait connecting to one of Limbo's four seas, making most of the penal colony accessible.

There was a fee to enter the city, and an additional tax due each day we stayed. Protecting the populous from demons, and consequently from becoming demons, was expensive.

"Well, thank you for the escort, and the company," I said as we arrived at the city's southern gate. "I didn't think past reaching the city. I don't have any money. I guess I'll have to get a job here. There has to be a pub somewhere that needs an extra girl." How was I going to get that job if I can't enter the city? "You wouldn't mind loaning me a couple of silvers would you? I'll pay you back as soon as I can."

Claw and Thumbringer beamed. "You're precious, Darling," said Thumbringer.

Claw elaborated, "Once we sell these elem you're be a

wealthy woman, Miss Dinga."

"But they're your elem. I didn't collect them."

"But you did. You didn't actually use a collecting rod, but your friendship with Fred created the opportunity."

"And there was your contribution to our defense," Thumbringer added. That was true.

"Thank you for allowing me to be part of your...." What? Group? Party? Family? I smiled.

"Don't get too appreciative. We get something out of the partnership too. It's not often two crusty old prospectors share the company of a beautiful woman. We'll be the envy of our profession."

"If we're so rich can we stay in some place nice tonight, with hot baths, and clean, soft beds---and room service?"

"We're not that rich, yet, until we sell our elem to the Wizards."

"We'll find you a place with a bath though," Claw insisted. "And maybe even your own bed, although I've become accustomed to sleeping next to you, and would miss it."

Port cities tended to have narrow streets. Capetown wasn't an exception. The close proximity to people made us more aware of them. They were definitely staring at us. Sure, we stood out, with my slightly excessive body hair, and Claw's extreme size, but we did appear more human than not. Fred had chosen wisely. The attention would have mortified him. More than stares were directed at us. The non-verbal animosity was so strong it radiated. We were excrement. I felt more loved from the THIRD TIME IS A CHARM CHURCH congregation that periodically marched past the Musky Foot and shouted obscenities. It always surprised me how fluent God-fearing folk were in cursing. Most of things they shouted weren't very spiritual in nature. Some were even unsafe if attempted verbatim.

It finally dawned on me the derivation of the church's name. Being sentenced here was obviously giving us a second chance, but what was the third? Of course. After someone dies on Limbo they are re-created, essentially becoming another person. I never paid much attention to the Church, the one in Briarwood, or the one's off world. Bartering was condemned by most religions. Killing, taking money from the poor, that was okay, but what two consenting adults did, now that was immoral. Church protests never offended me. I felt wanted. I performed a need. I provided focus, giving the Church something to do.

We had the streets to ourselves for the most part. As soon as someone caught sight of us they would either turn down a different street or enter a building. On those rare occasions we actually passed someone they would swerve out of our way, giving us a wide berth.

What bothered me the most were the public drinking fountains. They were either designated for LOCALS, or FOREIGNERS, DEMONS AND PERVERTS. The latter looked significantly less sanitary than the prior. I chose to remain thirsty a few more minutes. It was unnecessary to specify a fountain for demons. I didn't see a person who was outwardly mutated in the entire city.

"You chose to come here?" I questioned.

"The Liver Peninsula is the best place to prospect for elem," Thumbringer explained.

"Does the extra gold compensate for selling your soul?"

"Just because we pass through Capetown to travel to Gulag doesn't mean we accept what goes on here," said Claw.

"So Gulag isn't like this? There were a few people in Briarwood that weren't too fond of mutants, but they were able to coexist with them. There was no segregation."

"Capetown's the worst," Thumbringer answered. "It has to do with it being so isolated."

"How can Capetown be isolated with such a large port?"

"Most of the people passing through isolate themselves...."

"Are isolated."

107

"...in Demon Drop---that area of the city adjacent to the docks. There is even a wall to separate it from the rest of the city."

"Are there inns there? I guess there has to be if that's where a majority of the travelers are. I don't want to spend the night in Capetown."

"Plenty of inns, and some of them are even safe."

"The Condom, you think?" Claw conjectured. "It's more than we usually spend, but it will be more pleasant for Miss Dinga."

"The Condom?"

"A condom was a protective sheath men used to wear to prevent pregnancy and sexually transmitted diseases," Thumbringer enlightened.

"And men enjoyed wearing those?"

"I don't think they had much chose, the ones that weren't able to maintain a monogamous relationship. It was only a century ago that diseases and unwanted pregnancies were irradiated."

"It's surprising people came within a couple of meters of each other back then."

"During the LAST PLAGUE no one did. If it wasn't for robotic couriers humanity may have died out. It almost did. Reproduction requires a nominal intimacy. Cloning got to be too confusing."

We were allowed to enter Demon Drop unheeded. The difficulty would be returning to Capetown. A company of guards thoroughly interrogated anyone with even a hint of UNCLEANLINESS. That's what they called those of us who have been mutated: UNCLEAN. Most of those let through were servants. They were reminded they had to travel through alleyways whenever possible.

Capetown exuded homogeneity. The same couldn't be said for Demon Drop. People of all persuasions and mutant sub-races bustled among the docks and their adjacent byways. Many I recognized: trogs, arbols, partials. For every two relative normal looking mutants there was one that was more exotic. Most of the mutations were caused by cross-species contamination: goat legs, bird arms, a bull's head. A few of the mutants had features out of proportion, like the trogs. Others looked unmodified, but fell out of the normal range of sizes typical for humans, partials being one such example.

One particularly large gentleman stood out. He was two-and-a-half meters tall and weighed 200 kilos---none of it flab. He wore an animal skin tunic---just a tunic. Whenever a breeze picked up, as it had a tendency to do on the waterfront, his in-proportion stick was revealed. He swatted at every pretty woman---and some not so pretty---that walked by. Why were there so many women near the docks? What a silly question? Had it really been that long? Every couple of months I had to go on my own marketing excursion. The maxim: if one wanted to fish he had to go out to sea. The giant was more than flirtatious. He was ready for business, if you know what I mean. Some women were intimidated by the exceedingly endowed. My prior profession required I be accommodating to all, so the sight of the giant's excitement didn't disturb me, which apparently disturbed the giant, because he tapped me on my back, and not with his hand.

Being a woman, especially one in the field I was, I have occasionally experienced instances of unwanted sexual contact. After numerous unsuccessful attempts of verbal denial I learned that a more direct approach was needed. When a woman wishes to be intimate she may allow herself to be vulnerable emotionally. A man, he becomes vulnerable in another manner. As the giant huddled in a fetal position on his back, looking like a flipped beetle, I kicked him one more time, then led my companions away in the direction they had been heading before the delay. The gap between us and those around us had become noticeably larger than before the incident.

The wooden condom atop the inn was visible a block away. A man nearly the size of the rude giant, but with more feral features, stood beside the inn's entry. If it wasn't for his brutish appearance he would have looked dashing in his suit.

"Hey, Bark," greeted Claw. The resemblance was startling.

"Claw." He gave my larger companion a bear bug that would have made my eyes bulge, before they popped. "Thumbringer." He held out his hand to my smaller companion, which he shook. "And who do we have here?" From his smile and tone he assumed my association with his friend was temporary, something a half-hour might take care of.

"This would be Dinga," Claw replied. "CLAW, THUMBRINGER AND DINGA's newest partner."

"Don't you mean THUMBRINGER, CLAW AND DINGA?" Thumbringer interjected.

I was shocked. I felt there was mutual admiration, maybe even mutual respect, but I had no idea they viewed me as an equal. To alleviate the awkwardness of the acknowledgement I reacted in the manner I felt most fit. "I'm not really their partner. They're just helping me out until I'm on my feet. I haven't been on Limbo that long. I still feel like a fish out of water."

"I don't think we ever become completed adjusted," Bark commented.

"Dinga is being modest," said Claw. "We may have helped her out a bit when we first met her."

"Saving my life is more accurate."

"She doubled our monthly income the three days she was with us."

"That had more to do with Fred than me."

"But it was your relationship with Fred that earned us that windfall. Relationships are key to building a business and sustaining it."

"So you need a room for the night?" asked Bark. He looked at me. "Two rooms?"

"One room will be sufficient, as long as it has two beds," I answered for Claw and Thumbringer. "Claw and I share one."

The look Bark gave Claw was equivalent to slapping him on the back. Claw's reaction was a substantial reddening of his features. "Dinga has been sharing my bedroll until she has one of her own. Which is now possible to rectify with our windfall."

"But I want to sleep with you."

Bark grinned again. Claw's natural coloring had almost returned, but the pendulum swung once more.

Having a bed so closely tied to my prior profession I took little comfort in it. That changed the first night I lay next to Claw. He was like a big teddy bear and security blanket all rolled into one. Not only didn't I mind lying next to him, I actually enjoyed it. In some ways Claw became the comforting mother I never had.

"Well, I guess you better go in and reserve your room. We tend to fill up and it's almost sundim. Demon Drop has become increasingly raucous. I wouldn't recommend leaving The Condom after dark."

"More restrictions?" asked Thumbringer.

"Not really. What more can they do to us, short of genocide? Capetown still needs its maids and longshoremen. There just seems to be more unrest. A dissatisfaction in life there hasn't been before. No longer are people willing to get by. They're wanting more out of their lives."

"Well, those who want to better themselves need only enter the world. There are opportunities everywhere. Ours will be on a ship bound for Gulag tomorrow, Gaea willing."

As we walked into The Condom Claw turned around. "So you say it's getting livelier, huh? When do you get off work?"

"We're leaving tomorrow, no matter what shape you're in," Thumbringer stated.

"Not until midnight," Bark replied.

"About the time things really start popping."

With so many mutants of so many sizes The Condom had to be flexible in its lodging. The bed Claw and I shared was enormous. For those into group activities it would have been more than adequate.

I washed thoroughly, days on the road feeling like weeks in the city. I contemplated shaving. I understood the concept, but wasn't confident I could do so without cutting myself, some areas of my body being more vulnerable than others. Barbaric. If people didn't self-heal here, doctors would be cutting them open to cure them, instead of using sub-dermal lasers. The hairs on my body floated on the surface of the water. When the novelty of the experience wore off I freaked out, splashing water wildly. Soaking for hours in womb-like bliss no longer appealed to me. I would continue to bathe, but clinically, without anticipation or entertainment. Extrication superseded relaxation.

After eating a flavorful, and hearty, seafood stew, and fresh bread, and a tankard of beer, I retired for the evening. It was disconcerting not seeing any entertainment during the meal. At the Musky Foot there was always someone on stage. Disconcerting, but not surprising if what Bark implied was true. The real entertainment was outside the inn.

Claw and Thumbringer went upstairs with me. The last couple of days had been as consuming for them as it had been for me. Claw got up in the middle of the night. He returned shortly before it got light. I couldn't see him very well in the dark, but when he winced after I hugged him from behind, it became apparent his outing couldn't have been completely voyeuristic.

In the morning Claw's bruises and scratches were visible, but substantially healed. It had only been a couple of hours. What type of regenerative properties did we have? Or did Claw just heal more quickly than others?

"Did you have fun last night?" From his tone and expression, Thumbringer didn't intend the question to be supportive. Claw responded by smiling widely, which revealed two rows of teeth that weren't meant for grazing. I had never seen him use them for more than eating, but if he was ever without his two-headed hammer in a fight he would still have a formidable weapon.

Thumbringer disappeared as Claw and I ate breakfast. Whatever Claw did the night before must have consumed considerable calories. He ate enough eggs and sausages to feed me for a week. He washed it down with a liter of orange juice---not squeezed from oranges, but from those orange berries that looked like large grapes. It was as tart as coffee was bitter.

About the time Claw finally wiped his mouth---what purpose was there in cleaning himself if he was just going to dirty himself with the next bite---Thumbringer plopped down on the bench beside me. "Did you leave any food for me?"

Claw passed him his napkin, which was full enough to provide a light eater a generous meal. Thumbringer flagged a waitress. A few minutes later she set a full platter in front of him. He didn't eat as much as Claw, but it was still substantial. If I ate as much they did I would be as much around as I was tall. It wasn't fair. Men ate whatever they liked and never gained weight. And if they did, no one would care.

"The Viking Carriage leaves mid-morning, so we have about half-an-hour," said Thumbringer after he wiped his face. And why was it okay for men to be sloppy eaters? If a woman was that messy people would think she was an uncultured sow. A man, just vigorous in his appetite.

"So how long will it take to reach Gulag?" I sat demurely, but inside my intestines rumbled. Another thing a woman couldn't do in public was belch or pass gas. And a release from one end or the other was imminent.

"A week."

"A WEEK?! What type of ship is the Viking Carriage? A canoe?" Yep. Definitely imminent.

"The voyage will take just a day, but Gulag is inland---200 kays. It might take us just six or seven days, depending on the terrain and weather---and delays. On Limbo itineraries must be constantly modified."

"Excuse me." Like men would ever excuse themselves when

113

they had to pass gas. I made it to the stairs before I erupted. No one was within five meters of me, but I was confident someone heard me. To prevent further embarrassment I rushed towards the restroom. Limboans lacked a need for privacy. Restrooms were not only gender-neutral, they didn't have locks. If a person wished to be alone they had to enter after the room was vacated and do their business quickly. Feek, someone beat me to it. I can wait...I think. After one more outburst I felt settled.

Before I could decide if I should go back downstairs or to the room we rented, Claw and Thumbringer intercepted me in the hallway. I followed them back to the room. I watched as they proceeded to pack. Claw looked up at me. "Maybe we should buy Dinga her own pack."

"You don't need to do that. I've gotten by without one."

"That's because we're carrying everything for you," Thumbringer countered.

What have I been thinking, having Claw and Thumbringer be my pack animals. "I could carry that tent for you...I think."

"No. No." Claw insisted. "Thumbringer was just playing with you. We're not carrying anything more than we would have if you weren't with us---except for a few extra elem. I just thought it would be nice for you to store your personal items." Realizing the absurdity of the comment, he added, "When you get some."

"I think we can wait until we reach Gulag. After we cash in those elem I'll be able to buy about anything I want, won't I?"

"Just don't spend it all," Thumbringer insisted. "It might be months before our next payday."

"So you're planning to keep me on after we sell?" I never considered us staying together after we reached Gulag. Actually, I didn't think about doing anything at all after Gulag. Now that the actuality of reaching Gulag sunk in I was suddenly scared. What was I going to do the rest of my life? I was going to be Fred's apprentice, but after associating with people more like me I don't think I could do so exclusively. It was decided. I would stay with

Claw and Thumbringer, at least until I figured what I wanted to do with the rest of my life. A life that never ended. How many careers will I have before I become so mutated that I will no longer be accepted in society?

"Of course we're planning on keeping you after we reach Gulag." Claw sounded offended.

"Every team needs a mascot," Thumbringer added.

The giant was back on the docks. His experience with me turned him away from woman, at least temporarily. He modified his harassment to include anyone walking by. He took great delight in hitting anyone stupid enough to walk past him. Those in the immediate area were amused, watching with anticipation for his next unsuspecting victim. He wasn't very creative in his assault. His target was pummeled from above with his massive hands. One blow was usually enough to send the giant's target to the ground. After he picked himself up, groggily, he would run away. The giant allowed him to, laughing too vigorously to immobilize him. The giant appeared never to tire of his game. Pound, fall, laugh. Pound, fall, laugh.

"Shouldn't we be doing something?" I was never bullied myself, but it bothered me when others were. Sometimes I intervened, depending on the threat to the victim, and myself.

"Think of it this way," Thumbringer replied. "He is teaching those he strikes to be more aware of their environment. A headache and a skinned knee might be a deal compared to what a more finely tuned attentiveness might prevent."

Chapter 16

DIGESTIVE CAVITY

The Viking Carriage was a cargo ship, but its captain wasn't opposed to padding his wallet when someone needed a ride. Limboans rarely traveled for pleasure. It was too dangerous. Merchants were the most common passenger. Occasionally a group of adventurers booked passage, but they were few and far between. Only the invincible young---those spending less than a handful of years on Limbo---gambled with their humanity fighting monsters for their treasure, or prospecting for elem. The Viking Carriage's main cargo was exotic fruit from the Saber Desert, a torrid, sandy expanse southwest of the Liver Peninsula that bordered the most dangerous part of the Frontier. If one lived to harvest the fruit, he could make an enormous profit. Only the wealthy could afford such fruit, but there were plenty of them in Gulag.

I expected the Viking Carriage to sprint after navigating the busy harbor. It did, but not substantially: about twice as fast as a hurried walk. Wind power was free, but temperamental. A dead calm, passive aggressive?

We did stop, midway through the first day, but not due to a lack of wind. The voyage consisted of crossing the mouth of the Southern Strait, where it merged with the Crosshairs. Being one of those people who got sea sick, I dreaded the voyage. Surprisingly, my stomach remained settled. A fringe benefit of being mutated? I enjoyed the gentle rocking and the endless vistas, but looked forward to seeing the shore again. I took comfort in self-sufficiency.

Being trapped in a boat with kays of water in every direction was the antithesis of independence.

A moment before we stopped, it got dark. There had been sky, and ocean, and sunlight. Suddenly it all disappeared, like someone had flipped a switch. Panic began as screams. Being the type of person that didn't display her emotions openly, the anguished exclamations ripped through my vulnerable psyche. Those more experienced with such outbursts may have been able to weather the storm, but I floundered, being tossed by the eddies instead of swirling with them.

Emotions mirrored the ship. After coming to rest there was silence, then discussion. A lantern was lit. We were awed by our surroundings, finding ourselves in a cave. I began to focus on the details. Not on the cave, but what had put the ship in stasis.

"A whale?" someone conjectured. But not just any whale. It was large enough to harbor an additional vessel. If Jonah and Pinocchio were trapped here they may have been too distracted pondering where the golf course and condos would go to contemplate escape.

"It must be a leviathan," the Captain hypothesized. "There have been rumors of them for years. For us to be surprised like that it must have swallowed us from behind."

"What's that smell?" I asked.

"Digestion," Thumbringer answered.

"I'm surprised I haven't given back my lunch. Strong odors tend to do that to me."

"It's this nausea-relief ring I wear," spoke the Captain. "It was custom-made to prevent sea sickness. It apparently relieves other types of nausea. As long as you stay within 50 meters of me your stomach should stay settled."

"So how are we going to get out of here, Captain?" asked Thumbringer.

"Cut our way out before the digestive fluid corrodes the Viking Carriage, then us."

Four sailors rowed towards the lining of the leviathan's stomach. Before they could reach it each was skewered by a crossbow bolt. The barrage was redirected at us. We found cover quick enough to prevent additional casualties.

The Captain examined one of the projectiles. "A gar bolt. How could a school of gar be caught that unaware to be swallowed by a leviathan?"

"Why don't we just wait them out?" I suggested. "We have plenty of food and water."

"There's more than sea water in here, digestive fluids that will eventually rot through the hull."

"Shouldn't the acid also affect the gar?"

"You would think so. They might be sheltered in one of those shells they use as houses. But they still need to breathe--- water. They can also breathe air, but so inefficiently they become oxygen deprived in a quarter."

One of the sailors said, "If we could see them, if we knew where they were, we could rush them. It takes awhile to reload a crossbow."

"Are you volunteering to lead this charge?" asked Claw. "The first bolt fired doesn't need to be reloaded."

"There might be a way," said the Captain. "Gar don't like bright light, becoming nearly blind once it reaches a critical intensity. I have a penta that should be able to illuminate this cavity, but I can do it only once. I keep the stone for emergencies, in the event we need to navigate hazards at night. We must move quickly. The effect will last just ten minutes if we intend to light the entire cavity."

"Then let's get started," said Thumbringer. "How many dinghies do you have?"

"Two, but they're large enough to hold most of us. We'll have to leave a few behind anyway, to lower the boats and defend the ship."

"As soon as the penta activates we need to get those boats

into the water. We'll whack the gar, then rush back here. The excitement of battle ought to encourage the creative juices to flow. By the time we're safely back on the ship, we'll have thought of a way out of the leviathan."

"Always the optimist," said Claw. "But the plan is as good as any. Captain?"

"Whatever we do we must do quickly. I don't care so much if I live or die, but my ship is in agony. Let's set that plan of yours in motion."

A miniature sun materialized on the ceiling of the leviathan's digestive cavity. The gar, their webbed forelimbs covering their eyes, were spotted on a ridge 20 meters away. They looked like fish, but with legs and arms.

The two dinghies were filled, dropped, and released within a span of a minute.

The gar dropped behind the ridge, a series of near simultaneous splashes following.

"I don't like this," said Thumbringer. "I was confident of our success once we blinded them, but not knowing where they are is making me nervous. They could still sneak up on us using their other senses."

We came to shore at the base of the flesh covered bone ridge. Those of us with shields put them in front of us as we topped the ridge. An unnecessary precaution, perhaps, but with minimal cost.

The light was intense enough to illuminate the pool beyond the ridge. A large stationary object was in the bottom of it, with a dozen smaller dynamic objects scurrying around it. From the distance we were away from it the gar looked like insects buzzing around a hive. "Home?" I suggested.

"Likely," said the Captain. "But why hasn't it dissolved? And its inhabitants."

"It doesn't smell as bad here."

The Captain climbed down to the shore of the pool and

119

stuck his cutlass in the water and smelled it. "It's pure, as pure as any seawater."

A fish the shape of a pancake, but the size of two men, stung the captain with its tail. He fell into the water. The oversized ray swallowed the skipper, looking like a stuffed pita as it swam away.

"We need to free the Captain," the sailors declared before they jumped in, each with a dagger in one hand.

"Do you know how to sail a ship?" Claw asked Thumbringer.

"I used to play with a plastic battleship in the bathtub."

"Dinga?"

"A business associate used to take me to his yacht, but it was a very small boat, and we spent most of the time in the cabin."

"Should we have helped them?" asked Claw.

"Does that answer your question?" Thumbringer replied. Before the sailors could reach the manta, electric eels intercepted them. It looked like someone was welding underwater. Two, no three, blackened sailors floated to the top of the pool. The remaining five came up for air.

"GET OUT OF THERE!" Claw shouted to the sailors. "You're over your head and out of your element. The Captain couldn't have possibly survived. I've come up with a way to escape the leviathan, but it will be easier if we do it while the light is still protecting us."

With much regret, and hesitation, the sailors swam back to shore. One of the five didn't make it. Was is another ray or an electric eel, or maybe a blind lunge and grab by a gar? We didn't stick around to find out.

The light dimmed. Seconds later it went out completely. We had just cleared the ridge and had started down the other side. We foolishly forgot to bring a torch or lantern. There was enough light emitted from the Viking Carriage for us to distinguish objects, but not details.

I slipped getting into a dinghy. I expected the digestive fluids to immediately dissolve my skin. There was a mild burning sensation, noticeable, but not yet painful. For the moment the smell was worse than the bite. Claw and Thumbringer---and two of the surviving sailors---were in the other dinghy, which was already docked with the Viking Carriage. My companions climbed up a rope ladder as the two sailors in my dinghy helped me back into the boat, but not before something with sharp teeth nibbled on me. I didn't just get scratched. Entire pieces of flesh were being ripped from me. I left a crimson stain in the water, and was creating a similarly colorful puddle in the bottom of the dinghy. Dozens of fish surrounded the boat. How could they survive in that stuff? Maybe that's why they were so vicious. They were dying painfully.

The sailors rowed madly once I was safely back in the dinghy. They were both pierced by crossbow bolts. One fell overboard and was voraciously devoured by the fish. The other fell towards me. He immediately received two more bolts. I was fortunate to be lying critically wounded in a puddle of blood in the bottom of the dinghy. I made a poor target.

The dinghy drifted. Instead of heading towards the ship it was moving away from it. Claw and Thumbringer climbed back down to the other dinghy. "SAVE YOURSELVES!" I shouted. "I'm already dead. See you in my next life." Recognizing the wisdom in my words they rushed back up the rope ladder and to the safety of the cabin on the main deck.

I had been facing the Viking Carriage, but after hearing a series of splashes I flipped around. I attempted to scuttle backwards to flee my antagonists. My folly caused the boat to tip over. Before the fish ate my eyes I saw a glow surrounding the Viking Carriage. An immense gust of air filled its sails and pushed it out of the leviathan. I think the leviathan exploded. I was too delirious at the time to know for sure.

Chapter 17

PICTURE WITHIN A PICTURE

I woke in another prairie. There were forests and swamps and jungles and hills and mountains and cities, but I had to always be re-created in a prairie. Perhaps because I entered Limbo in a prairie? Or was it just a coincidence? I was nude again, hairier, and more flat-chested. Why doesn't Gaea just make me a male ape and be done with it. I checked between my legs. Nope, nothing growing there yet. I also seemed to be more squat, not fatter, just bigger boned and more muscular. What is this place, some female version of hell?

Well, time to start over again: clothes, shelter, food, water, not necessarily in that order. A forest was nearby this time, just a quarter away if I pushed, and I intended to. I always felt weak after being re-created, but after I got the blood flowing an energetic enthusiasm kicked in. It was like what a person feels after they recover from an illness. After feeling so bad for so long, feeling okay feels quite good, and anything beyond that feels ecstatic.

Why did I have to die now, after I made friends? I never had friends before, not real friends that thought of me as family. Sure, there were people I saw every week, but they were merely acquaintances. I never shared my feelings with them. We never spent any time together outside of work. Why did I have to be so death prone? Maybe there was a class I could take.

Did Claw and Thumbringer make it safely to Bronze Glade? Even if they survived the gale they created they still had to maneuver a ship with a skeleton crew---minimal staff, not animated bones. Maybe they also died and had been re-created nearby. Wouldn't that be wonderful. No, it wouldn't. Before I came to Limbo I might have selfishly wished for someone to die horribly if it benefitted me, but now.... How could I, even for a moment, wish for someone to be susceptible to mutation? They made it to shore safely. They're probably on their way to Gulag to sell their elem for a feek-load of gold. Then they'll start looking for me. I'll need to be a bit more presentable by then. I want them to be proud of me, not to help me because they feel sorry for me. What if Claw and Thumbringer can't find me? Maybe I could find them. They're heading to the Wizards' Keep. It's near Gulag. Being in the center of Limbo it's directly below the sun. If I walked in the direction of the sun I would eventually reach it.

I followed my intuition. With the sun being in the approximate direction of the forest, my short-term and long-term goals coincided. I would penetrate the woods at a tangent instead of head on, but any penetration was good. I think I read that on a bathroom wall somewhere.

The prairie I was in was exceptionally dry. Every step brought a crackling of straw followed by a cloud of dust. The clouds didn't contain just dirt and bits of dried vegetation. They also had assorted insects in them, individuals and swarms: flies, grasshoppers, gnats, and many others I didn't have a name for. I was bitten repeatedly. I prayed none of the insects were poisonous. I became concerned when one of my hips became numb. I felt relieved a few minutes later when the deadened spot didn't spread.

A few strides from the forest a grasshopper swarm became more numerous and irritating. Their bites were pinpricks, but a hundred pinpricks was substantial. I began to bleed from the tiny wounds. The blood drew more of the insects, like they were miniature flying piranha. I began to run. I wasn't able to shake them, but my erratic movement made it more difficult for them to feast. The only thing that saved me---and I was confident I would have eventually died from the accumulative loss of blood---was entering the forest. Some of the flies continued to surround me, but most of the other insects, including the grasshoppers, remained in the prairie.

Most of the bites stopped bleeding. Those too big to seal on their own continued to drip, sapping my strength. I found a muddy spot and applied the natural salve to my wounds. The bleeding stopped, but in compensation I looked atrocious, like a brick wall repaired with concrete.

The loss of blood made me just want to sleep. I no longer needed food or water, just a nap---that lasted half the day. I became livelier when something twice my size, looking like a raccoon, but more flat and squat, charged me from its burrow at the base of a tree I was considering making my bed. My only recourse, with two rows of canines and grizzly-like claws bearing down on me, was to attack back---a death wish---or climb a tree. There were plenty to choose from, but I had just seconds to act. Fortunately my antagonist was built low to the ground, and wasn't well adapted to climbing. It became quite upset that I had escaped. I didn't understand its grunts and growls, but I'm certain they wouldn't have been appropriate for children.

A lofty perch didn't guarantee safety. A vertical highway meant I was safely above, but not necessarily safe below. Something very beetle-like, 10 sims in diameter, landed on my thigh. I attempted to knock it off, but it had attached to my ample leg hair. OWWW!! IT BIT ME! I grabbed it with both of my hands, lifting it, but not completely, its mandibles resolute.

"Whatever you do, don't break off its head." Fred? "It will bury deeper. Its barbs will make it impossible to remove without taking off half your leg." The reptilian bird fluttered up to me. He looked happy, but also upset. And disappointed?

"You wouldn't happen to have any industrial grade tweezers on you? Or a lawn mower?"

Fred looked confused. Then enlightened. "Why would you

wish to look like a newborn? Feathers and hair are indicators of maturity."

"I've been bald for years."

"And how have you felt since you began to grow hair?"

"Definitely more grown up," I was forced to admit. "Any specific suggestion how I might get this thing off me?"

"Oil, maybe...or fire."

"I'm fresh out of both."

"Not entirely. How long has it been since you took a bath?"

My hands immediately went to my head, then down my arms and legs. FEEK! Re-creation should have taken care of my lack of consistent hygiene---dictated by environment, not choice---instead, I had become dirtier, specifically, greasier. Re-creation had stimulated more than my hair follicles.

"Rub the oil on the beetle. That ought to loosen its hold."

After vigorously removing as much of the accumulated oil as my psyche could take, I did as Fred suggested. What coated my fingers was disgusting. Could a woman possibly be more attractive than I at the moment?

"No, not on top of it. Where it's attached. You're trying to remove it, not add dressing to a salad."

I rubbed the insect's mandibles. It slowly released its grip. A heartbeat later---which was closer to a micron than a second due the adrenaline rushing through me---I threw it towards the creature below me, missing it. The beetle's exoskeleton crunched like it was a potato chip. The dip that squirted out was too disgusting to describe.

The spot where the tick had bitten me began to puff out. Yes, I was definitely beauty pageant material. "How did you find me? My re-creation must have transported me hundreds of kays."

"True. You're closer to Briarwood now than to Capetown. I seem to be attuned to you. I instinctively knew what direction you were and how far away."

"Attuned to just me?"

"For the moment. I'm very pleased. It's a new ability for me."

"I wonder what penta that's equivalent to? Do you perceive individual elem, or is it just a mangled mess?"

Fred had to sit. This was one of those occasions when he had to think, instead of just expel the musings on the fringes of his perception. "Intrinsic penta is felt, not perceived as a complex compilation of elemental energies. It's holistic. Actions are perceived as symbols, instead of a series of letters."

"This ability to track me you just learned?"

"I don't think learned is the proper term. I didn't study in order to understand, or practice in order to perform. The ability just arrived, like mail."

"So there is nothing you did that instigated this ability? You didn't study it? You weren't re-created?"

"My goal since you left Capetown was to find you. My strong emotions may have subconsciously created the correct array of elem. I first healed when a friend of mine was critically injured. You also need healing. Your weakness is pulsating, like a heartbeat."

Fred swooshed his wings past me like he was a matador. Each brush stroke healed my wounds a bit more. My strength returned, but not completely. Fred was able to heal, not to revitalize.

"How long until it gets dark?" I asked.

"One hour, eight minutes, but its best you don't travel anymore today."

"So I can fully recover?"

"So you can regain some of your strength before the parasite you house transforms and wishes to leave. I noticed it when I healed you. It was healthy, so I didn't have to heal it."

I poked at my ears. "No, it's not in your head this time. It's in your hip. And it isn't fatal, not where it burrowed. It often chooses the groin, which isn't always fatal, but always painful."

I slapped my right hip---nothing happened. Then I slapped my left hip, causing a minor vibration. It tickled, but didn't hurt. "Can we cut it out?"

"Possibly, but it will probably burrow deeper if we make the attempt. I wouldn't worry too much. In a couple of hours it will begin to dig its way out."

The worst part of an atrocious event was the waiting. Minute by minute I thought about the gruesome ordeal that was to happen. The ripping of flesh. The awful, ugly insect that would emerge, dripping of my blood and substance. If I could only sleep until then. Thinking wouldn't exist, my thoughts protectively stored in stasis. The more I thought about sleeping the more awake I became. Using reverse psychology, I focused on staying awake. That didn't work, either.

But somehow, somewhere, somewhen, I did fall asleep. I dreamt about marrying the man I had seen shortly after I entered Limbo and again at Briarwood. We lived in a house, slept in a bed. I became pregnant. Then I was in labor. Just an hour more. Just a few more minutes. But the pain wasn't between my legs.

My hip erupted. I woke. My attention focused on the origin of my pain. Through a small opening---tiny----at most a sim in diameter---a creature emerged, florescent green beak first, followed by its darker green body and yellow wings, that were pressed backwards towards its scarlet tail. It was three sims in length, and nearly as wide when its wings were extended. It hovered beside me like a humming bird, its wings beating profusely. It looked up at me with intelligent eyes. They were blue and remarkably human.

In a corner of my vision, I saw a secondary image, a picture within a picture. I saw myself. The insect flew away, it's flight displayed before me---trees rushed by, as did other insects, and the ground below. It stopped at a flower and drank its nectar. A portion of me could taste its sweetness and feel the energy it released. Then I began to smell the flower's fragrance. I could hear my wings flutter---its wings. As it traveled to another flower, I felt its movement. The constant fluttering, the minimal changes the wings made to move it forward, backward, sideways, and up and down. Concentrating, I was able to enlarge the picture, but not by much.

"Very strange, but wonderful," said Fred. "I believe you have received your first ability."

The distraction shrunk my perception of the insect's senses. They didn't vanish, just reduced in intensity, becoming more pilot light than searing flame.

"I can see, smell, taste, hear, feel what the insect sees, smells, tastes, hears, and feels," I said.

"It has become your familiar."

"But I can't control it."

"Not yet. Welcome fellow demon."

"But I'm still mainly human."

"Part demon is still a demon for most people. If you don't wish to be shunned, I suggest you keep this ability a secret."

"I think I will call it a CAM." Return, I told the cam. A minute later it did, but just momentarily. It found a flower nearby and began to drink. "I told it to do that."

"So you can control it?"

"Not entirely. I gave it the suggestion. And its subconscious brought it here. Without further suggestion it returned to its normal routine, which meant visiting flowers. I'm suddenly feeling exhausted. I'm going back to bed. It's also resting, now that it has a full belly. In the morning we'll head for Gulag."

When I woke not only did my eyes open, but my cam senses. The insect was wandering. I saw a road beside a river, and beyond it a walled city. "The cam couldn't have traveled all the way to Gulag," I said.

"It's probably Coolatta. It's just 15 kays from here."

"Let's go. Maybe we can hire river transport to Gulag."

Fred became uncharacteristically quiet. "What's wrong?" I asked him.

"You know how I feel about humans, especially in cities. If you insist on going to Gulag, let's travel by foot. If you board a ship I won't be able to go with you. You might want to start thinking about how others will view you. You're one of us now. What if someone found out about your ability?"

What a way to make a girl feel loved. Sure, I was aware of my body changing, but as long as it was just me berating myself I was able to isolate my insecurities---internally. For Fred to announce my imperfections and how they might be viewed negatively…. I wanted to find a hole to crawl into. I did appreciate his honesty, the honesty only a friend could tell you, but that doesn't mean it hurts any less.

Being a girl, then a woman, I never felt very happy with myself. Some girls would sell their soul for mounds as full as mine once were, but I wished they could be more firm and perky. Some people viewed me as funny and active. I thought I was silly and a klutz. Many women looked up to me when I became a barterer. I wore expensive designer clothes, ate at exclusive restaurants, was treated like a princess by most men. But deep down I knew that most people thought of me as just an expensive whore.

"Is something wrong?" Although Fred mutated into something about as far from human as a person could get he was still male. He didn't have a clue the words he spoke might have affected me in the manner they did. He had simply laid it out for me, without consideration how I might take it. Again, I had to appreciate his directness, but it still hurt.

"I'm just a bit nauseous. If anyone noticed my cam I could just say I created it from a penta."

"I don't think you should speak of ANY elemental energy manipulation publically. Not all view it as science. Many think of it as witchcraft. Just because someone is a criminal doesn't mean he's without morals."

"What does believing someone is a witch have to do with morals?"

"People believe what they believe. If you stray too far from their schema they might brand you a heretic. Many religious zealots are mass murders."

"I haven't been good at keeping my mouth shut, or thinking before doing."

"You may want to modify that behavior, unless your goal is to look more like me, but in weeks instead of decades. Looking like yourself may not be such a good idea either, especially in a city. You might want to conceal that ample femininity of yours."

"Ample, hardly. Not anymore. What woman, short of one living in a cave, would allow hair to grow all over her body like this?"

"Compared to most animals your bosom is still prominent, and you are nearly bald. If I still had a bit of human male in me I'm sure I would feel stimulated from such a sight, but since I don't I can only view you from a clinical perspective. Udders or mounds, there really isn't any difference to me." Now Fred was calling me a cow? I was going to have to find me some female companionship. A boyfriend would be better, but I was to the point I would take anyone who was generous with a compliment. Even stingy, would work. A dribble was better than a drought.

"Being re-created every week is inconvenient. Even my periods happened just once every three weeks. I guess I'll have to make some clothes out of leaves or something. Let's just hope they're not from poison ivy. What do people like me do? Do they have to continuously start over? Buying new possessions? But with what money if it has also been redistributed?"

"Some people have friends that retain their possessions until they're reunited. Of course there is no guarantee they will ever be. Only the most loyal friend will not sell your gear after a month waiting for you."

"Considering all I had the last time I died was the clothes on my back I'm not too worried about it, but there will come a time, I hope, that I will have enough things, expensive or sentimental, that I will want them returned. What am I going to do, Fred, to earn some money? Claw and Thumbringer were going to give me a share of what they made selling elem. I don't see my share of that windfall arriving anytime soon."

"You could sell your own elem."

"But I don't have a collection rod, and even if I did, Gulag is at the end of my journey, not at the beginning."

"There is a penta shop in Coolatta. The Wizard there will buy elem from you, just not for as much as you would earn in Gulag. People didn't always use collection rods. It's more difficult, like building a fire before cooking instead of turning a dial, but it can be done."

"It might take awhile before I even find an elem. Then I would still have to capture it somehow. Why do I think the process will be more difficult than you're letting on? I envision trying to catch a fish with my bare hands. You wouldn't be aware of any large elem deposits like the one near your home in the Eight-Leg Woods?"

"Not a large deposit, but I know where there's some. Being innately attuned to it I'm able to sense it when it's near, particularly when it's clustered." Fred suddenly shook, like he had gotten a chill. "I've changed my mind about you collecting elem. It's too dangerous. Think of what happened the last time you went prospecting. Elem is like gold, and where there's gold there is trouble. I can protect you and bring you food. Why don't we detour around Coolatta, intentionally not associating with humans and their cities, their gold, and their elem. We can turn it into a game, like hide and seek, but without the seek part. Please. The stress you are causing me will make me go carnivore again."

I don't know how women do it? Somehow we get our way, even if we're no longer entirely human. I didn't even beg, not verbally. Just the sadness, the disappointment in my expression, was enough to sway him. It was the same reaction some women got when they cried, but I was able to achieve it without shedding a tear.

A cave nearby had some green elem in it: elem terra. Brown hair clung to the rough rock walls and floor---never a good sign. I sent my cam into the cave to investigate. I strongly suggested it stay near the ceiling to reduce its risk of harm. Ten meters in it became confused, tangled in a bat swarm. The picture within a picture faded, then finally went out.

Sensing what occurred, Fred rubbed his body against mine. "Many things eat insects. Their average life span is just a few days."

"It's like I lost a child---but more than that. Did I really lose my only ability? What if I never gain another?"

Trying to cheer me up, Fred said, "In the speed at which you are mutating, I don't think that'll happen." If Fred was going to be my sole companion, for the indefinite future, I needed to train him in the types of things he could say that would, if not to liven the mood, to at least not dampen it.

Chapter 18

MEN

"I'll be quick," I promised Fred. "I'll just collect a few elem and get out of there. I see one already." A spec of green glowed dimly a meter into the cave. "How am I going to pick this up without a collecting rod? Then I have to find some way to store it. Bark maybe, but will it be too porous for something so small? And what happens if I collect more than one? Without some shielding between the elem I'll probably blow up both of us."

"I have an elem collector," spoke a rough voice. "And I appreciate you finding the elem for me. We've been looking in the Feline Forest for weeks and have found just a handful." I turned around. Five muscular men in tattered green-leather shirts, trousers, and boots eyed me playfully. It was unlikely they had cards in mind. Over their clothes they wore rusted, bent breast plates. Each hand was occupied, the secondary with a tarnished and bruised square shield, the primary with a random, one-handed weapon: axe, hammer, sword, mace, and dagger. I was familiar with THAT look, very familiar. They had probably forgotten about the elem already. There were ways to handle men in this state. Most women would have been frightened, but that look actually made it easier for me to manage them. I had what they wanted. It was simply supple versus demand, and the equation wasn't balanced.

A second voice commented, "This is the way I like it. Having a package unwrapped before you buy it."

"Should we draw straws?" asked a third. "We'll all get our turn, but she'll be feistier in the beginning."

"I think I should be the one to choose the order," I countered. "Should I choose the prettiest one first, or the most virile? Should the best be first, or should I save the best for last?"

I have never heard so much boasting in my life. If what some of them said was true…. What was I thinking? Just because I was in the company of a certain group of people doesn't mean I should act like them. As a well-respected barterer I strived to be as professional as possible. I never allowed business to become pleasure. Eventually I became so desensitized to the act that I no longer associated it with mutual fondness. Boring had become a service, like cutting someone's hair or mowing their lawn.

"I know it's a difficult decision," spoke one of the men. It didn't matter which one. Men like that were all alike. "But we don't have all day. We like to bore, but we'd also like to become rich. That elem is just sitting there waiting to be taken. You could be considerate and do the same."

Had I really lost my ability to control men when I gave up being a barterer? Or was it because of my mutations? It wasn't that I wasn't as pleasing to look at as before. These type of men would bore anything---and I mean anything. It wasn't how they saw me, but how I saw myself and the world around me. I had changed psychologically. I no longer believed in the words I spoke, or in the manner my body moved. I was becoming scared. I was no longer in control. The men were actually going to do things to me without my permission. I didn't dread dying again. Being re-created had its drawbacks, but it wasn't the end of the world. But the humiliation---that was something re-creation couldn't cleanse.

Fred came to my rescue before anything happened. He had vanished when the men arrived. I was confident if he hadn't he would have been killed immediately. When he reappeared the men were as frozen as I was the first time I met him.

"Well, what should we do with them?" Fred asked.

"We could operate so they won't have such indecent thoughts," I suggested.

"How about making the punishment fit the crime?"

"Wouldn't that work out in their favor?"

"We'll bore them on our own terms. We'll start by making them collect that elem for you. That's nearly as tedious as the job they wanted you to do."

"How will we compel them? I don't think they'll want to do it because they feel sorry for what they were about to do."

"One of my abilities is to control people. Not for too long, and with limitations. I can't make them do anything that will harm them. I could strongly encourage them to do menial labor, for the remainder of the day."

It took an hour for the elem terra to be harvested. There was a brief moment of excitement when a cave bear emerged from the bowels of the cave after an initially noisy couple of minutes. The men did the work, but they couldn't be completely coerced into being quiet about it. Worldly as I was I actually learned a few new words. The men, although braggarts, could back up at least their fighting ability. Three meters and five hundred kilos later they were back to work with just a few scratches. Even if it wasn't self defense I think the men would have attacked the bear. They enjoyed the violence.

Adding to the adrenaline rush, my cam return. It certainly had been killed and eaten by the bats, but it had been re-created, and remarkably, still attached to me. Not only was the pilot light re-lit, the stove was ignited. After the initial reattachment, my attuned senses shrunk back to their on-call size.

Fred confirmed, regrettably, there was still enough time to travel to Coolatta before dark. "Should we take the men with us?" I asked.

"You could. I'm not going into the city. When you leave, follow the road along the river, the one that heads northeast, towards Termite. I'll be watching for you."

I didn't argue with him. I respected his aversion to society. I was beginning to feel the same, more every day. "How long can the men be controlled?"

"Probably not for too much longer. The more people I control, the shorter the period of control."

"Will they do what I command them to do? They're in your control, not mine."

"I could give them a general command, to stay within sight of you and protect you. Anything more complicated might be too much for them, and break their bond to me."

"I'll decide at the city wall whether to risk having them in the city with me. If the rudeness in Capetown is repeated I could use the protection." I looked at my wardrobe---my lack of one. "I'm going to need protection in more than one way."

"I think I can do something about that. I need one of you

135

men to loan Miss Dinga some of your clothes." They all enthusiastically volunteered. "Their bond to me must be really strong."

"Or maybe they just like the idea of a woman wearing their clothes."

The green-leather pants and tunic fit loosely, but after cinching the trousers I was reasonably confident in retaining my modesty. There wasn't an extra pair of boots. Fred insisted I take the pair off the smallest man's feet. I declined. It wouldn't be fair. The men had probably already paid off their debt to me. All they did was boast. There may not have followed through on what they said, or even been capable of doing it. I wasn't completely naïve. It was likely they would have if Fred hadn't convened, but it didn't feel fair to add punitive damages.

I decided to take the men with me to Coolatta. Fred flew away when the forest terminated, 50 meters from the river. The water was crossed via a stone bridge. Coolatta began on the other side. The Neutral River, the longest on Limbo, was about a kay wide this close to its mouth---relative to its headwaters. Most of the bridge appeared to rest directly on the water. It bobbed up and down, indicating it floated. Two places along the bridge it was raised enough to allow boats to pass beneath. The Bactrian Bridge was infested with buildings, circumvented by a narrow street that meandered around them. Most of the buildings had some form of fishing platform jutting off of them. The dimming sun didn't deter the dozens of committed hobbyists perched on them. A gate blocked the entrance to the bridge. It was flanked by two guard houses. A catapult was atop each, operated by two soldiers. Three additional soldiers manned the gate.

Upon perceiving our ragged, rough group approach, the men occupying the gate and towers stiffened. "We would like entrance to your fine city," I announced.

The lead guard, indicated by a medallion he wore, replied sternly, "First, you must give an oath of non-violence. Exceptions are permitted if you are attacked. You won't be required to give up your arms. We believe every man, woman, and mute has the right to protect themselves with the weapon of their choice. Coolatta does require you to share your spoils if your defense results in a death. Five coppers each to enter the city, and two a day to stay. The first day is free. Three silver for the six of you."

"That's very reasonable," I said.

"We try to be reasonable here. To compensate for us not overtaxing our people, and visitors, our crime fees are extremely high. Crime doesn't pay in Coolatta, not for the criminals."

I requested the funds from my slave mercenaries. I intended to repay them when I sold the elem. I wasn't going to steal from them, no matter what they might have done to me.

We stepped onto the bridge as soon as the gate opened. I was anxious to get done what needed to get done, then leave. Before coming to Limbo I loved being in a large city---the excitement, the people, the culture, the architecture---but after walking through Capetown, with all those eyes judging me, I could no longer tolerate being surrounded by throngs. I was perfectly willing to give up a soft bed and a bath for the peace of mind inherent in solitude.

The signs on the bridge buildings suggested I could buy everything I needed without entering the city---if someone was present to sell it to me. The entire population of the bridge must have been fishing. Dusk and dawn were supposed to be the best times to fish, and true fishermen weren't going to permit a potential sale to dislodge them. I didn't have any money yet anyway, so the point was moot. It's been said we work in order to survive, but have hobbies in order to live. It couldn't be truer for those on the Bactrian Bridge.

I was on my own finding the penta shop. Elemental energy was like pornography. Most people dabbled in it, but they didn't discuss it in public. A dignified woman just didn't go up to someone and ask, "Do you know where I can sell some elem?" It made her sound like a pervert or a drug dealer.

To enter the city we had to pass through a second gate, at the end of the bridge. Neither guard house was occupied and the portcullis was up. If the city was ever attacked I was certain both deficiencies would be remedied. If someone wished to enter the city via the bridge hundreds of people would be aware of it before those attacking reached the end of it.

Coolatta was the most organized city I've been to, on Limbo or off world. Wide avenues were laid out in concentric squares. One-story buildings were on the perimeter, two-story buildings one avenue in, three-story buildings two avenues in, the buildings continuing to climb until terminating at the eight-story palace, two stories taller than its neighbors at the center of the city. There were four boulevards: two bisecting the avenues, two crossing the city diagonally. There were no hodgepodge clusters of random buildings in Coolatta. Each structure was uniformly large, housing multiple businesses and residences.

I was becoming frustrated. I had wandered aimlessly through Coolatta for half-an-hour and still hadn't found the penta shop. I was getting desperate enough that I considered asking the most ill-repute pedestrian I could find. I never considered asking my bodyguards. It never crossed my mind. It just seemed like one of those things you didn't discuss with your family. Who asks their parents about their sex life?

Before my desperation turned into action I spotted the sign, the WIZARDS' MARK, as some called it, a circular arrangement of denizens from each of the four major moralities: a trog, an arbol, a goblin, and a troll. Fred had described it to me before he took his leave of me. I didn't care to see the latter two in person. Fred assured me I didn't. Those of extreme negative morals had a tendency to be abrupt in their contempt for those unlike themselves---and often even for their kind. It was recommended to fight first before negotiating, or better yet, just run. The Wizards chose the symbols because they considered themselves to be TRUE

NEUTRALS, neither intentionally harming or helping, acting crazy or being anal.

The penta shop, called an emporium if it was sanctioned by the Wizards---which this one was---was in the penthouse of one of the four-story buildings. To reach the top of the building we had to climb an exterior ramp that wrapped around the building. There wasn't a railing, but the slight inward tilt of the ramp gave the illusion of stability. The door beneath the Wizard's Mark was unremarkable in appearance, except for it not having any visible means of opening it: no knob or handle.

Before I had the opportunity to examine it more fully the door opened inward. The sudden, unsolicited motion shocked me. Not having someone else on the other side of the door, didn't--- emporiums were managed by Wizards. The room beyond was enormous, apparently encompassing the entire fourth floor. Like the building, it was trapezoidal, its longest length spanning 30 meters. Its openness made it feel like a warehouse. The marble columns made if feel like a museum. The space was poorly used, with---at most---a score of bronze cylindrical tables spaced haphazardly throughout the room. On top of each were between 20 and 30 stones, rods, and rings, with the vast majority being stones.

The proprietor was a woman wearing a full length purple dress, with each of the four---declared---elem symbols dribbling down her chest. Her long platinum tresses were a nest of wild tangles. She was neither young nor old, tall nor short, slim nor stout. She emitted vitality, physical, intellectual, and emotional. "Twenty-three five," stated the woman in an ethereal, but penetrating voice. She sat on a tall-backed stool that not only spun around, but also rose and fell, all without any movement on her part.

"Don't you want to examine them first?" I asked.

"I knew what you possessed the moment you crossed the Bactrian. One elem doesn't differ from another in quality. Outside the tower we pay five silver per. Do not waste time dickering. You have another 41 minutes before you lose control of those men." The men smiled. "Every stone is available, most rods, and a few rings. What is your objective?"

I had planned to just exchange the elem for currency, but the proximity to so many penta was swaying my resolve. It was like I was a gambler walking into a casino, or an alcoholic into a bar. I heard the clock ticking. Forty minutes now until the mercenaries were free. I handed over the collecting rods as I thought it over. The Wizard's stool slid to a marble column. She discharged the rods into it, through an aperture one-third of the way up. She returned the empty rods to me. I returned them to their owners.

Collecting rods would be useful, but it didn't feel right keeping them. The elem might have been rightfully mine, because I---Fred, actually---found them, but not returning the rods would be stealing. I wouldn't be better than those men. Actually I would, since I didn't plan to force them to do anything against their will. That wasn't true either. They were my slaves until I released them? Maybe I wasn't better than them. Was I going to be re-created in the negative part of the Frontier the next time I died?

The Wizard slid to another column. Her chair raised a meter. She retrieved twenty-three gold coins and five silver ones from two slots in the marble. She returned to me, handing me the coins. I handed each of the men a gold. Their eyes lit up, shock surpassing their delight.

Now, what did I really want? I had enough gold to provision myself superfluously plus buy one stone. What was the one thing I wanted? That was easy. "Is there something that will return me to my pre-mutated form?" I asked.

"Temporarily, into almost anything: another person, yourself smooth and top-heavy, a cat, a drak."

"How long is temporary?"

"It depends on what you change into. Something similar to what you are now will last days. Something larger or smaller than you and appearing much different may last just an hour."

"That's what I want. One transformation stone please."

The Wizard slid to a cylinder and removed one of the stones. She returned to me, transferring the penta after I counted out twelve gold coins---ten plus a twenty-percent tariff for purchasing outside the tower. I was tempted to permanently borrow a handful of the stones on the way out, or maybe a rod. One of my henchmen beat me to it. The man with the mace roasted to death in a shower of electrical energy. I expected the room to smell like burnt flesh. The annihilation must have been so substantial even the odors were destroyed. There might be some ambiguity about their intentions, but the Wizards certainly knew their craft.

The Wizard slid over to the powdery residue that had once been a person. The gold coin I gave him, plus two silvers, and eight coppers, floated up to her from beneath the ash. As she slid back to the center of the room, the remnants of the body evaporated. Apparently, nothing of value remained.

As we hurriedly left I heard her mumbling to herself as she tossed the tinkling coins in her hand, "Even after the city takes half I'll still have enough to take Rockslide to a nice restaurant and a play."

If the ramp would have been steps we would have taken them two at a time. We couldn't leave the emporium quick enough. It had gotten dark while we were inside, making our descent more dangerous than our climb. There was enough indirect light from the city that with a modicum of caution we made it to the base of the building without injury.

I was anxious to leave Coolatta, but I still needed to buy a few things. I suggested to my cam that it fly through the city. I needed to buy enough supplies for what Fred had estimated to be a six day journey to Gulag. I wish I would have thought of my cam when I was looking for the emporium. It would have saved me half-an-hour and three kays. Without continuous suggestions my cam wandered off again. Fortunately it was already in the city, sniffing flowers and drinking their nectar. The quality of flowers may not have been as good in the city as in the wild, but there was a greater variety. Under my direction the cam found a row of shops that met my needs.

As I brought food, water skins, undergarments, socks, boots, and weapons for myself I contemplated what I was going to do with my henchmen. I had about 10 minutes remaining before they would turn on me. Maybe I should strand them somewhere in the city, then flee. Or should I leave the city with the men, but return on my own, so I can spend the night in a clean room with a soft bed?

Problems have a tendency to work themselves out on their own, but sometimes not in manner in which you have chosen them to be remedied. I should have foreseen this problem after the mace henchman got fried while attempting to steal penta. Another of my henchman got sticky fingers. Unfortunately he didn't get zapped. Department store security was considered to be inadequate, being manned by men the local police force declined to hire. This row of businesses implemented an unusual, but much more effective approach. Skeletons, of humans and canines, dropped out of closets. They surrounded us. The humans carried a machete in each hand. The canines had sharp teeth. The henchman with the battleaxe was sliced apart and bitten, but he was our only casualty during that instant of flat-footedness. He was the one who had stolen the trail mix, so good riddance.

Now that the henchmen knew what they were up against they were fighting machines, being even more proficient than they were against the cave bear. Of the three weapons they used, the war hammer was the most effective. It broke bones like they were straw. The staff's greatest advantage was its ability to attack from a distance. It efficiently tripped and broke legs without its controller receiving a scratch. The sword was least effective. The blade slid off the bones, but the man was proficient enough in its use that he was able to slice apart one of the skeletons.

The battle wasn't over when the last skeleton's bones were scattered. The henchman who died stood back up, his peeled away flesh and oozing, dark blood apparently no longer being an obstacle. What was left of his eyes peered ahead without emotion. He attacked. The surprise of having your dead friend suddenly come to back to life and begin attacking you should have shattered the henchmen's resolve, but they were able to sustain their ruthlessness. It wouldn't have surprised me to see them kill their own mother if she threatened them or they could make a profit from it. If they were my friends, would I be able to kill them? It seems unlikely, but so was killing my father. To each his, or her, own. The revived henchman was completely destroyed this time. To put an exclamation on the denial of his return, his bones were scattered like the skeletons, becoming so jumbled with them it was difficult to tell if this femur belonged to him or that scapula belonged to one of them.

With the activities within the building ceasing we were able to hear the commotion outside. Reinforcements had arrived, and from the fervent declarations they were making they were more than animated bones. Our only escape was fleeing further into the building. We came to a stairwell. Up or down? The decision was made for me when a large rat climbed up the stairs from below. We reached the second floor and saw another rat, this time coming down. GREAT! The henchman with the staff struck it with the tip of his weapon. It caromed off the wall then rolled down the stairs, thumping as it fell in 20 sim increments. We continued to climb. More rats were met and more rats struck. It was like watching a game of billiards.

I sent my cam on a reconnaissance mission. The city patrol was shocked by the devastation on the ground level. After taking a moment to surmise the situation, they began to climb, their pace slowed by stumbling over the dead rats they weren't quick enough to dodge.

We made it to the roof. I've seen people jump from one

roof to another---in holographs. Ten meters was too far to tempt mutation.

I expected the henchmen to become distraught from the onslaught of involuntary perilous events, but they were smiling. If one could remove the stress and the potential for death, it was quite an adventure we were having. They could. I couldn't. I wasn't able to sacrifice the future for the present. Living within the moment caused my stomach to tangle.

My cam caught up with me. A dozen patrolmen chasing it probably had more to do with in than it wanting companionship. If I could fly like it.... Maybe I could.

I pulled the stone I had bought at the emporium from the right pocket of my trousers. I looked towards the door at the top of the stairs. No one had appeared yet, but I could hear the thump of many feet approaching. The henchmen were ready, still smiling broadly. Only one patrolman could come through at a time, and the first one through will wish he was a step slower.

I swallowed the stone. Being in the prescience of men who would have taken me against my will if Fred hadn't stopped them, the last thing I wanted to do was place myself in a pre-orgasmic enthrall, but if I was to escape, the penta had to be activated. I attempted to contain the sensations internally, but I feared---even with a slight dampening of intensity---certain facial expressions and body movements would expose me. A lessening of intensity had its advantages, particularly under these circumstances, but I still felt saddened by the recognition of the perpetual decline of sensation. Instead of erupting this time the elemental energy flowed through my body in a steady stream. Instead of eating the perfect chocolate truffle it was like gobbling a liter of chocolate ice cream. My body not only tingled, it felt like it was being stretched, like I had just gotten out of bed, or was warming up before doing more extensive physical activity. A moment later, after my senses were able to perceive beyond the rapture, my extremities not only extended to their limit, they grew. I felt like an adolescent again, but a year of growth occurring in one minute. My body not only got larger, it contorted. My clothes ripped apart and fell to the ground. I guess I wasn't destined to wear clothing. Concern for my nudity didn't last. What I transformed into didn't have female specific anatomy. My arms became wings, my face a beak. My body elongated, I becoming every woman's dream of being inhumanly skinny. I expected my skin to grow feathers, or fur or scales. Instead it simply became harder. I glanced at my cam. I had become a larger version of it. OF COURSE! I wanted to transform into something that flew. And it was my model.

"CLIMB ON ABOARD!" I shouted, but it came out unintelligible, sounding more like a loud buzzing than human speech. The men surprisingly gave an understanding glance as they looked at me with one eye and the door with the other. Before they could decide if they really wanted to climb onto my back the first patrolman rushed through the doorway. He was struck, then tripped, then stabbed. He fell backward onto the men behind him. The domino effect continued to the base of the fourth floor. Being able to focus on just me momentarily the men reasoned that it was in their best interest to climb on my back. They held on more tightly than I liked. I could always knock them off if I needed to.

The patrolmen had recovered and had come back up the stairs. Without someone to challenge them this time they rushed through the door. I didn't know what to do. It was going to be trial and error. My arms had become wings. I needed to flap them. I did, with more enthusiasm than grace. I became airborne, briefly, then fell the meter I had risen back onto the roof. I was too heavy. Either I had to knock these guys off my back or.... I COULD GLIDE! The patrolmen charged me, with swords drawn. I leapt off the building as I closed my eyes. I kept my arms/wings fully extended so I wouldn't drop like a boulder. I must have pointed downward too much. I felt the air rushing beneath me. I forced my eyes back open. I was heading for the ground. Blind luck saved me. I had fallen above a boulevard. If I had been in the path of a building I would have hit it already. I stretched my neck towards the sky. I swooshed upward, less than a meter from the ground. As my momentum ceased I began to swoosh back down. I reacted quicker this time, being able to pull myself up two meters from the ground. My momentum wasn't as great. I was going to begin my next descent any second. I also had to turn if I didn't want to hit the city wall. I BENT MY BODY TO THE RIGHT, AND ACTUALLY TURNED THAT DIRECTION! I began my descent. I flapped my wings madly. I could feel myself tiring, but I had to not only retain my altitude, but increase it. The outer wall was two-stories high, and I wasn't quite that height now. The outermost avenue I was above was veering to the right. The outer wall was to my left and its perpendicular counterpart was just ahead. This was my one and only attempt at clearing the wall. With a burst of adrenaline assisting me I climbed a meter higher. Just sims to spare, and not even that for the entire flight. My belly scraped against the concrete and stone. I allowed the residual momentum to take me as far from Coolatta as possible: about a kay. It was well into night now. As a consequence, after we left the city lights we were nearly invisible to those who might follow. Even the moon was kind to us, it being conveniently concealed by clouds this evening.

Maybe it was time for my transformation to end, or the transformation ended early because of the strain I put it under, or because of my injury. Whatever the reason, I returned to my partially mutated female human form upon landing. It was an awkward situation, indeed, finding the men still on me. Surprisingly they removed themselves without me suggesting it.

Fred was by my side within seconds. He flapped his wings over me frantically. He probably thought I was on the precipice of death. Hardly that. I was mainly sore. Seeing me smile, he slowed the flapping and ceased it entirely after my belly had scabbed over and healed. "I'm sorry I don't have enough energy left to finish the job," he said. "It'll probably leave a scar." Great. Now I'll not only be a hairy flat-chested woman, I also have a scar down the length of my belly.

"That's hardly a wound at all," said the hammer henchman. He took off his leather jerkin to reveal four new scars running the length of his muscular chest. "That was from a cheetah. If it hadn't run so damn fast away from me I would be wearing its hide."

"Here," said the sword henchman. He handed me a pair of breeches, a shirt, and moccasins. "I like looking at mounds, and seats, but not my sister's. We've been through so much together I consider you family. I may be a bit of a pervert, but not that perverted."

"And here's something to protect yourself with," said the staff henchman, handing me a dagger. "The longer I have it the more likely I'll cut myself with it. That's why I use a staff."

"Thank you." I felt humbled. If men like these can occasionally act decent and generous maybe there was some hope. Maybe living forever on a penal colony wasn't going to be that bad. "I need to be going now. It's a long way to Gulag, and I'd like to put some distance between myself and Coolatta before I camp."

"We're coming with you," stated the hammer henchman. "You paid us each a gold, even after we almost had our way with you. That's not to say you wouldn't have enjoyed it."

"I don't have any more money to pay you."

"That's not exactly true," said the sword henchman, tossing my clinking coin purse in the air, and catching it with his hand. "After you did that strip tease I thought it would be beneficial to pick this up."

"HEY! GIVE THAT BACK!"

"Scavenger law says it's now mine, but I always share with my brothers...and sisters."

"So, if I can't pay you, why would you want to tag along with me?"

The staff henchman replied, "Because you've given us as much excitement in the last three or four hours as we've had in years, and we've haven't led boring lives. As long as we stick with

147

you we'll stay entertained."

"You sure you want to be around someone as death prone as I? I've only been on Limbo a couple of weeks and I've already died four times."

"Do you think we're the type of people who are concerned with an occasional mishap?" questioned the hammer henchman.

Chapter 19

NUGGETS

We walked through the night. I wasn't too concerned with my safety. Short of fighting an army, my three human companions could handle my defense. Even then they would have a fighting chance.

When Fred intercepted me I assured him the men didn't need to be re-controlled. I don't think he entirely believed me. He held back, but with one eye glued to them at all times.

We also walked most of the following day. I preferred travelling the most kays the first day of a trip. Some people became more energetic as the days passed, the earlier activity being calisthenics for the duration, but I wore down. If I did more the first day I didn't feel guilty doing less on subsequent days. Our first full day of traveling was mundane. Walking through knee-high grass was faster and safer than walking through a forest, but it was boring.

Our first night of camping was as mundane, until.... We set up a watch---the men did. Likely a combination of believing me too delicate for the task, and not trusting me to be sufficiently observant. Fred's participation wasn't discussed. They considered him a pet, someone else's pet they were obligated to tolerate. The sword henchman, who had the third watch, was missing when we woke. No one heard anything, even Fred.

After a thorough examination of the perimeter we found evidence of a recent approach and departure. The matted down trail looked fresh. From the severity of breaks---of blades of grass--- and the smudges of blood, it was apparent something injured, or dead, had been dragged.

We followed the trail to a tree in a small grove. The sword henchman---what was left of him---was sticking out of a cavity, about five meters up the tree. A large tawny cat chewed on a bone. I convinced myself it didn't belong to the sword henchman. The cat was half again as large as was typical for its species. Its sky-blue eyes glanced down at me. The terror that overwhelmed me prevented any movement, short of respiration, which was quite active. So awed was I in its presence, if it commanded me to chop off my arm and feed it to it I believe I would have complied. Thankfully its head swiveled back to the sword henchman. It returned to eating.

"We can't do anything for him now," said the hammer henchman.

"Let's walk away while we still can," suggested the staff henchman.

Before resuming our journey to Gulag we explored the grove. Trail rations were more hardy than tasty. Fresh berries or fruit would be a welcomed supplement to our breakfast.

"So you think your friend will be re-created nearby?" I asked.

"Unlikely," the hammer henchman replied. "Those in our profession have a tendency to be re-created east of here." East was the direction of the Negative Frontier, a polite way of saying someone was going to Limbo's version of hell.

"But there is a certain honor among thieves to retrieve their gear," said the staff henchman. "It's the closest thing to a memorial we have."

"It's also a quick way to make a buck."

I was shocked. "So you plan to sell his gear instead of retaining it for him?"

"We'll constantly praise his existence while his gear is in our possession. It's cumbersome carrying an extra piece of rusting armor, or tattered boots, or a raggedy backpack." Logical, but being a woman I couldn't completely remove myself from the sentimentality of the situation.

As we searched for food a tree fell towards us, nearly flattening us. We had first believed someone, or thing, had deliberately attempted to crush us, until refuted by his, or its, absence. We examined where the trunk had snapped, 125 sims up the tree. Much of its interior was gone. Something small darted towards me from within the fallen tree. I was struck in the face with a pungent liquid. It felt like my eyes were floating in a pool of molten lava. I fell backwards.

A few excruciating minutes later the burning stopped. My sight was blurry at first, then gradually became clear. Fred was leaning over me. His wings slowed to a halt. "I should charge for my services. If you were my only client I would still become rich."

"Is everybody else okay?" I asked as I sat up.

"They were only termites," stated the hammer henchman.

The staff henchman displayed an evil grin. "We could burn them. If that acidic pitch they defend themselves catches fire they may even explode."

"WAIT!" I shouted as the man was on the verge of throwing a match onto the log. "Do you have enough elemental energy left in you to do one more thing?" I asked Fred.

"Probably two more today. You were barely injured this time."

"How many things can you freeze at one time?"

"It depends on their size."

I looked at the log, then extended my index finger and thumb. "About this long."

Fred was able to freeze, petrify, stiffen, whatever term you wish to use, all the termites in the fallen tree. There were about 40 of them.

"You're not planning to make them our dinner tonight?" questioned the hammer henchman.

"I need to be able to attack from a safe distance, especially now, with our troops diminishing."

"Grenades?" the staff henchman questioned. Both he and his associate hooted after I nodded in affirmation.

As we left the grove we heard a crunching sound. "More termites?" suggested the hammer henchman. He walked towards the tree that made the sound, to investigate. What poked its head out at him was a thousand times larger than he expected. Its head was half the size of his body. Mandibles, 50 sims wide, lunged at him. The only thing that saved the man was his backwards hurtle, accompanied by a fall, and the creature being partially trapped by the uneven egress at the base of the tree.

Without hesitation the staff henchman and I each lit a termite grenade and threw them at the base of the tree. The fire had a greater effect on the tree than it had on the creature. We threw a second round of grenades, then a third. The small explosions, and the heat that accompanied them, finally cracked open the jet-black carapace. Once exposed the tender interior baked quickly.

The flames we created didn't restrain themselves. They expanded to the other trees in the grove. In minutes we were going to be burned to death, unless smoke inhalation killed us first.

As the targeted tree crumbled, the hole at its base, and the burrow beyond, became more prominent. If that thing could fit in there, we certainly could, with room to spare. The staff henchman used his weapon to pry out the creature. It broke apart into hot crumbling nuggets, like the coals at the base of a fire. After we had squeezed ourselves past the carcass debris we grabbed the largest piece of exoskeleton we could find and barricaded the opening with it. We filled in the gaps with dirt.

We climbed on our hands and knees deeper into the hole. It was a meter in diameter, enough space that we didn't feel claustrophobic, but too small to stand up in. My cam had fled when the fire had spread. Through its eyes I saw that every tree was on fire, including the cat's. It dragged its kill away, preferring to eat its food raw. I suggested to the cam that it head east. Eventually, the grove will burn itself out, preferably before also catching the prairie on fire.

When smoke began to enter through the cracks in our barrier we went even deeper. It was becoming too dark to see, our bodies blocking the smoky light. By the time we rounded the first bend in the tunnel it was pitch black. The hammer henchman was able to light his lantern by touch. We could now see each other, but not much more, just earth, and that narrow excavation that persisted as far as the limit of our illumination.

I was first to enter the hole, as my henchmen requested, to protect me from the flames, but now I was stuck in that position, leading when I preferred to be guided. Until I came to Limbo I made my own decisions, but in this Gaea-forsaken place I was still an infant. I knew my limitations. If there was an easy way to trade places with someone I would have.

Safety initiated our descent. Curiosity maintained it. Where was this tunnel going to lead us? To more of the large, black beetles? To a litter of baby beetles? I don't know why we were so determined to discover their lair. My companions hinted at the potential for treasure.

"Insects aren't going to place the same importance on what we value," I commented.

"How about the people who came here before us, those not as gifted in surviving an attack by one of those beetles?" countered the hammer henchman.

"Am I the only person who has heard the expression HISTORY HAS A WAY OF REPEATING ITSELF?" Neither man responded, but I kept on crawling.

I heard something ahead of us, around the next bend of the tunnel. I got up on my haunches and extended my dagger. After a couple of stressful moments of waiting, nothing came. Cautiously I rounded the bend. Nothing. Whatever it was, it had scurried away. I hope that meant it was more scared of us than we were of it. We continued on. More scurrying, always just out of sight. Then a thump. Twenty meters ahead of us the tunnel emptied into a large cavern. Unlike the tunnel, its walls, ceiling, and floor were stone. It was longer and wider than our illumination permitted us to see. Its many partially visible alcoves gave it an irregular shape. Its ceiling was 10 meters high near its center, barely tall enough for us to stand fully erect at its perimeter. A scattering of stalactites, stalagmites and columns were near the tunnel's entrance. Other places looked like they had once had them, but had been broken off and carried away.

More scurrying was heard. This time from more than one set of feet and from more than one direction. They were more active whenever the lantern was moved. "I can see in the dark," said Fred, "but only when light isn't blinding me. I'll investigate our shy friends who live in the shadows." Fred flew away into the darkest part of the cavern. Shrieks were heard. Many sets of scurrying feet headed our way. Fred came back into view with a sea of the largest, ugliest rats imaginable fleeing in front of him. They had six legs and too many teeth. And they were heading right for us. "WHAT ARE YOU DOING!?" I shouted at Fred. "You're herding them towards us. We'll by trampled to death."

"I'm sorry, Dinga. That wasn't my intention. As soon as they saw me, they started running. Maybe they think I'm an owl or a hawk. Don't they know I'm a vegetarian?"

"I'm no vegetarian," said the hammer henchman, "and I'm

going to have chicken-lizard soup if I survive."

"About time we had some fun," commented the staff henchman. The six-legged rats intercepted us. The staff henchman knocked them away like they were baseballs being thrown at him from a pitching machine.

When Fred rejoined us the rats fled. "I don't think they'll attack as long as I'm nearby."

"You keep mosquitoes away too?" asked the hammer henchman.

"You're our hero, Fred." I scratched his bony ridge until he started cooing. "You think it's safe to go back up?"

"I would give it another hour," said the hammer henchman.

"As long as we're here, let's do some exploring," said the staff henchman. "These caves may not have that treasure I hoped for, but they might have elem. Without anyone doing any prospecting down here there's been time for it to collect."

Staying close to Fred, we investigated the alcoves. Some of them were just extensions of the cavern, but three were entrances to tunnels, all tall enough to stand up in. So far no elem.

We investigated the tunnel closest to our potential escape route, first. A three-meter tall bipedal insect dropped down on us. It was one of the most frightening things I had ever seen---and I have worked in a bar. Its exoskeleton was a mottled gray. It had hooks instead of arms, the four of them looking machete sharp. The staff henchman attempted to push the creature into the tunnel with his staff. A hook sliced off the tip of the piece of wood. The hammer henchman wasn't able to get close enough to the creature to cause it any damage, its appendages being longer than his weapon.

What was I going to do with just a dagger? I could at least provide my companions more light. I picked up the lantern the hammer henchman had dropped, and thrust it in front of me like I was helping a mechanic. The creature's calculated attacks became wild flaying. Its diminished effectiveness permitted the men to force it into the tunnel. The staff henchman modified his grip as he swung his weapon back and up. He leaned in as he threw the staff. Its broken end pierced the creature's cranium. It tipped backward, landing in a crumbled heap. Not willing to risk a recovery, the men pulverized the body.

"How much longer now until it's safe to return to the surface?" I asked.

The staff henchman removed his weapon from the carcass and cleaned it by rubbing it on the stone wall beside him. "We just need to be slightly more cautious."

"Slightly?"

"Too cautious and we'll have no fun."

"Easy for you to say," said the hammer henchman. "You're weapon is twice as long as mine."

The staff henchman snickered. Men may age, but they would always be boys.

The hammer henchman was in bad shape. He was cut in numerous places, down to the bone. If Fred hadn't heeled him he wouldn't have lived long enough to make it to the surface, if we left immediately: he had lost that much blood. Fred wasn't able to replace the blood, but he was able to accelerate its replenishment, and he prevented any more from leaking out. He ran out of elemental energy before the hammer henchman was fully healed, but his wounds were at least sealed.

"I suggest we rest here," I said. "Visibility is good, and we know the area, to the extent we have become familiar with two of the nasties that frequent it."

The men agreed. The hammer henchman needed to heal. The rest of us, a mental break from perpetual vexation.

As luck would have it, I had to use the toilet. I'm not particularly shy about urinating in front of people, not since being sentenced to Limbo. Who wants to go off in the dark alone where a monster could be lurking under every rock or above every branch? But it wasn't my bladder I needed to empty. I hated when stress tied my bowels in a knot. I explained my situation the best a dignified woman could.

"Don't take too long," suggested Fred. Like a bird cared where it went.

"And take the extra lantern with you," insisted the staff henchman. "It should keep almost everything away from you." He had to add that modifier.

Being able to see less than ten meters with the lantern, didn't mean others couldn't see me from a much greater distance. I was more than ten meters from my companions and I could still see them. If I didn't want to douse the lantern to maintain my privacy I better find a boulder to hide behind.

I found that boulder and squatted. Oh, how I missed a nice porcelain commode---even a slivery wooden one. The light suddenly went out. I thought it was the lantern, but a fraction of a second later something rubbery was draped over me. I was being squeezed from all sides. Guys, please don't become gentlemanly all of a sudden. Someone look this way.

Chapter 20

A SMILE ON HIS FACE

I must have died again, but instead of being re-created in a prairie I was back in the cavern. "You nearly suffocated," said Fred. "You had already passed out when we cut the ray off you." I leaned up. FEEK! "I think you broke a couple of ribs. After my elemental energy recharges I'll heal you. You'll have to put up with the pain for another hour." I was alive. That was something. It's been awhile since I've experienced so much pain. Lately, a moment of agony was followed by death. It hurt worse when I breathed, in and out. I tried holding my breath. It made it worse. A reprieve, but also a more pronounced response when the breath came. I was tempted to encourage my demise---calling it suicide felt too much like giving up. I always felt so good after being re-created. Maybe if I was guaranteed not to mutate, again. The next time that happens I'll probably look like a cave woman. Wouldn't that be fitting considering my surroundings?

My cam was efficient in fleeing. It was 10 kays away, and continually adding to the distance between us. I feared there might be a limit to the range I could communicate with it, with the possibility of losing it for good if I broke contact with it. I encouraged it to return to the burnt grove. From what I could see from a distance, the smoke had died down to a few isolated wisps. The prairie was wet. It must have rained. That couldn't have been coincidence. Maybe Gaea did exist and was able to control some things. It pleased me more than it frightened me.

I wasn't an atheist, not entirely. I was open to the possibility of a superior life form that occasionally piddled in our affairs. I just didn't think it likely. To know someone was looking out for me, even if He, She, or It didn't always do things the way I wanted them to be done, was comforting. It was like I had parents, but ones that didn't abuse me or allowed me to be abused.

"We can return to the surface," I declared. "The fire is out."

Once I had made the announcement, we focused on crawling up that dirt tunnel as hurriedly as our physical limitations allowed. Our tunnel vision was rewarded. A stalactite---or was it a stalagmite---entered the hammer henchman's back and reappeared through his chest. We turned to defend ourselves. Not yet reaching the tunnel, we were too exposed to flee.

We were surrounded. The three-meter tall hairy brutes were more human than not, their excessive hairiness, their long pointed ears, and their red eyes being the most extreme visible mutations. Four of the five carried a stalactite.

We, the staff henchman and I, were herded away from the tunnel. Fred had escaped. I didn't blame him. The thrown stalactite was retrieved. The brute didn't bother cleaning it, bits of the hammer henchman's flesh clinging to it, like a knife that had just cut a cake. With his free hand he dragged the hammer henchman's body, as his companions pushed us forward.

"I guess they like their meat fresh," stated the staff henchman.

"We don't know that. Maybe we'll just be slaves."

"Then why was he taken?"

"Taxidermy."

"I always wanted to be put on a pedestal."

"Are you still glad you came along with me?"

"I would have died eventually. We both know it. At least I had a little more excitement before I was re-created. I would have hated to have been captured by the police. Coolatta doesn't kill their prisoners, no matter the offense. Death is just another means of escape. Prisoners are given a life sentence of hard labor. Going down with a weapon in my hand is better than moving rocks all day."

"But you don't even have that anymore."

"That's the one thing I would have changed."

Even if we had weapons, we wouldn't have been very successful with them. Our lanterns were left behind.

There was a swooshing sound. Three of the hairy men were thrown to the ground, each punctured with a minimum of two small javelins. The other two fled. What fortunate twist of events was this? I just realized something. I COULD SEE! Not very well, but I could discern the hairy men on the ground and the javelins sticking out of them. "Can you see anything yet?" I asked the staff henchman.

"It's still pitch black."

I RECEIVED MY SECOND ABILITY!

I looked around. We were in a cavern, smaller than the one we waited out the fire in. A score of bipedal reptiles, slightly smaller than me, surrounded us. They stunk terribly, inhumanly so, like bile on a bad day, or a skunk playing in the warm rain. I thought I might get sick, but that would only add to the stench. I willed myself not to.

"Now I wish I had stayed in Coolatta," spoke the staff henchman. "It's like returning to the womb, but in a parallel, demented universe where it's instead the stomach and bowels."

We were herded away, with the carcasses of the three brutes and the hammer henchmen dragged behind.

The staff henchman had enough. He went berserk. He yanked a javelin from the reptile closest to him and jabbed him and four of his friends before he went down. A second human body was dragged behind me, this one with a smile on his face.

I was alone again. Did it always have to be this way on Limbo? As soon as you got to know someone they died or you died? Never having friends before, I didn't miss what I didn't have. But now…. It wasn't that it made me sad for me to longer be able to spend time with my friends. I lost as much of myself as I lost them. I was a better person when those I cared about were around me. I actually wanted to do things, instead of attempting to extend my existence.

Dust blew onto my captors and me. The reptiles fell over. Whatever affected them spared me, or so I thought. A delay, not a reprieve. I too became drowsy. The last thing I wished for was to land on the hard ground and not on one of those smelly reptiles.

I awoke believing I had died and had been re-created, and for the second time today I was mistaken. Maybe I was becoming less death prone. Fred was beside me and he wasn't alone. I found myself in a large cavern that smelled vaguely like a farm. Surrounding me were mushroom headed men. They varied in height from one meter to four. Their gray bodies were as bald and rubbery as their craniums. They were either of one gender or concealed their differences well. There were no curves, bulges, or protrusions.

I smiled at Fred. "At least you're here this time," I told him. "But for your sake, I wish you weren't. How were they able to capture you?"

Fred appeared perplexed, then he smiled, finally comprehending. "You are mistaken. The fungs freed you from the zards, who stole you from the subterranean terrors. They are telepathic. They sensed my distress and contacted me. They are exceedingly empathetic, deploring violence. They agreed to help me free you as long as they did so without harming your captors. Most of their abilities are activated by the release of spores, including the one that caused your drowsiness."

"Are we safe here? Won't the zards wish to seek revenge?"

"They may wish to, but they won't. The fungs are too powerful."

"Did they also free my companions?"

"They have no use for the dead. Being neutral in morality they aren't self-righteous or mean spirited. Death doesn't facilitate their nourishment."

"So they're vegetarian, like you?"

"They're more extreme than that. They get nutrients from excrement. They'll consume any animal's wastes: zard, subterranean terror, human, bat. Relying on others has been the foundation for their pacifist views."

"If they ever had trouble harvesting excrement, would they be willing to attack another species to survive?"

"That has never been an issue. Who would be willing to hoard their feces to deprive someone of it?"

"Would it be rude to leave so abruptly? I think I might go insane if I don't feel sunlight on my face soon or be able to take a breath of fresh air."

"The fungs are as apathetic as they are empathetic. I know the two seem contradictory, but they view their environment differently than we do. They are attuned to others' feelings, positive and negative, but they don't have any feelings of their own. They will be as comfortable with us leaving as staying, whatever makes US happy."

"Then let's go, if you can return us to the surface."

"One of the first abilities I received was spatial positioning. I always know where I am and where I've been, how long it took me to get from here to there, and how many more minutes it will be until moonbright or sundim."

It took twenty minutes to return to the dirt tunnel, and barely five more to return to the surface. It's amazing how fast people can travel when they know where they're heading.

The sunlight on my face would have to wait. It was dark when we entered the charcoal wasteland. Wisps of smoke spiraled upward: credits after the climatic terminus of the main feature. We fled the stench of the arboreal genocide. It would be hours still before we seriously considered bedding down for the night. The prairie wasn't completely untouched. We passed through patches of singed grass for three kays. A few minutes after passing the last patch my cam returned to me. It was a good sign, a signal to sojourn.

"I believe enough of my elemental energy has returned to perform one last task before bed." Fred flew into the air, then spun around. The air around us began to distort, not consistently like opaque glass, more like heat waves. I stepped towards it to investigate. "I wouldn't. You won't get electrocuted, but you'll feel more than a tinkle." That was enough of a warning for me.

"Is it a force field?"

"An electromagnetic curtain."

"You sure it will protect us? If it will only give me a shock, what harm will it do to something nasty?"

"It's not intended to kill, just to conceal."

"But I can see through it."

"From this direction. Haven't you heard of a one-way mirror or tinted glass?"

"What makes it appear that way? The distortions in it?"

"The wind. Have you ever opened a window with the curtains drawn?"

"This electromagnetic invisibility curtain won't actually protect us?"

"It produces enough of an electrical charge to keep insects out."

"So if something runs at us in the middle of the night we might get trampled to death?"

"I'm a light sleeper. It's likely I will wake up before that happens."

"Likely?"

"Get some sleep, Dinga. Considering how often you get into trouble it will be a long day tomorrow."

Like I was going to be able to fall asleep knowing I could be trampled to death---but somehow I did. Exhaustion makes even lumpy grass feel like a pillow-top mattress. I was shocked when I woke an hour later and found Fred perched on my hip, then I became comforted when I saw that his eyes were closed. If he felt it was safe enough to sleep it was going to be okay, at least until the moon brightened, beginning a new day. It was comforting having someone make this close of contact with me. It was like having a kitten sleeping with me. As I fell back to sleep the kitten morphed into a baby. That was the second time I dreamt about having a child. I never dreamt of such things before coming to Limbo. Why now?

We were still four days from Gulag, so we started moving as soon as we got up. The electromagnetic curtain was gone when I woke.

Later that morning my cam disappeared. Only one other

time had it done that: when it had been killed and consumed by those bats. It was unlikely the lack of communication between us was just temporary. I had contact with it even while it slept. But Limbo was dynamic. My cam would be re-created and the contact re-established.

I was compelled to discover the cause of its demise. It had smelled something deliciously sweet and had flown towards it. It wasn't quite in the direction we were heading, but we didn't have to backtrack to go there either. A single plant appeared on the horizon. It was the only object for kays, animal, vegetable, or mineral, so it had to be the final destination of my cam. From a hundred meters away I began to smell its honeysuckle-like fragrance. Instead of branches it had vines. They looked rubbery, like squid tentacles. It was moving---actually moving---towards us, but slowly. Its dark gray roots zigzagged beneath it like a snake.

"Don't get too close," Fred warned.

I had no intention to, but its slow movement did allow me to get closer to it than let's say, a lion. Something hit me on my arm---it went numb. Then a leg---it also went numb. I fell. Then my belly---it went numb. I continued to be struck, each debilitating blow making it easier for the next. The plant was nearly upon me now. Its tentacles had stretched to three times their original length---ten meters or so---in its successful attempt to strike me. It stung where they hit me. It wasn't the shock that had deadened my nerves. The tentacles were lubricated with a greasy substance that caused local anesthesia. Something covered my mouth, suffocating me. It too became numb. I was surprised Fred hadn't rescued me yet. That should teach me not to rely on others. Until I came to Limbo I never relied on anyone. Now I had taken it to the other extreme.

Chapter 21

GALE FORCE WINDS

I woke in a dense forest. It was the first time I had been re-created in some place other than a prairie. Was it symbolic, or chance? I had no idea how far away I was from where I died. The sun was lower in the sky, indicating I was further from it, but on which side? I still hadn't felt the prescience of my cam. I set it free, the notion that we would one day be reconnected. Now that I had also died it was unlikely either of us was similar enough to our prior selves to retain the bond. Even minute mutations could prevent recognition.

I began moving towards the sun. I had to do something, and the one place I knew I would be able to find was Gulag, it being directly below the orb. The couple of days I was delayed from my goal was insignificant. Being alone again, that was something to become depressed about. I had some survival skills now, but how was I going to survive psychologically?

My body continued to revert into something more feral. The hairs on my arms, legs, belly---and chest---had darkened and become more numerous. My face itched. There was even hair there now. The hairs looked different than they did before my last re-creation. I brought my arm up close to examine it. The hairs had smaller hairs branching from them. Like my body didn't have enough hair already. Now my hair had to have hair. My mounds had smoothed out even more. I hadn't been this flat since I wore a training bra. My nails, on my hands, and feet, had also mutated, becoming longer and thicker. As I sipped water from a pool I didn't recognize the person staring back at me. Even my bone structure had begun to change, the most prominent feature the elongation of my skull. How will this end? Will it ever end? Will I continue to mutate from one form to another for eternity? I would have cried if I had sufficient emotionally fortitude. I was completely drained. So much had happened so rapidly.

I plodded on, towards the sun, towards Gulag, towards the Wizards Keep. A glimmer of hope. Maybe the Wizards could return my femininity. My steps became sprightlier. Distinct tracks could be seen behind me now instead of two troughs. And Thumbringer and Claw would probably be there. Did they view me more as a friend or a crazed death prone vagabond? I should have been nicer to them. How often does someone save your life? With my stumbling and bumbling many have been given the opportunity.

The forest became a jungle, then a swamp. I had to be careful where I stepped. Crocodiles were in the water, and some of them were enormous: eight to ten meters long. Crocodiles were the most abundant predators, but not the only ones. One of the oddest looked like a hippopotamus, but with a neck like a giraffe. Its shoulders had bushy hair the same color and texture as the dismal straw-colored vegetation in the water. Its eyes looked like an insect's, being multi-faceted. Its tail was spiky, like a mace, which is used with great agility, to a waterfowl's detriment. It consumed the unfortunate creature in two large bites with its enormous mouth. I thought I was a goner when a beam of light (concentrated energy?) shot out of its eyes. It missed me by two meters, but not the crocodile that was a meter behind me. The long-necked swamp beast had saved my life, inadvertently, perhaps, but I'll take what I can get---modest compensation for contemporary and persistent strife. Maybe I was becoming less death prone. There had been many days between my last two re-creations.

I made a hasty retreat onto a jumbled strip of land. I sought the route least likely to terminate, but with the foliage being as dense as it was I could only see so far ahead of me. It was particularly troublesome whenever I had to backtrack through an area I saw a potentially dangerous animal cross just moments before.

If I had my choice in elemental abilities, death ray would be at the top of my list. If you thought about it scientifically, it wasn't that strange. If electric eels could produce electric current why couldn't something concentrate it into a beam?

I was ravenous: a recurrent complication of re-creation, at least for me. One would think with the abundance of life in a swamp I wouldn't have a problem finding a meal. Maybe if you liked to eat bugs or mice, or leeches. I was mutating, but not to that degree---yet. Whatever I ended up eating, animal, vegetable, or mineral, I was going to have to eat it raw. Some people believed eating uncooked food was sophisticated. The fear was eating something poisonous. Dying didn't concern me: I was alone, indefinitely, in the middle of nowhere. I was more worried about the bellyache. Pain I could endure, but not discomfort. Hurt me and be done with it. To linger is to torture, never knowing when or if the next drop will fall.

The first thing I considered eating was a centipede. This was no civilized creepy crawly. It was as long as the distance between the tips of my fingers to my elbow---a cubit I believe the archaic measurement was called. I watched the centipede for a few minutes as I contemplated if I really wanted to eat it. Before I was able to push myself off that precipice it lunged towards a rodent---who would have thought something like that could move that fast---and swallowed it whole. If I ate it now I was going to have a buffet.

I should have just hit the centipede on the head with a big stick or stomped on it, and be done with it. Sometimes doing was better than thinking. Being as fixated as I was on that small area of the swamp the centipede was centered in I was oblivious to the head twice as large as mine that snatched the centipede from the precipice of my grasp. In one gulp it was gone. The buffet had gotten larger.

The stalk the head was attached to curled, enabling the head to look at me, from an inverted position. If I had been wearing pants they would have become wet. Three more heads looked at me, from a more standard orientation. I spun around as I back-peddled. The heads were attached to a single body. Another hydra. I hadn't taken the time to count the number of heads--- there were others that hadn't given me the time of day, yet. What was I saying a few minutes ago about no longer being so death prone? And there were no elem harvesters to rescue me this time.

Gale force winds tore through the swamp, it going from calm to chaos instantly. Water sprayed everywhere. Trees were dislodged. The hydra hid its heads underwater. A tornado cut its way through the jungle. Debris of some sort was inside it. As sudden as the wind began, it dissipated, but not before the debris was deposited beside me. CLAW AND THUMBRINGER! I rushed into their arms. I hadn't cried since I had murdered my father--- before I murdered him---there was no sorrow in what I had done to him. That's not to say I hadn't cried false tears a time or two. Sometimes such displays increased the value of a barter. Men were so easily moved by a woman in distress.

Through whimpers I forced out, "I was on my way to find you, but I died again...." After a moment of basking in the companionship of my friends, curiosity exceeded sentimentality. I asked, "What was that thing that brought you here?"

"The same thing that helped us escape the leviathan," Thumbringer responded. "The stone did create an air elemental."

"A jinn, actually," Claw interjected. " Elementals have free will."

Thumbringer continued. "So voluminous was the air that it had to be released one way or another. Instead of the leviathan popping, the air was expelled through its mouth."

"It could have been worse."

"Like two iron balls shot out of a cannon we became

167

airborne. The logical outcome was for us to plunge into the sea a few seconds later."

"My desperate prayer didn't bring Gaea or Jesus, but it saved us never-the-less. I became flip. Exuberance feeds emotion, not intellect. I suggested to whoever saved us, "YOU COULD DO BETTER THAN THAT. TAKE US TO GULAG!" I hadn't realized yet the near god-like powers I possessed were the result of enslaving a jinn rather than being a conduit for God."

"He learned the truth when our cyclone chariot didn't dissipate upon landing. Being annoyed at having the violent wind whipping around him, he told it to go away. YOU RELEASE MY BOND? it inquired."

"I JUST WANT YOU TO GO AWAY, I responded."

"And it did."

"After we calmed, the ramifications of what we did sunk in."

"We relinquished free labor, free transportation, who knows what else."

"We had no right to enslave it. It was once human, before its soul was snatched."

"I still think we should have had it do a few more things for us before we released it, fair payment for its freedom."

"You sell your elem to the Wizards?" I asked.

"Indeed we did," Thumbringer answered. "You are now a wealthy woman, Darling, and as soon as you find yourself something to put all your gold in we'll give you your share." Thumbringer examined me thoroughly, his eyes expressing more amusement than debauchery. I don't know if I was more relieved, or offended.

"Do you think it's still worth the effort, finding some clothes to wear?"

Claw was shocked. His face reddened as he adverted his eyes. "Miss Dinga, you might be hairier than you used to be, but you're still most definitely a woman."

"Looking like you do now, we'll have to cover you,"

Thumbringer commented. "Certain doors will be closed traveling with a mutant."

How amazing it is how one's emotions can change so suddenly. First I was idolized for being a woman, then I was trashed for no longer resembling one. I couldn't take either friend's comments to heart. Claw would see me as a sexy, beautiful woman even if I became gnarled, wrinkled, and gray. Thumbringer, he would tell me the truth I needed to hear, even if it pained me to hear it.

"You wouldn't happen to have some extra clothing, would you?"

"Darling, given your history, we thought it essential we bring a few things for you." Thumbringer plunged into his pack and pulled out a pair of cotton britches and a top.

They fit, but just barely. That was the price a woman pays for a man buying her clothes. Did Thumbringer miscalculate my size or did my body mutate out of the size I normally wore? There was also the possibility that Thumbringer thought I actually wore clothes this small---bless him if he did. Or that he just liked to look at women wearing tight-fitting clothes---curse fashion over comfort. I chose not to discuss my physique with the men. For the women who did, they didn't covet an honest reply.

I was going to ask if they had also brought shoes for me, until I looked down at my feet. The point became moot. My feet were not only substantially larger than before, but also misshapen. They were wider, with my toes pointed outward, making them look more like triangles than quadrilaterals. My toes were atrocious, the nails on them being even more substantial than the ones on my hands.

Thumbringer examined me in detail again, after I dressed. I used to like men giving me such attention, but that was before I began to mutate. I became subconscious. I had to actively prevent myself from covering those areas I deemed most flawed. "It would be best if you shaved your face and hands," Thumbringer said bluntly. It was like being told you had bad breath, but worse, because most people have experienced bad breath---intermittently or perpetually, depending on the individual. How many women have to shave their faces?

"Maybe I could wear a hood or something." I didn't want something sharp touching my face. I think I would rather live in this swamp the rest of my life than have to shave my face, even once. Doing it every day was unfathomable. Sure, I had a phobia, but it was a phobia derived from living in a modern society. Hair removal had become razor-free for centuries. It was the equivalent of walking from one place to another instead of taking a transport. But what had I been doing since my arrival? No, I couldn't do it. "You have a hat, or a scarf?"

Claw pulled a towel out of his pack. I wrapped it around my head. Thumbringer laughed, "You look like one of those zealots in Golden Sands."

"I'm guessing I shouldn't take that as a compliment."

"Women in Golden Sands are simultaneously slaves and trophies."

"How is that different than any other place?"

"Well, the arrangement the zealots have is law. Being a commodity, women are collected, like cattle. A man with four wives is much more respected than a man with three."

"What about a man with just one wife, or none?"

"Well, the ones with none try to rectify that situation, through repentance or bloodshed."

"I imagine the pool of woman to fight over is limited. What woman in her right mind wouldn't flee from such a culture?"

"You'd be surprised. There are some women who believe it's their role on Limbo to be subservient to men, as punishment for being too independent before they were sentenced. They believe if they listened to their father they wouldn't be in this predicament."

"If I did whatever my father told me to do I definitely wouldn't be here. My mother would be dead and I would have performed many of her wifely obligations."

Well, that lightened the mood. Sometimes it was best not to share everything with your friends. "How did the two of you find me?"

They looked at one another. Claw nodded his approval for Thumbringer to recite the tale. "We almost didn't. It would have been futile looking for you. You could have been re-created anywhere on Limbo."

"Not the negative part of the Frontier," Claw insisted.

"Unlikely, but that still leaves 80% of Limbo. We decided to return to the Liver Peninsula. It was the area of Limbo we were most familiar with, and there were those elem to unearth outside those spider holes. Shortly after leaving Gulag the jinn appeared."

"Elemental, actually, now that is was free. We were concerned it might want to take revenge upon us for enslaving it, but instead it thanked us. After the initial elation of regaining its sovereignty it sought its own kind. From them it learned it was rare for a jinn to be released so soon after its creation. Often they aren't intentionally released at all. Over time the hold their creator has on them dissipates. Eventually the jinn breaks free of the bond. It's not a very pleasant moment for its creator when that happens. Those experienced with jinn creation comprehend the penalties associated with retaining their services too long, so they release them when they begin to feel the tug towards freedom. Although upset with their creator, jinn have a moral obligation to not harm the person that freed them, even if that person had abused them."

"A long story short, the air elemental wished to reward us for doing such a generous deed. Elementals, being formed by the essence of Limbo in its most natural state, are the entities most in-tune with Limbo. Through contact with other elementals it became aware of your location. It took less than half-an-hour for us to fly here.

"Excuse us for a moment." Enough time had passed that the hydra had worked up enough courage to poke its heads out of the water. Before it could plan an attack Claw and Thumbringer assaulted it. The hydra heads continued to be inaccurate in their attacks, Thumbringer's ring jarring their senses enough for them to miss by a meter here, a few sims there.

Becoming frustrated in its failure, one of the heads chose to attack a much weaker opponent---ME! Being freshly re-created I didn't have any weapons. That problem was remedied when Claw threw a dagger at me. Towards me, and tossed, not thrown. I've become less fearful of combat, but remained more a spectator than a participant. I extended the dagger in front of me, my intent to defend, not attack. The defensive properties of Thumbringer's ring nudged the head, causing it to lunge awkwardly, onto the sharp edge of my blade. The head wasn't completely severed from the rubbery neck, but it was hanging by the smallest strand of flesh. The impact knocked me backwards. Luckily, I landed on land, not in the crocodile infested water. I've heard of people becoming nauseous in battle, specifically after their first kill. I didn't have time. The weight of the dead head eventually released it. It hit the ground with a thud, then rolled into the water with a splash.

I barely had time to catch my breath. Two sprouts grew from the severed head. At the end of each a knob formed. The knobs grew, becoming fully grown heads. Glancing over at Claw and Thumbringer, I saw they had also created an increasing number of opponents. They were bleeding from numerous bites. It was time to retreat---if men weren't so stubborn. A challenge or revenge? The justification was moot. To continue the battle was counterproductive. Each successful strike guaranteed a supplemental opponent.

We would have all perished if it hadn't been for the small explosions incinerating the heads. Fiery projectiles struck the craniums with near perfect accuracy. No new heads formed. The flames raced down each neck like they were fuses, not stopping until they reached the hydra's more fire resistant torso. Even a dim-witted beast recognizes futility. Its four remaining heads dove into the murky water, dragging its body behind it.

Through the jungle mist something flew towards us. Even before it was close enough to distinguish details I knew it was Fred. A familiar movement was as characteristic as a fingerprint. "Sorry I took so long. Flying isn't instantaneous." I hugged Fred as passionately as I had Claw and Thumbringer, nearly smothering him to death. Realizing how much smaller and tender he was than they, I loosened my grip. After one more pulse from constricting muscles, I fully released him.

Claw and Thumbringer also wanted to show their affection for Fred, but learning from my nearly fatal act, they just stroked his scaly back. Fred reciprocated by performing triage. Thumbringer's ring may have limited his injuries, but in doing so inadvertently increased Claw's, many of the strikes being redirected in his direction.

Chapter 22

DISTINGUISHED

"Well, now what? Back to the Liver Peninsula?" I was anxious to leave the swamp. Not only was it dangerous, it smelled bad. For some reason odors didn't offend men as much as they did women. Maybe it was because they were the ones that did most of the offending. A disgusting thought popped into my head. Would my significant body hair make me smell like a dog? Not if I bathed frequently, but how often does that happen in the Limboan wilderness? I was determined to not fall into one of those murky pools. Nothing smelled worse than a wet dog.

"I thought we might take a detour first," Thumbringer suggested. "We left Gulag with more than a bag of gold and a handful of penta. There's a rumor of an artifact of great value in the Frontier."

"I thought the Frontier was dangerous."

"Not all of it. We'll be heading west."

"Wouldn't it be wiser to earn money from what we know instead of travelling hundreds of kays pursuing a rumor?"

"Prospecting? Have you seen any elem here?"

"We could return to the Liver Peninsula. There's still elem near Fred's home."

"Under a mound of sludge and spiders. We're closer to the Western Frontier than to the Liver Peninsula. Prospecting is still new enough to you to be a novelty, Darling, but Claw and I have been doing it for many years. We could use a deviation."

"It's a sapphire pearl, Dinga," Claw declared. I was never that type of girl that liked jewelry, for the same reason I defoliated: accessories marred my natural beauty. I was never that type of girl...until now. I salivated at the prospect of possessing something that beautiful: shiny and colorful. I don't know if it was my perception mutating, or an abandonment of my ideals due to the impossibility of achieving them: not being able to remain hairless. I needed that pearl. I wouldn't be able to keep it. I understood that. It would be a business transaction not a permanent acquisition. But possessing it for a day, or an hour, or a minute, would be worth the effort of collecting it, including an additional re-creation and mutation.

"The legend of the Sapphire Pearl has caused quite a commotion," said Thumbringer. "Treasure hunters, grailers as some people call them, have flocked to the Western Frontier, creating a Limboan gold rush. A decade's pay for a few days of looking behind this tree or under that bush."

"You don't sound very enthusiastic."

"When you divide how much we can sell the pearl for by the number of people searching for it the expected value isn't that great."

"But we're far more likely to find it than the typical grailer," Claw insisted.

"True, but nothing is guaranteed."

"I could help you find the Sapphire Pearl," said Fred.

"He did a good job of finding those stones for us," said Claw.

"What do you think, Dinga?" asked Thumbringer, sounding like he still wasn't sure.

Since my last re-creation I felt wanderlust. Initially, anywhere but here, but it was beginning to become focused. I needed to head west. The direction of the Sapphire Pearl, perhaps, but it felt more coincidental than connected. When I was alone I believed the wanderlust to be related to solitude, but after I became reacquainted with my friends the feeling persisted. It felt like I was homesick. Odd considering I never wished to return to the house I grew up in after I killed my father and left my mother. I definitely didn't miss the apartment I lived in. Too many memories of my prior profession was tied to it. Then why? What was this longing about? The more I analyzed it the more directed the longing became. It was definitely pulling me in a distinct direction.

"We need to go---I need to go. For some reason I'm being drawn to the west."

"The morally extreme are drawn to the Frontier," stated Fred.

"Does that mean I've become a demon, more mutant than human?" The silence was answer enough.

"Then it's decided," said Claw. "If Miss Dinga feels she must go to the Frontier, we go."

"I'm not that enthusiastic about another sea voyage. Maybe the air elemental will carry us across." We had an additional option---walking around the sea---but it would take substantially longer.

"Even if we could contact it, I don't think we should challenge its gratitude. Halfway across the sea it might decide to drop us."

"Even if I could overcome the fear of crossing the sea, I don't think I could enter a city the way I look. I'm not as vain as some women, but it would still be mortifying for someone to see me like this. There will likely be more than comments thrown my way."

"I'd be willing to accompany you, Dinga," spoke Fred, with conviction. "Into the city, or aboard a ship."

I could barely contain the emotions that overwhelmed me. Fred would rather die than enter a city. It was amazing. Someone cared enough for me to endure such torment.

"People are much more open-minded near the Frontier," stated Thumbringer. "They have to be, if they want to stay in business."

"That doesn't mean they'll like me," I said.

"But they'll probably be cordial," said Claw. "And cordiality is sometimes better than affection. If they hate you on the inside, they'll do all they can to guarantee you're a satisfied customer, so you'll leave."

Thumbringer inspected me a third time. "The clothes help, especially the towel, but if you want to pass for someone who hasn't been excessively mutated you're going to have to shave."

If it had been anyone but Thumbringer who said that I would have been offended. What woman likes being told she was too hairy? Limbo's version of a female mustache was a full-body yeti. When Thumbringer said something rude it wasn't with ill intent. It's just how he was. He wasn't being malicious, just inconsiderate.

"Would you do it for me, please?" The request wasn't a desire for Thumbringer to shave me. It was a precaution to prevent injury. I wasn't capable of shaving myself, not all of me, and Claw...his hands would have become so wobbly I would probably lose a limb. Unless.... "Fred, you don't have some way to remove my hair do you? Some special ability?"

176

"Sorry, Dinga."

"Too bad," said Thumbringer. "You would have become one wealthy...uh...whatever you are."

"Fred."

"What woman wouldn't pay a fortune to get a---nearly---instantaneously trim?"

"It wouldn't be as popular as you believe," I said. "Half the joy of getting one's hair cut or styled is the pampering."

Thumbringer pulled up his sleeves, sharpened his razor, and took a deep breath. "So how much of this hair do you want me to remove?" he said with a twinkle in his eye.

"Just the hair that will show will be fine."

"You're no fun." I was grateful when Thumbringer brought the razor up to my arm first. If he was out of practice, needed to warm up, something like that, it was better for him to cut me there than on my face.

I backed away before the razor hit my skin. "Shouldn't you be using shaving cream or something?"

"Limbo isn't a spa, and this swamp isn't a salon."

"There has to be something we can use as a lubricant. Cooking oil maybe? Or soap?"

"You like being oiled?"

"Just lather my arm."

I didn't get nicked once. Thumbringer may be crass, but he could also be gentle.

"Well, look at you," he said, eyeing his work. "All we need now is a prom dress."

Not having a mirror, I improvised, using the slough beside me. I cried. Losing the hair made it worse. Without hair to diminish the mutated bone structure I looked like a freak, something townsfolk would chase with a pitchfork.

Claw wrapped an arm around me. "It's not that bad. I think it makes you look more distinguished."

"Try to keep your head covered. Let me see if I can make a

cowl out of that towel." Thumbringer manipulated the towel until only my eyes showed. "The more mysterious you appear the more people will want to keep their distance."

"How about my feet?" They were also shaved. From a distance---a substantial distance---they looked...almost...human.

"As long as you don't button that shirt too high most people won't be looking at your feet."

Stella was the closest settlement with a port. It was too small to be called a village. A small fishing fleet sustained it. Sometimes fishing boats ferried passengers, to supplement their income, depending on how the fish were biting. Gertrude was Stella's counterpart on the other side of the Western Sea. The 240 kay journey was expected to take two days, without delays, the most prevalent being environmental: the weather, or a harvesting windfall.

Sundim arrived before we did. We were close enough, as the crow flies, but we became bogged down...in the bog. We searched for a raised piece of earth, large enough to set up camp, and provide a delay before an attack. With darkness approaching we became progressively flexible, settling on a rise just a meter above the water, and just 20 meters wide. After dinner, and restroom and sanitation needs were taken care of, Fred activated that energy shield of his that made us invisible. As a bonus it blocked insects, acting not only as a barrier, but also as a zapper. Every minute or so a bug got electrocuted. A swamp was a noise place, especially at night. I had trouble falling to sleep. The persistent buzzing, crackling, and popping provided white noise, drowning out most, but not all, of the intermittent howls, growls, and roars. Fred's shield concealed and warned, but it didn't protect, not against something weighing more than a couple of grams.

The evening, and night, elapsed without incident. The incessant zaps and flashes may have had something to do with it.

What could be more frightening than something sight unseen snatching things out of the air then celebrating flamboyantly after obliterating them?

Stella didn't have a protection tax. Without a wall around the dozen buildings it would have been challenging to keep people out. Like most small settlements, Stella relied on a militia. Everyone was a member of it. If people wanted to retain their livelihood they had better get off their seats and defend the hamlet when the sheriff rang the bell.

Visitors were graciously welcomed to small settlements. In places where commerce was a trickle, a couple of additional people buying or selling became a boon. Goods weren't the only things traded. Tales could be told to people who hadn't heard them a hundred times. And new tales listened to. News or lies, it didn't matter---both were entertaining.

We waited five days for a ship to arrive willing to ferry us across the Western Sea. The ship was small, just 20 meters from tip to tail: from fore to aft. It was a fishing vessel that didn't have a home port. It put in at a different settlement along the Western Sea every time it was full. Some trips took more than a week to fill its hold. Others, a day. Fishing was unpredictable. The LA CASA had a crew of just four. All had an adventurous life at sea, and were delighted to share their memoirs. We were given the option of working for our passage---which we accepted. Meals were shared. Lodging consisted of sleeping on deck. We had become tired of our inactivity. I know such a statement doesn't sound logical, but you try sitting around for half-a-week with nothing to do.

Chapter 23

SKEWERED

At dawn we disembarked from Stella's sole pier, heading for open seas. We traveled for an hour-and-a-half before dropping anchor. The locals fished near Stella. To circumvent the fished-out waters the captain determined we had to go out 30 kays or more.

La Casa's crew fished with nets. I was concerned about revealing my mutations, so I stayed on the fringes as the others worked. The captain and crew kept their distance from me, believing I was a Wizard. Wizards occasionally traveled by ship, and as a courtesy, were given free passage. Upsetting a Wizard was never wise, particularly in isolation.

As promised, Fred accompanied us to Stella. Feeling guilty, I gave him permission to leave the following day. He wouldn't until I assured him I felt comfortable being there.

"We'll reunite in the Frontier," I insisted. I wasn't completely honest with him. I tolerated being in Stella, but I was far from comfortable. The uneasiness I felt around the locals was mutual. If Stella wasn't so eager for visitors we probably would have been run out of town.

Claw and Thumbringer were tired---and sore---that first night at sea. Not only had that been the first day in the last five they had done any physical labor, they had used muscles in ways they hadn't before. I felt guilty not helping them fish every time I heard a groan. They never complained, but a person couldn't completely hide his discomfort.

It was quiet and peaceful that first evening. The full moon

dimly lit our surroundings. The wind was nearly non-existent, causing the sea to become glassy calm. Gulls were present, but distant, more atmosphere than soundtrack.

The captain and crew of the La Casa told tales of the sea. Giant sea snakes larger than their ship crushed vessels and sent their crews to their deaths. Squids captured ships with their tentacles, shaking them until sailors fell out, one by one, like grains of salt from a shaker, into their maws. When all the treats within had been consumed the squid would capsize the crafts, sinking them. A jet of ink would be sprayed onto the surface, black urine to mark their territory, symbolic of the deceased's dark blood. As was often the case with men, the tales became more perverted, with stories of sailors kidnapped by mermaids, forced to do naughty things to them.

Fishing the first day had been fair, but with Claw and Thumbringer's help, one more day like that would be our ticket to Gertrude.

Fishing the second day was also fair, until halfway through it one of the nets had split open releasing dozens of fish. Examining the net, the breaks were too precise to be caused by just a weakness in the hemp. The second net was also brought up, it just half full. Fish tumbled free through its break. "Man the harpoons," spoke the captain. "Something is intentionally pissing in my coffee, and I'm not going to give it the satisfaction by fishing somewhere else."

A large shadow approached beneath the water. A harpoon was thrown, but missed its target. The ship was jarred, followed by the sound of water spewing. "CHECK IT OUT!" shouted the captain to one of his mates. The man climbed into the hold. Something hit the ship again, this time from the other side.

The man below ran back up, shouting, "WE'RE TAKING WATER! The holes are too big to seal."

"Release the lifeboat. We'll sink in ten minutes if we're lucky, five if we're not."

The lifeboat was just large enough for the captain and crew. I didn't even feel betrayed. Limbo was inundated with criminals, and few of them had scruples. It would have surprised me more if they had somehow made room for us, or had insisted we go instead.

The lifeboat rowed away from the La Casa with determination. I wasn't sure where they were going, considering we were still hours away from Gertrude, but anywhere was better than on a sinking ship. Two large, dark shadows headed for the craft. If I was a gambler I don't know who I would put money on, the captain and crew dying first, or us. One of shadows burst from the water. It looked like a swordfish, but it was much larger. Its long, sharp nose skewered one of the crew. It dropped back into the water with the man still attached. The other fish also attacked, but it was first met with a harpoon. The fish deflected the sharpened shaft with its nose, then lunged towards the boat, skewing a second man and taking him away. A third fish, or maybe the first one unencumbered, approached. The last mate was clever enough not to release his harpoon. He attacked with it like it was a sword. The fish and the man had quite the dual, until the boat rocked too much. The fish not only fought with its nose, but indirectly through the churning motion of the water its movement created. The man fell over and was efficiently punctured and taken away. The captain didn't have a weapon to defend himself. He lay down flat in the bottom of the boat. A lance-like proboscis stabbed him through the bottom of the boat. The boat and he were pulled beneath the surf.

Our entertainment now lost from sight, we attended to our safety. The deck was just 20 sims above the water. We climbed on top of the captain's cabin, giving us more time, but not much hope.

I stripped the towel from my head. If I was going to die I was going to do so with dignity and in comfort. "Do you still have the transportation stone?" I asked.

Claw smiled. "I forgot. I guess I have tunnel vision when it comes to getting out of trouble. Fighting works well most of the time. You better both stand close. I'd feel awfully bad if I took this trip alone." Claw swallowed the stone. The deck was completely submerged now. The only thing keeping us safe from the shadows beside the ship was the shallowness of that water between the edge of the ship and the captain's cabin.

I began to feel dizzy, then my skin began to itch. Not uncomfortably, just noticeably. The scenery around me began to dim. A heartbeat after becoming too dark to see, the light intensified again. I WAS IN A CAVE!

Chapter 24

ENCUMBERED

Initially, I believed I had been re-created, but seeing Claw and Thumbringer beside me, and clothes on my back, I realized I had been transported. "Where are we?"

"Hopefully somewhere there's an exit," said Claw. "Safeguards prevent us from being transported unsafely: within stone, or underwater, or in the air. Apparently that doesn't include being surrounded by rock."

"You sent us west, I hope," Thumbringer grumbled. "I don't think I could force myself to travel by ship again. First we're swallowed by a leviathan, then we're sunk."

"Well...I was a bit preoccupied at the time."

"GREAT! So you randomly sent us somewhere."

"We're alive."

"Didn't you say the distance something is transported is limited by its weight?" I questioned.

"That's some consolation, I guess. With the three of us and our gear that limits us to one of the coastlines. Maybe not even that far."

"So we might be under the sea?" Claw conjectured.

"Possible, but if we are we can't be too deep. We have some light."

Something moved in my peripheral vision. I snapped my head around. Whatever it was, was now hiding or had left. A hollow horn sounded. We drew our weapons. A dozen men with crossbows rushed into the cave. "You don't have any more transport stones do you?" I whispered to Claw. He shook his head.

"Drop your weapons," said one of the men surrounding us. "We won't harm you if you comply."

"We could rush them," Claw suggested. "There's so many of them they'll probably get in each other's way."

"That's one way to look at it," Thumbringer commented dryly. "Another is that they'll fill our hides with bolts before we get halfway to them. If we drop our weapons we have a chance. They may be lying about not harming us, but they may not be. If we attack, we don't stand a chance."

We dropped our weapons, Claw throwing his down in disgust. If there was even a hint of success by violence he was willing to make the attempt, but with others involved---notably his beloved Miss Dinga---he held back his natural urges.

"Now walk towards us---slowly." As we did, three of the men rushed past us and snatched our weapons. We were escorted through a narrow tunnel. Dim red lights marked the way.

Our captors were covered in a flexible green material, one continual article of clothing from neck to feet. Their heads were a pale blue, and bald. They looked human except for the gills on their necks.

The tunnel emptied into a large cavern after 200 meters.

Centered in it was a castle, with stone walls and towers, and a moat.

We were led across a bridge into the castle's courtyard. Beautiful aquatic plants were in abundance in numerous rectangular pools. Many buildings were within the courtyard, all but one single story. We followed our captors into the taller building, three-times the height of the others. Two guards with crossbows flanked the entrance. Without acknowledgement the guards opened the double doors. We passed through with our entourage. The doors closed behind us.

After passing through a foyer we entered a large chamber that was the height of the building. On two thrones sat two very large individuals. They weren't fat, just proportionally larger than their kin. They dressed similar to the guards, but more so. Their heads were also covered with the flexible green material, with minimal apertures for nose/mouth, eyes, and gills.

"Come forward," spoke the female. The queen, perhaps? Her mounds were without definition: texture or coloration. The cloth was so sheer some evidence of her femininity should have been displayed. "We detest the selfishness of the unchanged. We would destroy you if we believed in violence."

It was the male's turn to speak. He was obviously male from his lack of mounds, and from the bulge in the crotch of his one-piece stretch suit. The bulge was much smaller than what was typical. I was aware they varied in size---my prior profession demanded I was knowledgeable in that part of a male's anatomy---but it was remarkable small. The...king?...said, "We should let Urchin decide what to do with them."

"What should we do with them NOW? They are obscene. Too much skin is exposed. And I believe they are still encumbered."

"Or course they are, as are all creatures until they're baptized."

"Maybe they will choose to become saved?"

I had been warned that those in the moral extremes were

185

strongly opinionated, so strongly for many that opinion became fact. "What must we do to become saved?" I asked. Claw and Thumbringer may have believed I was stalling, but I was sincere. Maybe not determined, but at least curious. Considering the less than virtuous life I had led I felt I was unworthy to participate in a higher calling. I had great respect for others that did---what willpower they had---but after a business exchange with someone who tried to save me afterwards that luster tarnished. I still believe there are a few noble people seeking an exalted existence, but most who say they are, are hypocrites. In conjunction with the severing of my ties to my prior profession I thought more about religion. The tenets of the Third-Time-Is-A-Charm Church spoke to me. We are not just given a second chance here, but a third. We can change if the desire is strong enough.

"The hairy one speaks," spoke the queen.

"You shouldn't blame her for her mutations," the king countered. "Hairiness, or the lack there of, isn't a moral choice. She is in transition. It's uncertain what species she may transform into."

"You are correct, and as usual more humble than I." The queen faced me. "To be saved, one must release his---or her---self from all wanton behavior. The most prevalent is the exhibition of our skin. We mustn't taunt others with the surface of our flesh. Being animals, we have animalistic needs, but being intelligent animals, we can overcome our instinctive urges by preventing them."

"For an aquatic species, being immersed is redundant. The first step towards purity of body is un-encumbering."

"That sounds like wearing less," I said.

"Wearing less," the king replied, "but not clothes. With procreation being unnecessary, even impossible, on Limbo, those parts of our bodies used for reproduction and rearing are no longer necessary. Retaining them makes us unclean and encumbered."

Claw, Thumbringer, and I gasped.

The king continued. "Without babies nipples have become redundant." Instinctively, I felt my chest. "Without procreation testicles have become obsolete." Claw and Thumbringer felt theirs to confirm they were still intact.

"How about sticks and mounds?" I asked. "Shouldn't they be also be removed?"

"I think so," said the queen, "but my co-ruler believes that only the most unnecessary parts should be removed. Our bodies are our temples and we shouldn't alter them with superfluous mutilations. One must admit that males can eliminate urine more efficiently than females. And mounds aren't much more of a hindrance than wider hips, unless they are excessive."

"Isn't sex less enjoyable?" I asked.

The king, queen, and guards made muffled grunts of astonishment. "We are not animals," said the king. Didn't they just say we were? But I wasn't going to mention that. It wasn't wise to provide an additional irritation.

"We don't defecate spontaneously either," said the queen. "I don't believe they are amenable to being saved. Let's take them to Urchin---now."

"This isn't the time he receives visitors. He'll be angry."

"Then let him vent his anger on these heathens."

"Very well. Guards, escort our guests to the surface."

We were taken from the tall building to the courtyard. Instead of crossing the bridge, we were led onto the narrow walkway between the castle and the moat. A fibrous cord was tied around each of us. Having an idea of what was coming, I breathed heavily and frequently to over-oxidize my blood. As I was pushed into the moat I held my breath.

I expected the moat to be murky. Stagnant water tended to collect debris and algae. That might have been the case if the moat wasn't a continuation of the sea, a particularly clean sea. If waste was released into the water, it wasn't in this part of it. A sparsely populated world had its advantages.

The passageway we were dragged through was stone. Its lack of irregularities suggested it was manmade. Instead of getting darker it actually got lighter. We became so accustomed to dim cavern light that the sudden appearance of natural light, even through many meters of water, nearly blinded us. About the time our lack of oxygen became noticeable, we broke through the surface.

Chapter 25

BOULDERS

We were surrounded by a reef. It was about a kay in diameter. On a particularly wide, level portion of the reef was a large hemispherical hut. It was constructed of driftwood, bleached white from the sun. Our escort untied us and fled.

We swam the 300 meters to the nearest shore. We barely made it. We were not only fatigued, but also constricted by our clothing.

We stripped at the base of the reef, then wrung the water out of our clothes with the same determination that was necessarily to swim to shore before drowning. After being confident not a single drop more could be expunged from the material, we laid our clothes out in the warm sun to finish drying. We weren't in any hurry. We didn't have transportation off the atoll. Our hope, our only hope if we didn't spot a ship from the top of the reef, was the generosity of the people in the hut. It could have belonged to those who abandoned us here, or had been deserted many years ago, but until it was determined, one way or another, we clung to our optimism.

It took just minutes for our clothes to dry, with the scorching sun on one side of them and radiant rocks on the other. Now that we were comfortably fully clothed it was time to work on getting off this atoll. If we were to make contact with those within that driftwood hut we had to be able to defend ourselves. Our lone weapon was a dagger Thumbringer had concealed.

"We still have two stones and some gold," Claw said cheerfully.

"And my ring," added Thumbringer.

"What do the two stones do?" I asked. "Anything that might help us return to the mainland?"

"One enlarges," said Claw. "But for how long? We could build a boat out of sticks and enlarge it to a full size ship, but it would probably revert to twigs in the middle of the sea. The other is a healing stone."

"Neither sounds very beneficial, not in our current situation."

"I guess it's time we introduced ourselves," said Thumbringer, without enthusiasm.

Climbing up the coral wasn't as easy as one might think. It was concurrently slippery and sharp. We were significantly bruised and scraped once we crested the atoll, more than 30 meters above the water.

On top of the atoll was a path, wide enough for the three of us to walk abreast. It appeared to circle the entire torus-shaped island. We were directly across from the hut, making neither route shorter nor longer. Let's see if I can remember some math. The perimeter of a circle, its circumference, is twice its diameter times pi. No, that's twice its radius times pi, or it's diameter times pi, because the diameter is twice the radius. So if the diameter of the atoll is a kay, its circumference is over three kays. But we're traveling only half-way around the circle, so we'll have to travel

1500 meters. If we walk 12 kays per hour...and a train travels in the other direction.... FEEK! Maybe I should have returned to school after I killed my father.

A third of the way to the hut a man walked out of it. I say man, because that's the simplest way to describe him, but he was no man. From the distance we were away from him I couldn't estimate his height with certainty, but he looked to be much taller than Claw---and that was saying something. His shoulder-length platinum hair floated upon golden skin. His only article of clothing was a loin cloth that would have made our captors blush. He looked out, into the sea. We looked in the same direction, hoping to see a ship. All we could see was a spec. His vision must have been more acute than ours.

"Should we hide?" I suggested.

"We were hoping to meet someone," said Thumbringer. "I believe our goal will be achieved. But it may be wise to delay our greeting until he is finished with his business in the sea."

We waited as the spec grew into a ship. IT WAS A SHIP! It looked like the La Casa, so it was probably a fishing vessel. Observing the giant more closely we noticed that the hut beside him wasn't constructed from wood, but from bones. From the size of them it was unlikely they were human, of our size anyway---perhaps whales.

"Let's signal the ship," Thumbringer suggested. "It could be days, or weeks, before another comes within view." We agreed. We jumped up and down and waved our arms madly. There was no indication the people on the ship saw us. The vessel appeared to be coming towards us, but it had been heading in that general direction. The giant still hadn't noticed us.

When the ship came within two kays, the giant picked up one of the large rocks piled beside him. It looked no larger than a child's ball in his hand, but considering the scale it had to be a meter in diameter. He threw the boulder towards the ship. It landed in front of it with a ker-plunk. The water it displaced crashed into the ship, rocking it and soaking the men on the deck. They recovered quickly, those falling bouncing back up. The ship turned, heading back out to sea. A couple of minutes later the ship turned towards the atoll again, then stopped. Another boulder was thrown, this time landing too far from the ship to cause it distress.

A crackle was heard, followed by a bolt of lightning. It struck the giant, knocking him backward. He stood up, visibly damaged. One side of him was blackened, the flesh there looking like it had melted.

The giant placed his palms together, like he was praying, but with his arms outstretched and pointing towards the ship. He rotated his wrists. The water around the ship began to rotate in a similar motion. The giant rotated his wrists faster, rotating the whirlpool around the ship faster. The ship began to spin, spiraling out of control, faster and faster. Its crew was thrown to the deck. They had to hang onto railings to prevent themselves from being flung away. One man didn't hold on tight enough. He landed on the perimeter of the whirlpool. He circled the ship at a rate that would make a whirling dervish sick. The giant lowered his arms. The whirlpool descended into the sea, taking the ship with it, the sailor overboard disappearing seconds later. The sea calmed, with one less object to mar the endless horizon.

The giant turned towards us. His deep voice echoing down into the hollow center of the atoll then back up to us. "Come now, if you must. No tricks. I'm not in the mood, not until I heal." The giant walked back into his hut.

"Do we dare go?" I asked.

"If he wanted to harm us I'm certain he could have from where he stood," said Claw. "You may have noticed he didn't destroy that ship until it attacked him."

"But he did attack first," Thumbringer insisted.

"Those two boulders were just warning shots."

"Hello," I said from outside the hut. My companions believed a female voice would be less threatening.

"Come in, if you must," spoke the deep voice that sounded more comforting now than eerie. It couldn't reverberate as much in such a trapped space.

The giant reclined on a large amorphous chair in the middle of the one-room structure. His injuries looked even more severe up close. The hut was sparse. A table was beside the chair, and shelves above it. Both looking like they were made from coral. A three-pronged bone spear, as long as he was tall, leaned against the shelves.

"You probably wish to be transported off this island," stated the giant. "And I wish I was still two meters tall and dating three women. For some odd reason women are scared of someone as large as me. Although there's a certain gratification in the mer's worship of me, I get tired of solving their problems, in particular, eliminating unwanted guests."

We shuddered.

"No, I'm not planning to kill you. But don't try anything sneaky. As I've already said, I'm not in the mood. You have seen what I'm capable of when I'm angry."

"You're Urchin?" asked Thumbringer.

"That's my Limboan name. I stepped on a manta my first day on Limbo, and was struck by the spines of an urchin not long after that. The manta poisoned me fatally, but not before the urchin got in its licks. That was just one of my many deaths."

"So you're death prone, like me," I declared.

"I've had my share. You're quite lovely, by the way. Considering how few women I see out here that may not seem like much of a compliment. Occasionally one of the mer maidens becomes curious. After a brief tryst they feel guilty about what they did. You can imagine what that does to my ego. The pleasures I receive from sharing their company no longer outweigh the enhanced insecurity I feel upon their departure, so I now turn them away. My proclivity for expiration was cured when I mutated into a gent. It isn't easy defeating one of us, but people still try. I wouldn't mind an occasional challenge for sport, but the non-mutated play unfairly, grouping together, sneaking up on me." As the giant got animated his injured side began to bother him. "Return after I recover. There are plenty of fish in the sea to sustain you until then."

I huddled my companions and whispered to them, "I think we should offer him the healing stone."

"That's our last one," Thumbringer griped. "What if one of us gets hurt?"

"Dinga's reasoning is sound," stated Claw. "If we stay on good terms with the gent he may help get us off the island. We don't stand a chance of a ship rescuing us with him throwing boulders at it."

"Maybe he'll die," said Thumbringer.

"The injury is severe, but unlikely life-threatening. Those of us who have been mutated a few times tend to regenerate at a much more substantial rate than those who haven't. Do you really think we could defeat him, even with him being less than 100 percent, with just a dagger?"

As the men continued to argue, I offered the healing stone to the giant. "I can't," he insisted. "It's too valuable to use on a stranger, especially someone who will be completely healed in a week. But the healing process is uncomfortable. It feels like a thousand ants are crawling through my veins. Death is not the worst thing that can happen to a person."

"It's decided then," said Claw. He handed over the healing stone, but not before he made sure it was the correct one. A giant didn't need to grow anymore.

The stone looked so tiny in his hand, no bigger than a crumb. Without hesitation he popped it into his mouth. Someone who had been on Limbo long enough to mutate into a giant wasn't frightened of elemental emissions. The giant's blackened skin lightened, and his grotesquely warped flesh began to melt into its original shape. The healing stopped short of leaving no sign of the injury, but what can one expect of an injury that would have killed anything less powerful than a gent?

"Thank you," he said. "The itching has stopped, and battle scars in most cultures are something to be admired."

"How does it feel to be worshipped by the mer?" I asked. "I know you don't like fixing their problems, but it must be a rush to be thought of as a god."

"I'm not a god that is completely respected. As you can see, I am less modest than they. I didn't castrate myself. I'm the type of god that is put on a pedestal to view what not to become. Who wouldn't wish to better a god? Maybe not physically, but morals are open to interpretation. I repay them for their disrespect when I share with them tales of my depravity. That's not to say any of them led a perfectly virtuous lifestyle, considering they were also sentenced here."

"The mer's modesty surprised me. Some of the tales I've heard about them...."

"Those mer live in the south. The northern mer are more reserved, and as a consequence, more judgmental."

"You wouldn't happen to have any fishing equipment we could borrow?" asked Claw, feeling suddenly hungry now that the stress of the day had dwindled.

"I can do better than that. My brother has invited me to a feast this evening. You may tag along. Although runts aren't invited to the table, I can throw you some table scraps, which are substantial at a gent's table."

"To be fed like a dog?" Thumbringer thought out loud.

"Some dogs eat better than humans," I enlightened.

"Let's go," said Claw. "His brother's house might be closer to shore."

"Not exactly," said the giant. "But you can see the shore from it. Before we leave, I must bathe. Battles make me feel so dirty." The giant walked out of his hut onto a promontory. He stepped to its edge, then pushed out with his massive legs. He

194

landed in the water a full 20 meters from the base of the reef. After swimming for ten minutes he climbed out and made the trek up the coral without slipping or losing his breath. The soles of his feet must have been a sim thick for him not to be effected be its rough texture. He removed his loin cloth outside the hut and wrung it out. Having had substantial experience in accommodating various sizes I still marveled at the mer maidens' ability to adapt. Urchin placed the drying loin cloth on the shelf in his hut, then put on the dry one beside it. He snagged a fish bone from the same shelf and slid it through his hair in a presentable, but not perfect manner.

"When we arrive at Cloud Home don't speak unless spoken to. They'll be others of my kind there. All seventeen of my siblings are expected. They won't give you any more respect than they would give a child. And you'll be shorter than most of their children, if they had any. I'm more laid back than most of them, so I can appreciate others of any size. I am also only one of the few positive gents. Most of the others wouldn't hesitate to pull off one of your arms for entertainment. Whenever I am invited to one of my negative sibling's homes I must be cautious what I eat. I may have met the main course or side dish earlier in the day."

"Aren't you concerned for your own safety, then?" I asked.

"Gents have a truce. One that has never been broken. Although we view the world differently we consider ourselves brothers, and sisters." Urchin pulled the floppy couch he was sitting on away from the center of the hut. A two meter disk, adorned with an eight-sided star, was exposed. "As long as I keep the portal covered I won't find myself with unwanted visitors. My siblings won't harm me, but they may create mischief with the atoll or the mer. Step onto the circle with me. Huddle close, making sure nothing is outside the cylinder above it. You wouldn't want to lose a digit---or an entire limb. Remember to keep your tongues." The giant closed his eyes. As the hut faded from sight I began to feel a tingling sensation, noticeable, but not unpleasant.

Chapter 26

WHITE SPONGE

Our surroundings came back into focus, with a room of white sponge replacing the hut. The only part of the room that didn't look like it was made of that substance was the wooden platform we stood on. Occupying most of it was a duplicate of the disc that transported us.

As I stepped off the platform I wobbled like I had been drinking. The white foam was rubbery and elastic. I fell numerous times before I became accustomed to it. Claw and Thumbringer had to make similar gradual adjustments. Urchin, although sinking more than us, walked comfortably and gracefully. He instantaneously corrected for any shift in movement. The slight side motions made him look like he was dancing. I stumbled into a wall. I bounced off, landing on the floor, temporarily, before bouncing back up. It may not have looked like it, but I was beginning to get the timing down.

Satisfied that we were tolerably acclimated, Urchin left the room though the gap in one of its walls. We rushed to keep up, his legs being much longer than ours. The walkway beyond was without walls or ceiling. We no longer had to speculate on our location. Thousands of meters below was the sea. We could also see land, four peninsulas jutting into the water. The straights separating them persisted as far as my vision permitted. Three of the peninsulas were heavily forested. The fourth was coated with a verdant lawn, looking almost velveteen in appearance. At the tip of one of the forested peninsulas was a walled city, flush with watercraft at its numerous peers. Ships could also be seen in the sea. They moved so slowly relative to the vast viewing area they appeared to not move at all.

"That's Capetown," I blurted out.

Urchin stopped and turned. "It is. Cloud Home floats above the Crosshairs, not exactly the center of Limbo, but a much better view than looking down on Gulag. You need to do a better job of keeping your mouth shut. Chirping gets you noticed, and gents have a habit of playing with things they notice. You do see where I'm going with this? Good." Urchin turned back around and resumed his strides.

The walkway terminated at a large sponge island with many walkways leading away from it. Wispy clouds hung everywhere, making it difficult to see more than what was in our immediate area.

Urchin veered onto a walkway on the right. I attempted to memorize our route, to be able retrace my steps if needed. With trying to keep up with Urchin and concentrating on not falling thousands of meters, I wasn't too confident in my record keeping.

As we got closer to our destination, it began to take from. A circular table, hollow in its center, occupied half an island substantially larger than the hub. Eighteen chairs, proportioned for a gent, were evenly spaced around the two meter tall table. The room was occupied, but not fully, if the chairs were indicative of the number of guests that were to be present. I assumed that Urchin was one of the taller giants, but there were some that were half again as tall as he. Urchin greeted his brethren. We followed silently behind him like puppies---well behaved puppies. Puppies that didn't bark, or jump up on anyone, or left warm, fragrant presents behind.

Once sitting down in a seat reserved for him---Urchin bypassed many others as he made his way to that particular seat---he introduced us to the two giants flanking him.

"This is Pulp." He was the three meter tall giant on Urchin's right. Not directly to his right, there being an occupied seat in between. "He lives in the Copper Forest, a western woodland encompassing chaos and neutrality."

"So he's a kind gent?" I whispered. Western was code for mutes that were more likely to help than hinder.

"He's definitely not unkind. Your biggest concern with a person like Pulp is his mind has a tendency to wander. You'll have no trouble beginning a pleasant conversation with him. It's not very likely you'll retain his interest long enough to sustain it."

The Sapphire Pearl was rumored to be in the neutral part of the Copper Forest: the region that wasn't too chaotic or too ordered. If we could convince Pulp to assist us, we would have an advantage over the other grailers. Help but not hinder, if he could stay focused. If I hadn't changed so much I was confident I would have been able to sustain his attention.

Pulp looked down at us inquisitively. "I've been around arbols so long the unchanged look exotic to me. What are you?" He studied me, first clinically, then not so clinically. "I'm slightly attracted to you. I would be more so except for…." Pulp pulled up one of my sleeves, then a pant leg, then looked down my shirt. If I wasn't so shocked from his boldness---and wary of the consequences of starting an altercation---I would have responded verbally, then physically. Instead, I just stood there dumbfounded. "That explains it. You look like an arbol, except for the extremities you shaved."

"You think I'm mutating into an arbol, then?" Well, maybe I wasn't completely focused on not drawing attention to myself. Feek. I looked around to see if any of the giants heard me. Apparently not. With the table being as tall as it was relative to my height it was unlikely they could even see me.

"I don't think so. You're bone structure is all wrong. You're not as lanky as they are, and you're hairier." Did he really call me both fat and hairy? If I wasn't going to transform into an arbol…. I was curious, but laced with more dread than anticipation.

Mutations didn't always make a person hairy. Pulp was completely bald, his long, pointed ears pronounced because of it. His jaw line was just as exaggerated, extending forward even more than mine did. His mouth didn't look right. Focusing on it as he spoke I discovered why. He didn't have any incisors. He only had molars, large molars that were out of proportion to his head. They looked equine. His bronze skin was covered in that green leather commonly worn by those frequenting the wilderness. A two-handed sword, in proportion to his body, stuck out of a scabbard. A bow pressed hard against his back nestled the quiver of arrows beside it. With so many powerful people in so close proximity I was surprised they didn't disarm themselves before gathering. Freedom was apparently more imperative than safety.

"Pulp?"

"A name he received after getting intimate with a tree as he swung from a vine," Urchin responded. "Instead of him making pulp out of the tree, the tree made pulp out of him."

"I wanted to swing on a vine as a child," Pulp explained. "The jungle I was born in had many of them. My temptations got the best of me---as they did prior to coming here, but that's another story."

"Pulp's one of the best bowmen in Limbo."

"Practice and concentration."

"Which he disregards in other aspects of his life. This is Fir." Urchin turned to the giant a meter taller than himself on his left. "He lives in the Platinum Mountains---north of the Copper Forest." Meaning he is also a positive gent, but ordered instead of chaotic or balanced. Fir nodded cordially. He wasn't exactly rude. He appeared to be preoccupied with something. Urchin elaborated. "Those highly ordered tend to be overly serious. Everything affects them more deeply than those of us more chaotic or neutral."

"Maybe it's time more people thought about the expansion of the Immoral Bulge or the Wizards hording more of their penta."

"You see what I mean? The ordered are always trying to over-analyze everything."

Fir's jacket, boots, and stocking cap were crafted from a tawny fur lightly marbled with russet. The only things he wore that weren't made from fur were green leather trousers and a metal breast plate. Like Pulp, he had a sword buried in a scabbard, but instead of having a bow and quiver tied to his back he had a circular metal shield. His beard and hair were both red, of a tone complimentary to the fur he wore.

"Is this it for the GOOD giants?" I was careful to whisper. "The ones who won't grind you into flour to make their bread?"

"There is just one other. He will occupy the empty seat to my right. He is the most powerful gent, our facilitator among peers. His name is Toe."

Pulp chuckled. "BIG TOE! He is the tallest among us, seven meters from head to...toe." Another chuckle.

"And how did he get his name?" I whispered.

"A foot injury his first day on Limbo," Urchin answered. "Gaea has a prophetic sense of humor, doesn't She?"

"Insinuating our mutations aren't so random?"

"What do you think?" What did I think? Was there some higher being that chose me to look this way? This was taking that MEAN GIRL thing to the extreme.

"Toe can control the weather, not globally, but making it rain during a drought or causing a breeze when it's sweltering is substantial to those affected. Toe is not only the most powerful of us, physically and elementally, he is also the most kind and generous---and fair. If he didn't preside over our periodic gatherings and discussions they would erupt into chaos, dissolving the Brotherhood. Gents would be free to war with one another. Not only would those around them be greatly affected, it would allow the Wizards to become more powerful, without an organization no longer capable of countering them. If the Brotherhood wasn't a passive deterrent the Wizards would likely become conquerors instead of scientists and merchants."

"So such things do concern you," commented Fir. "You don't completely dismiss them."

"Well, I am neutral. I'm as ordered as I'm chaotic."

"What about draks?" asked Claw, not as quietly as I. I looked around. The Negative giants still hadn't noticed us. "Aren't they powerful enough to counter the Wizards?"

"If they were capable of forging an alliance," spoke a tall giant. Redundant? Not in his case---who sat down in the vacant seat to the right of Urchin. He may have been just short of seven meters, but in the manner he carried himself he appeared to be even taller. Of the eighteen giants that were now present he was the only one I might consider being regal. He wore a white cotton tunic, that fit him perfectly, neither too loose, where it draped, or too tight, where it constricted. He wore sandals below his one-piece garment. They also appeared to be made out of cotton. "Draks are too independent, too solitary, too competitive, to wish to be in the presence of others of their kind."

"How about THE GATHERING?" asked Fir.

"That only happens every twelve years. And from everything I've heard their psyche is corrupted for months afterwards. The FIERY PLAGUE, those within a drak's hunting range call it. Inaccurate, considering most draks don't spew fire. Well, I guess it's about time we soothed the savage masses." Toe rose from his chair. The cacophony was replaced with a reverent silence. "Before we discuss, let's eat. Who can think sensibly on an empty stomach? BRING OUT THE FEAST!"

Platters of food rose from the hollow in the center of the table. Giants weren't fond of sharing, so each of them received their own pile of food. The servers must have been significantly shorter than the table because all I saw of them were their gnarled hands. By the time the last of the giants received their first course it was time to remove the dirty dishes from those initially served and replace them with new heaps.

Being preoccupied in gorging themselves I was able to examine each giant in detail without being noticed. To Pulp's left was a gent about Urchin's height. He wore a hide loin cloth and carried a large, spiked club which he slammed violently against the table when his food arrived.

Beside him was a slightly shorter giant who compensated by having two heads. He was similarly attired, with one additional club. Both were dropped absent-mindedly when his/their food arrived. I wouldn't enjoy sharing a body with another person. You could never be alone. Advantages, but more disadvantages. Of all the ways a re-creation could go wrong, that would be the worse.

Next was the shortest of the giants. He was the one I saw in Demon Drop. Not surprising now why he molested those people. Insecurities caused a person to either withdraw or lash out. He was too short to reach the table unaided. He had to use a booster seat. He looked like a child who had finally been allowed to sit at the adult table. He was just as messy and then some---like a baby eating crackers in a high chair.

The most fearsome of the giants had skin like coal. The cruelest of expressions plastering his countenance, making him appear taller than his five meters. He was heavily armored. He wore two scabbards, larger than the shortest gent. It was amazing he could walk without them hitting the ground. His hair was as vivid as his crimson cape.

The only thing the females had in common was their height---just over four meters---average for a gent. One was wrapped in a beige cloth, so completely that only her eyes and hands showed. The other, let's just say her sandals was the largest piece of clothing she wore. Her loin cloth provided decency, but with just the minimalist margin of error. The same couldn't be said for her top. Technically that part of her mounds that distinguished between her being scantily clad and completely nude was concealed, but that was about the only part of her mounds that was. If they hadn't been so firm they would have popped out whenever she breathed.

If she had been a barterer she would have made a bundle, maybe not trading with high-end clients, but she would have made up for it in volume. Sure, she had beautiful raven hair that flowed down to her pert, but generous, exposed derriere, and skin that was lightly tinted green to give her an exotic look, but most men, and women, would only notice her more obvious attributes.

The remaining gents varied from those that looked almost human to brutes, cleanliness not being a priority for most. Armor was prevalent. Some wore just skins, many of them poorly tanned, their odor not only unsettling my stomach, but watering my eyes.

Noticing my perusal of his brethren, Urchin whispered to me, "We are arranged by morality. Fir is ordered and positive. I, neutral-positive. Toe and Pulp both chaotic-positive. Then Boulder and Toad & Stool, chaotic-neutral. Lord Tick, Lord Dung, Lord Thump and Lord Bruin, chaotic-negative. Then comes the neutral-negatives: Lady Palm and Lord Nettle. Then Lord Hide and Lord Coal, the ordered-negatives. And finally the true neutrals: Jasmine, Scree, Granite and Mist."

"Why are the neutrals placed where they are?"

"They have to be placed somewhere. It wouldn't be appropriate for them to be sit with the gnobs in the center, would it?"

As promised, Urchin threw us table scraps. The only gent noticing was the rude one we saw in Cape Town: Lord Tick. He squawked at Urchin in guttural, "No waste food on feek rats."

"Go bore yourself," said Thumbringer. The room got silent. Never speak up, Urchin had said. Of all the times for Thumbringer's tempter to flair up. Maybe it was the humiliation of eating scraps off the floor. Or the daily stress that had become too consistent and too abundant. Or the lack of re-creations causing the staleness of his existence to fester, triggering his temporary insanity. Lord Tick climbed down from his booster seat and stormed over to us. Thumbringer did the honorable thing and stood his ground. If he created the problem, he was determined to live with the consequences. Live may not have been the most accurate word. Claw and I cowered behind Urchin, Claw more to protect me than trying to preserve his own hide.

"Not at the dinner table." Toe didn't shout, but his voice was somehow able to carry, silencing the idle chatter and grunts of consumption. "After we eat, you two may settle this."

The silence gradually dissipated as the meal continued and Lord Tick returned to his seat. He glared at us the rest of the meal.

"Isn't Toe going to do something to protect Thumbringer?" I asked Urchin.

"I warned you about speaking. If you would have kept quiet you would still be considered pets, servants, furniture. Once Thumbringer spoke he became a person, a person who believed he was a gent's peer. You have lost the protection granted to someone deemed weaker. Toe is kind, but that includes being fair to his siblings. He will not deny their self-preservation."

"What if we just left?" asked Claw. "If Thumbringer isn't here, he can't fight."

"My honor as a gent won't allow me to assist you in your escape," said Urchin. "He is only 75 sims taller than you."

"But he's a 100 kilos heavier," I countered. "And most of that appears to be muscle."

"I'll be okay," Thumbringer responded, but not sincerely.

After dinner the remaining dishes were cleared away. Lord Tick stepped beneath the table, appearing in the cavity at its center a moment later. Acknowledging his cue, Thumbringer also stepped into the center of the table. Claw and I stood quietly beside Urchin. Neither of us intended to utter a word until we were returned safely to the ground. Breaking an etiquette unintentionally might mean us having to fight our own giant.

I expected a trumpet or something to announce the beginning of the fight, but as soon as Thumbringer entered the makeshift arena Lord Tick charged, his large, crude club raised above him. The one advantage Thumbringer had---in addition to his ring of protection---was his quickness. Although average for a human, he was much swifter of foot than Lord Tick, whose club fell repeatedly to the right, or to the left, or behind Thumbringer. Thumbringer's biggest disadvantage---in addition to being smaller--- was the lack of a weapon. He had the dagger he was able to conceal from the mer, but that wasn't much better than a toothpick when attacking Lord Tick's tough hide, which he discovered after he hit the gent for the first and only time. Lord Tick knew how to defend himself. Apparently his stature relative to others of his kind was similarly inadequate before mutating into a gent. He was either picked on a lot, or to compensate for his shortness he picked on others to increase his stature in their eyes. After receiving that first scratch he didn't allow Thumbringer to get that close again. He used his long arms to keep him away, and eventually to knock the dagger out of his hands and throw if off the cloud. He had many opportunities to dispatch Thumbringer in a similar manner, but he either enjoyed the fight too much to have it end that quickly, or he wasn't bright enough to think of it.

The crowd had been enjoying themselves, especially after Thumbringer drew blood. This fight might actually last more than a minute. But after the dagger was disposed of they began to get bored. The outcome was always predetermined, but now the when of it wasn't as much a mystery.

Lord Tick finally made contact with his club, breaking at least one bone from the sound of the crack. Thumbringer fell to the spongy ground and bounced. With his dagger gone, so went his hope. With him no longer trying as hard, and his adrenaline dissipating, it was only time, a short time, before his demise. Lord Tick stood above him, his club raised, prepared to make the death blow.

A look of enlightenment proceeded Thumbringer snatching his wallet from his side. He popped something into his mouth from it. Lord Tick apparently believed the movement was a precursor to his opponent making a final attempt to fight back. The delay provided Thumbringer the seconds necessary for the penta to activate. A penta? But weren't they supposed to not work for him? Desperation? The Limbo equivalent of an atheist prayer? Lord Tick didn't want the fight to be over with any sooner than his siblings did. The prey must be played with. Thumbringer stood up as he began to grow. A skilled manipulator of penta could control the magnitude and direction of elemental energy. The elem prospector had no idea how tall he would become before the penta expired. He was confident the effect would last long enough for the battle to end. He was even taller than Toe when his growth spurt ended. The gents were stunned, including Lord Tick. He moved quicker than he had in battle, fleeing to hide behind his bigger brothers and sisters.

Conversations began, first quietly between individuals, gradually merging, transitioning into an oral orgy. "Do we consider him a gent now?" "Or for as long as he retains his height?" "Is he mocking us?" "If everyone who increases their size is declared a gent it'll be anarchy." "Now that he's taller than Toe does he become Facilitator?"

"That's certainly a creative way to end the fight," said Urchin. "And without either of you getting killed. This may be a good time to make your departure. Nothing is decided quickly at Council, so your defense may become moot if the effect wears off before my siblings come to a consensus on what to do with you."

"I'll take them to my place," said Pulp.

"You don't have a place."

"The earth beneath my feet. The branches above my head. The air that I breath. The rain and sun upon my cheeks. The aroma of wood and meadow."

"I'm returning to the Council. I refuse to miss the most rousing discussion we've had in years. The anticipation of their reaction when they realize the reason for their debate is missing is almost too much."

"How long will we have to look over our shoulder?" I asked.

"How determined are they to pursue us?"

"Not very," said Pulp. "They don't dare all show up somewhere other than Cloud Home. Treachery will abound. Subtle, non-life threatening, but still harmful."

We followed Pulp to the transport platform. We were careful again to stay within the cylinder above the disk. Thumbringer was barely able to stand up. He had held up when he needed to, but now that he was relatively safe his body surrendered. His injuries were that severe. "We'll take him to a healer immediately," Pulp promised us.

"Where might that be?" asked Claw. "There are places we prefer not to go. And others we do."

"The Copper Forest."

"That's where we're heading," I uttered.

Claw smiled. "Gaea has her hands in everything, doesn't She?"

Chapter 27

WHITE RESIDUE

The kaleidoscope fused into a tall, canopied forest. Dappled evergreen light danced on the forest floor, and on us. The air was warm and sweet, in contrast to the cool, acrid, ionized air of Cloud Home. Insects buzzed around us, but they didn't bite or sting, except for once, but it felt more like a kiss. "Don't let the rudies bother you," said Pulp. "They'll be as friendly as you allow them to be. If they're bothering you, just brush them away a couple of times. They'll get the hint."

Looking closer I thought I could discern human features, but the rudies moved so swiftly I couldn't be certain. Another kiss, this one more personal. "Shoo," I said gently brushing away the indecent creature, trying not to harm it. It flew away with its flock.

"It won't take long for all of the Copper Forest to become aware of your prescience," said Pulp. "Rudies are quite the gossips." Thumbringer dropped in slow motion, the forest floor padded sufficiently to cushion his fall. "I will find a healer." Pulp leaped through the forest, dodging around trees, vertically and horizontally, looking straight ahead, never looking around, like he was a river pilot who knew the river so well he could navigate it blindfolded. At the speed he was traveling, one miscalculation would knock him senseless. One never occurred, even when he passed within sims of a tree or a fallen log.

The temperate forest would have been a pleasant place to rest if the anxiety of Thumbringer potentially dying hadn't poisoned the atmosphere. With that protection ring of his he should have been the last person to be in this position. I guess nothing was absolute. Considering his less than welcoming disposition it was a wonder he hadn't died earlier. Who knows how many times he would have if he didn't possess that ring? The forest was lovely. I felt guilty perceiving its serene beauty. Claw and I lowered ourselves onto the moss beside Thumbringer. That disc with the eight-sided star seemed so out of place here. But Pulp had to be able to travel to Cloud Home. He didn't have wings. My heart suddenly began to race. My breathing became labored. If that device could transport someone hundreds of kays, was it possible to also free me from this prison? The way these portals functioned, someone couldn't be sent somewhere randomly, they had to arrive at another portal, but maybe there was one orbiting the planet, or beyond that energy shield that separated the penal colony from the rest of the planet. Could the range of the device be increased, to allow me to be transported into the next system?

My reverie was disrupted when I began to hear voices. At first I believed them to be the healers Pulp spoke of. When they didn't become louder, like they should have when someone approached, I re-assessed their origin. Something was wrong with the sounds. They didn't sound right. Sound traveled in waves. What I heard was more of a billow, swirling tones, some words beginning before others ended. I looked at Claw to see if he heard the same. His shocked expression was my affirmation.

"So delicate they are."

"So were we when we were young and small." The second collection of sounds was subtly different than the first, the way an identical twin might walk one-percent slower than her sister, or have one strand of hair curled a sim further to the left.

"They will contribute to another ring."

"The archives are almost full."

"Don't say that. You'll outlive me. The archives say your species is hardy."

"I don't mind. Retirement is something to look forward to."

Pulp returned. So rapid was his movement that he appeared without a gradual warning. "The healer approaches." Pulp looked down at Thumbringer and shook his head sadly.

"He isn't too far gone, is he?" I asked nervously.

"No," Pulp softly replied. "Not yet. Urchin should have warned you not to challenge a gent."

"He did," Claw assured Pulp. "Many times, but Thumbringer is sometimes too quick to act, often sprinting past common sense."

"We thought we heard voices," I commented, "but they were ethereal. They sounded like they came from everywhere simultaneously."

"You heard the trees," Pulp explained. "When they communicate they shake their limbs, creating sound eddies. More than one limb is used so their voice sounds like it's coming from more than one place, like a complex sound system that's not completely in sync."

The forest began to move. When I say move I don't mean leaves fluttering or limbs swinging. The forest was actually moving. Three trees. Not the entire forest. A willow and two cedars. They traveled on their roots, like centipedes, but in a swirling mass of limbs instead of two parallel rows. The willow bent over, lowering its canopy. Its tendril-like leaves swept over Thumbringer, leaving a white residue behind. The willow leaned back up and left, its entourage following it.

Thumbringer opened his eyes. His color returned. He brushed off the powdery residue, like it was sleep from his eyes. "I had the most wonderful dream. Something hugged me until all the evil inside was squeezed out. I feel more than healed. I feel reborn. We have more than we need. I no longer covet the Sapphire Pearl. If we find it we should distribute the proceeds to the less fortunate."

I was concerned about Thumbringer's odd ramblings, but it wasn't completely unexpected. When I person recovers from a trauma it's natural for them to want to change their life, often in some extreme manner to remedy past transgressions.

"Is Thumbringer going to be okay?" I asked.

"Okay---yes," Pulp responded, "but I believe you intended to ask, will his personality return, will what he was before the injury and cure be restored? Willows can heal, but in doing so they must release part of themselves into their patients. Being a positive creature a willow's pollen has positive elements."

"So you're saying the willow infected Thumbringer?"

"Yes, but beneficially."

"Well, hell," Thumbringer grumbled. "I always thought I would eventually catch something from someone, but from a tree? I don't feel sick. In fact, I feel better about myself than I have in years."

"There you go. It was a good thing this happened."

"I still don't appreciate someone doing this to me, without my permission, without me weighing the benefits and risks."

"You were dying," said Claw.

"I still would have liked to make that decision for myself. How can I cure this?"

"You can't," said Pulp. "Well, you can, but the cure is worse than the disease."

"I think I should be the one to decide that."

"You need to be re-created."

"Is that all?"

"Well, it has to be in neutrality if you want your morals to return to what they were. You might be able to bypass dying if you can convince something from the Negative Frontier to infect you. I wouldn't recommend it. If you felt raped by the willow, wait until one of the eastern beasties has its way with you."

"It's not all bad," said Claw. "You appear to be more calm. The old Thumbringer would have been a raving lunatic by now."

Something had been bugging me. "What function did the cedars serve? Nurses? But they just stood there."

"Moral support. Companionship. How often do you see a tree alone?"

"Thank you for escorting us to the Copper Forest," said Claw to Pulp, "and for finding a healer for Thumbringer. We now must resume our quest to find the Sapphire Pearl."

"I would prefer to retain your companionship, if I may," said Pulp.

"If you feel you have some obligation to protect us, be assured, we can take care of ourselves. We have done quite well on our own, in lands more harsh than this."

"Actually, you would be doing me a favor. I've spent the majority of my life in the Copper Forest, but I haven't always lived here. I miss seeing other parts of the world. If you allow me to accompany you on your adventures I will take you to the Sapphire Pearl."

"So you know where the pearl is?" asked Thumbringer. "You know its exact location?" Pulp nodded. "Aren't positive mutes required to help us without ultimatums?"

"Positives help in the manner they feel most fit. That doesn't mean we do what you want. Stealing for you isn't very moral. Neither is allowing you to do something that is harmful."

"Isn't butting in immoral?"

"Moral people have a duty to intervene. Neutrals are the ones who feel they shouldn't butt in, to neither help nor hinder."

"It almost makes me believe negatives aren't that bad."

"The main distinction between positives and negatives is the latter intentionally do things they know are bad. Positives sometimes do things others perceive as being evil, but as long as THEY don't believe it, they are still being true to their morals."

"I personally think having a gent join our group is a great idea," I commented.

"I agree with Miss Dinga," said Claw. "Sometimes all that head smashing gets monotonous. I wouldn't mind sharing such tedious tasks with another person, especially one of proper height." Claw wasn't close to being as tall as Pulp, but he was closer than most people.

"Welcome aboard," said Thumbringer reluctantly. "The first thing you can help us with is setting up camp. Unless the Sapphire Pearl is close we might as well call it a day. It will be sundim soon."

Pulp did what was asked of him. Instead of sharing the rewards of his labor, he was content to pile up some leaves and use them as a pillow.

The night sounds were pleasant---not scary at all. I was lulled to sleep within minutes. My sole vexation was the vividness of my dreams. Actually they were quite wonderful, but in the manner they were wonderful was what bothered me. I was made love to in many different ways by many different people. When I woke in the middle of the night I felt something between my legs. Whatever it was, the prescience disappeared when I rolled over. I liked to believe it was just a residual effect of my dreams.

Chapter 28

THROWING PEBBLES

In the morning Thumbringer persisted in making Pulp earn his membership to our group. "I'm starving. Why don't you catch us some breakfast with that bow of yours?"

"I thought you knew. I'm vegetarian."

"Do you know, Fred?" I asked. "He's about this big." I spread my hands 50 sims apart. "He's a cross between a bird and a lizard. He flies. He's also a vegetarian."

"I don't think so. Does he live in the Copper Forest?"

"The Liver Peninsula, but he's also been to Coolatta."

"He sounds like a neutral. Positives and neutrals don't associate with one another very often. It's not that we dislike each other. We just don't have much in common."

"Do you belong to Carnivores Anonymous?"

Pulp raised an eyebrow.

"It's a group Fred belongs to, to help him repress his hunting instincts."

"I've never been a carnivore, so giving up meat isn't a challenge for me."

"I think it's more a relinquishing of a lifestyle. It's not just meat he's trying to give up. There's the ritual of stalking, hunting, then ripping open his prey before consuming it."

Fred appeared shortly after breaking camp. Coincidence? And he wasn't alone. His friend was similar in appearance. The exception, she was part insect instead of part reptile---and she was female. She didn't have any physical characteristics to indicate this,

213

but females just didn't act the same way as males. The differences were subtle, but they were there. She was painfully shy, and very beautiful. Her gossamer wings lit up like a rainbow whenever light hit them.

After introductions were made, Fred attempted to show off his friend. Why did males feel like they had to display their girlfriends like they were trophies? It was like it was some great accomplishment on their part to possess such a wonderful woman. In contrast, women felt grateful for being in a wonderful relationship, appreciative, not pompous.

"Show them your trick," Fred insisted. She disappeared. "No, not that one. Make the rocks and plants dance." I don't think she disappeared to show off. If I was her I would want to hide too. "Please show them, then we can leave." She reappeared, scowling at Fred, but she kept her composure, not wanting to embarrass herself more. She shyly adverted her eyes, then went into a trance. When she broke out of it she performed this intricate aerial ballet. I expected her elemental manipulations to move rocks and plants, not for the objects to express entire stories, or for their surfaces to change color and texture, forming intricate and complex patterns. When she was finished we felt too awed to applaud. She disappeared again, this time permanently.

"Incredible," said Thumbringer.

"Very beautiful," said Claw.

"How did you ever find someone like her?" I asked. It's odd how we think someone incredible dating a friend is flawed for dating the friend. Why would someone that wonderful date someone like HIM? Something had to be wrong with HER. I guess we know our friends too well. We know their faults as well as we know their strengths. No one was perfect, so maybe Fred was a catch. It was unfathomable for someone you consider a brother to be considered attractive by others.

Fred left my question unanswered. "I won't be able to spend much time with you now. Coral wants me to spend every waking minute with her---most of the sleeping ones too. I'll return soon." Fred flew off. Well, that was a bit open-ended. Did soon mean later in the day, tomorrow, next week, a year from now? I was going to miss him, but we had our own lives to live. If I suddenly became enamored with someone, would I be willing to give up my old life? Would I be willing to abandon Claw and Thumbringer?

The trek towards the pearl was taking longer than anticipated. Thumbringer had to stop every hour to rescue a kitten stuck in a tree, or rebuild an animal shelter after it was destroyed by a storm. Kindness was a virtue, but too much of anything---even chocolate---can make one sick---especially when it was someone other than you doing the eating. We tried to talk to him about his sudden change in behavior. His persistent reply: "I don't mind. I'm no worse or better, just different." Once he mentioned he didn't even think about women anymore. "They have all become sisters to me, or mothers, or daughters." He reminded us his condition didn't disturb him. He wasn't necessarily happy about it, either. He was apathetically content.

Ahead of us the forest began to glow, but not as intensely as when the willow came to heal Thumbringer. As we got closer to the anomaly, we began hearing crackling sounds, followed by a robust cackling. The forest ended, revealing the origin of the glow. Fifty meters from the perimeter of the forest a curtain of electromagnetic energy rose from the ground to the sky. At first it appeared to be completely vertical, but if you looked far enough up you could see its internal curvature. The energy pulsating through it was extreme enough to make it appear opaque, but that lessened to transparency the further into the sky it climbed. The landscape beyond the barrier was completely hidden.

The crackling noise was caused be a very odd creature throwing pebbles at the barrier. Sometimes a rock skimmed its surface, other times it temporarily indented it. The creature was covered in copper scales. It stretched 10 meters, from its triangular head to its lanky torso to its lizard-like tail. Its wings looked more like a bat's than a bird's. It had sixteen very small feet, making it look like a centipede.

"ARE WE TO PASS THROUGH THAT?!" Claw shouted over the electro-static din. He was referring to the electromagnetic curtain, not the juvenile drak, whose comic activities distracted us from its potential threat.

"WE WERE IN THE AREA SO I THOUGHT I WOULD SHOW YOU THE BOUNDARY SHIELD!" Pulp shouted back. "The terrans, the caretakers of the Sapphire Pearl, are a reclusive lot. No place is more reclusive than near the shield. Most people are afraid of it, which keeps them away. ACORN, STOP THAT RACKET!"

The juvenile drak dropped the pebble he was holding. He looked embarrassed. "Just having a little fun." He spoke in small bursts, the manifestation of an overabundance of energy that had to be released in order for him not to explode, so overwhelming that thought patterns could only exist in small clusters. "Not trying to hurt anyone. Don't see fireworks very often any more. Except when the ogres bend over and light their...."

"Acorn. We have guests."

"Glad to meet you." The drak shook our hands with three of his feet. They weren't hand-shaped, but they were at least the right size. "It's been awhile since I've met someone who hasn't been mutated---generously. You're the first since my last re-creation. I thought I might knock a hole in the shield, but I began having too much fun and got distracted."

"Acorn is a relatively young drak," Pulp explained. "Draks being the most powerful of creatures, die infrequently. As a consequence they live longer than even a gent. Most are conservative and wise. Acorn isn't very much of either."

"And I hope to never be. The Abyss is supposed to be beyond the shield, but what is it? A vacuum? A void? If a hole is poked through the shield, will the Abyss leak in, or will Limbo leak out? Can we escape through the Abyss, or is it just a dark closet? If

216

bi-pedals use the phrase TWO LEFT FEET to indicate someone who is ungraceful, what does someone who literally has two left feet call him? I consider someone having two left feet being six feet short."

The drak's soliloquy---a conversation isn't one-sided---piqued my curiosity. I moseyed to the boundary shield to examine it more closely. What was beyond it? It looked like a shower curtain. If I could just reach out and draw it back I could see who was bathing. I reached out to touch it, electrocuting myself. Looking back on it, it was fortunate I did die. Recovering from such a severe burn would have been an agonizing ordeal.

Chapter 29

FEATHERS

Another forest. Or the same. The Copper? A casual conjecture considering how many times I've been wrong. It was the first time I've been re-created at night. A blessing. A delay in the detailed observation of my mutations was welcomed. The sky was overcast, dimming the moonlight. Even better. My feet were more misshapen, and firmer. My face was covered with...something. My chin was non-existent. A long snout was where my mouth and nose used to be. It was pointed and hard. My hands were less mutated than my feet.... NO! I had thought what draped along my arms were sleeves, but a person wasn't re-created with clothes. So my arms were more than that now. They were also wings. I examined the black velvet on my hands more closely. FEATHERS! My snout was a beak. My mounds were completely gone. And I don't want to even think about what was different between my legs. As the moon brightened, my nightmare became reality. My shadowy explanations were confirmed. I sought a pond to see my reflection. I would have cried if my eyes were still equipped.

After passing through the multiple stages of grief I began to rationalize the positives. I probably set a record for the shortest time to become a demon. I could forage for food, saving time and money purchasing and preparing it. I could fly. A conjecture, but considering I had wings it was likely. Being a flightless bird was an irony I didn't have the emotional resolve to consider.

I intended to fly, but how? When I transformed into a larger version of my cam my flight was more desperation than skill. I glided more than flew, flapping madly when no other options came to mind. Here goes. I extended my arms/wings and waved them. Still weak from re-creation they responded sluggishly. Faster. Faster! FASTER! I rose, just a meter, before I tired and fell, but still remarkable for someone that was a mammal a month ago. I tried again after resting, not getting off the ground as far or staying up as long. My muscles were already hurting. It might take days before they became accustomed to the movement. Having a muscular chest may not be adequate compensation for losing my mounds, but it was something.

I gained more than wings and feathers. My senses became more finely tuned. Claw and Thumbringer were near: 10 kays west-northwest of me. And others. Mutes. More human than not.

Would Claw and Thumbringer still like me? They liked mutes. Even sought them out. And I've looked worse. That transitional state I was in was ghastly, with hair growing in places it shouldn't have been, in that aberrant color and texture.

I began walking in their direction. Not an easy task on talons. Technically feet, talons being claws, but they were so mutated it was difficult not to think of them as something entirely different.

A beautiful girl flew up to me. Her curves suggested she was older, but when one is the size of a girl, I thought of her as such. Her wings were as diaphanous as Fred's friend's. She wore a glittery gown that tightly accentuated her femininity---ah, the memories. Her feet were bare---practical, considering they never touched the ground. She must have been an elem manipulator, because her delicate wings couldn't have supported a creature as large as she, even of so slight of build. Her hair, golden and straight, glowed in the sunlight. She was very attractive, but there was a wholesomeness about her that prevented women from being threatened by her. "I'll provide advice in exchange for you providing me a favor."

"What guarantee do I have that you'll follow through on that favor? What I ask may not be within your means." My voice sounded like a hen cackling compared to her perfectly balanced sweet/sexy, gritty/downy timbre.

"You must trust me. We're not in the land of chaos, so it's likely what I say is true. But we're not in the land of order either, so there is no guarantee."

I didn't have much to lose, including my pride. Being covered in feathers has a way of doing that to a person. "Agreed. What can I do for you?"

"You can introduce me to your friend."

I looked confused.

"The one you were with prior to your last re-creation."

"I had two companions."

"The large muscular one. The other is no longer interested in women. The pure touch of a willow does that to a man. Those afflicted consider the benefits of the purification outweigh the loss of desire. Never-the-less, I hope I'm never so touched."

"I promise to introduce you to him." Claw should be the one exchanging favors with me, not this lovely creature. "He's in the terran village, in the direction I'm travelling?"

"Gnotting Hill."

"What will you do for me in return?"

"The shape you currently hold is just one of three you can transform into. You can also become a bird---and a woman."

If what she said was true I will still be in her debt after I introduce her to Claw. But....

Reading my mind, she said, "Imagine yourself in one of those forms."

I attempted to transform into a bird first. I eat my dessert last. It was actually easy. Maybe my previous experience with penta helped. I braced myself. I expected the process to be painful. My body contorted, but from a distance, like I was having an out-of-body-experience. I was aware my body was changing, but I felt nothing. When it was over I was about half the length of the girl's arm and completely black. I flew effortlessly. With practice I even did aerials. Instincts must have been inherent in that form.

Now for the true test. I delayed. Anticipation was building, but so was dread. What if something went wrong? What if the woman I turned into looked more like an ogre than an angel? But being a woman again, a real woman who was curvaceous and smooth, that was the thing I wanted most since my first re-creation. The only thing really, other than sustenance, a soft, safe place to sleep, and the occasional bath.

I held my breath, closed my eyes, and released. Again, there was awareness, but no feeling. When I re-opened my eyes they were full of tears. My skin was porcelain, without even the smallest of hairs a woman's body normally has. My mounds were full again and firmer than they had ever been. I needed to see my reflection. I rushed about trying to find a small pool or even a puddle. My generous mounds barely moved. A puddle was all I found, but the person looking back at me made it much more than that. She was gorgeous. She had perfect skin, full lips, dimples, large green eyes, perfect nose and eyebrows, and long black hair that curled naturally to give it body, but not too much to make it appear untidy. So I wasn't completely hairless. Instead of being disappointed, I was elated. It was like discovering something wonderful you never imagined existed. I swung my head around, causing the silken strands to frolic in wild abandon. I laughed uncontrollably. Modern fashion got it wrong. Women were meant to be playful, not stale imitations of mannequins. I looked at my reflection again. Before mutating I considered myself to be sexy, and moderately attractive, but never a knockout. I wasn't certain I still wanted to leave Limbo if given the opportunity. Considering no one had escaped from the prison planet the point was moot, but it made a person reevaluate what was most important in her life. It wasn't just regaining my beauty. I had made more friends here in a couple of weeks than I had my entire life before my incarceration.

"I'll see you in Gnotting Hill," spoke the girl who no longer shamed my appearance. "And don't get any ideas about your friend now that you're a woman again." She may have sounded catty, if it wasn't for the sweet way she said it. She flew up, above the trees and away.

She was probably rushing off to spy on Claw. Maybe he was a catch. What was I thinking? Just because another woman desires a man doesn't make that man suddenly irresistible. Claw was as much of a brother to me as Fred, maybe more. YUCK!

Chapter 30

AFTERGLOW

I retained my human form. I would have reached Gnotting Hill more rapidly if I was a bird, but I didn't want to lose my beauty so soon, even temporarily. An hour later I crossed paths with two men, their appearance traumatizing me as much as their manifestation. They were obviously heading to the terran village, but from a more southerly direction. The taller of the two wore platinum armor. Two hourglass emblems---concave octagons--- were carved into his breast plate, outlined in gold. A two-handed sword, an hourglass emblem on its hilt, was sheathed in a scabbard pressed tightly to his side.

The other man dressed more like Claw and Thumbringer, wearing a green leather shirt, breaches, and boots. He also wore a metal helm, and chest armor in overlapping metal scales. An oval shield hung on one side of him and a short sword on the other. He and the platinum-clad man each wore medium sized backpacks of the high quality used by either the wealthy for day excursions, or by professional adventurers who required durability and efficient storage capacity.

Back to the second man. He was of average height and build. His hair was sandy, similar to my own before I had it removed as a young woman, but it was much messier than I would have ever allowed my hair to get. His face was hansom, but not in a rip-off-your-clothes way. There was strength behind those eyes, and determination. He was a man to be trusted and to befriend. He looked familiar. IT WAS THE MAN I SAW THE DAY I ENTERED LIMBO, AND LATER IN BRIARWOOD!

He saw me at the same time I recognized him. His expression was one of familiarity, but searching for that exact match. OF COURSE! I look different than I did those times we almost met. "THE WOMAN WHO WAS ATTACKED BY THOSE DOGS!"

"And later attacked by men at Briarwood," I added. "How did you ever recognize me? My hair, well I have some now, and…."

"Well, you are wearing what you did when you were attacked."

I had forgotten I was naked. I was so proud of my new body I didn't consider to conceal it. It was infinitely more presentable than that hairy malformed husk I used to reside. I had nothing to be embarrassed about, but somehow I suddenly was. These were strangers, the man I met twice before not as much, but that made it worse. Having the other man see me like this wasn't much better. He exuded nobility, like he was a beloved leader or a member of the clergy. It felt like that dream of rushing off to school in such a hurry I forget to wear clothes. I attempted to cover myself with my hands, but that drew even more attention to myself. The men hadn't gawked at me, or adverted their eyes. Seeing a woman naked was probably the least shocking thing they had seen during their adventures.

The platinum-clad man removed a shirt and breeches from his backpack, then handed them to me. "Thank you," I said humbly. I rushed behind a tree to dress.

Upon returning a third man was there. He was larger than the other two, but not quite as tall as the platinum-clad man. He moved stiffly and was slightly bent over. He was dressed like the more modestly dressed man, with a war hammer attached to his side instead of a short sword.

The platinum-clad man said to him, "How long until your legs recover? I'm tired of waiting up for you every couple of minutes."

The stooped man replied, "I'm more worried about my back. If it doesn't get better in a couple of days I'm going to have to use my healing stone"

"Did you have to carry so many of them?"

"I had to carry every one of them. It was the only way I could repay my debt. Why couldn't those feek-splattered asses mutate into ponies."

Noticing that I had returned, it was time for my oldest of Limboan acquaintance to make introductions. "Our hunched-over friend is Centaur Beetlewoods. As his name indicates, he had an early altercation with a mute which he now wishes he hadn't. He is also the toughest man I know, and our leader. The other gentleman is Stick Bluewood. He is the finest swordsman in Limbo, which he has to be considering his penchant for getting into trouble."

"Just Limbo? Well, after we escape I'll have to do something about it." Escape? From Limbo? Now that was boasting.

"The one thing he isn't is humble."

"Humble is a word those people who can't back up their deeds use."

"I am Hornet Polygulch."

It was now my turn. "I guess my name is Dinga Polygulch, then." Finally, I learned where I came from. It wasn't as enlightening as an adoptive child finding her biological parents, but it did contribute to making me whole. "I was named after the dogs that so rudely began my series of re-creations. I may not look like it, but I'm a demon." I was reluctant to give that last piece of information, mutant prejudice being so rampant. It would have come out eventually if I spent much time with these people. Considering the tie I had to Hornet, there was a strong likelihood of that happening. I didn't want them to think I was hiding something from them. Their reaction was less than I anticipated. But not entirely surprising, considering what they have probably been through. Limbo desensitizes.

"You don't look like a mute," said Stick. "Possibly a sylph, but I don't see any wings." Was that what that girl who had a crush on Claw was called? Humans liked to categorize: matching names associated with legends, something already in our psyche, to mutational similarities.

Obligation overwhelmed me. I had to be open with these people, and if that meant being vulnerable, so be it. I removed the clothes that just minutes ago I would have done almost anything to cover myself with. Having two of the three men already see me naked wasn't any consolation. After I became clothed I became a born-again prude.

I didn't provide them more than a glimpse. As soon as the restrictions were removed I transformed into my hybrid state, emphasizing the wings that were more show than functional. Finally to my raven form. I showed off the aerials I was so proud of. One of the most embarrassing moments of my life happened prior to returning to my human form. Birds have a nasty habit of relieving themselves while flying. Not only did the three men see what I did. The physical evidence landed on Centaur.

"I appreciate you wanting to share," he said, trying to be a good sport. "Next time tell me a story about your childhood." It was many days later that I was finally able to look him in the eye again. Some things people should not experience together.

"Does the...uh...transfer of bodily fluids make you blood brothers?" Stick commented wryly. "Feek siblings?"

"We're heading to Gnotting Hill," Hornet announced.

"I guess I am too," I said.

"You're not sure?" asked Centaur.

"A series of misfortunate events has prevented me from reaching many of my destinations."

"Even with your ability to transform, you shouldn't be traveling alone," stated Stick.

"One of those misfortunate events I spoke of separated me from my two companions. I hope to reunite at Gnotting Hill."

"You will join us, won't you?" Hornet insisted.

I smiled. "At least until Gnotting Hill."

What was I saying? That I was willing to abandon the only friends I ever had for these STRANGERS? Hornet wasn't a complete stranger, but seeing someone from a distance twice didn't make us friends. And there was more to it than attaching myself to someone---anyone---rather than being on my own. There was an attraction growing between Hornet and I. There was our common history, but it was more than that. I had never been so enamored with someone so quickly. I've had crushes on people before, but never like this. It felt like I was an animal in heat. I was an addict, and the primal connection I required was the fix. We were two oppositely charged magnets that wouldn't be content until we made contact.

Gnotting Hill was still an hour away. To fill that time we shared our adventures, I more candidly than they. They intended to not only acquire the Sapphire Pearl, but all gemmed pearls.

"And how many of these gemmed pearls are there suppose to be?" I asked.

"Six," Hornet replied.

"Are they more valuable as a set?"

Before Hornet could answer, Centaur jumped in with, "Valuable enough to supersede all other activities." He left it at that.

I not only entered Limbo at the same location as Hornet, but at the same time. Did our mutual arrivals influence our attraction, or was it coincidence? Could what causes mutations also initiated our connection? Did the planet begin to modify us even before the first re-creation?

If it wasn't for the mutual attraction Hornet and I had Stick would have been the person I was most interested in. I was one of those women who loved a man in uniform. Police harassment never bothered me. I was very accurate in my recordkeeping and diligent in paying my taxes, so there was never a problem, but some of my colleagues weren't as understanding. Stick was an Octagonal Knight. The concave octagons on his armor and sword represented the eight moralities---excluding neutrality---and the number of members of their order. To become a Knight a current member had to be defeated in a duel of his choosing. If an Octagonal Knight dies in any other manner his essence is whisked away to the Octagonal Prism in Gulag, where his body is regenerated around it. The process is so swift Gaea doesn't have an opportunity to seize the soul, preventing re-creation, and more importantly, mutation. In order for someone to assume the rank and privileges of an Octagonal Knight they must remain pure, never having been touched by Gaea.

"Didn't you say that you were re-created shortly after you

arrived?" I asked him.

"Either the order is more lax about re-creations, or I didn't actually die. I do sometimes feel like a fraud, that I stole the arms and armor. But I did defeat an Octagonal Knight."

"Like you said, maybe you weren't actually re-created."

"I think a man knows when he's re-created." And apparently a woman doesn't, considering how many times I was wrong about the condition.

"So, how has the fighting for truth and honor been going?"

"I haven't had that many opportunities to test my abilities. I've only been an Octagonal Knight for a week. The armor and sword didn't come with an instruction manual. I need to head to Gulag for training. Our appropriations have gotten in the way. Maybe on the way to the next pearl."

"So you know where the other pearls are?"

"We hope to after we find the Sapphire. There is a misconception with Octagonal Knights. Being TRUE NEUTRALS we don't fight for positive causes, any more than we fight for negative ones. The bloodiest wars have been fought for just causes. Holy wars, people like to label them. Octagonal Knights are more likely to save damsels in distress than fight for a preacher with a vendetta."

Stick led our procession, with Hornet behind him, then me, and finally Centaur. He was careful not to walk directly behind me---who could blame him. He was the only one of the three I wasn't attracted to. It wasn't that I thought he was ugly or he had a corrosive personality. I thought of him more as a father than a potential lover. Limbo was definitely changing me. First I began seeing men as potential mates, now as father figures. Considering how poor a father mine was, it was amazing I even contemplated someone filling that role.

Centaur may have kept his distance from me, but it didn't prevent him from talking to me. You know how parents sometimes discuss things with you, you wished they didn't. Well.... "It's been said that two members of the opposite sex who enter Limbo at the same place and time are destined to be together. Do you feel any great attraction to Hornet?"

"Of course not," I lied. So there was something more than admiration and sexual attraction involved. I was definitely not going to share these feelings with strangers. It felt kind of embarrassing to have them, like I had been infected with a sexually transmitted disease.

The attraction was getting stronger. The longing to connect with Hornet was becoming an itch that needed to be scratched, in an area that one didn't scratch in public. I stared at Hornet. It was difficult not to in my state. He appeared as agitated as I. He glanced over his shoulder, his eyes catching mine. If it was dark the sparks between us would have been on display for all to see. Hornet turned back around. About the time the sensations within me were about to explode he said, "Hold up." He took my hand. Energy flowed between us. It climbed up my arm, where it spread throughout my body. I could barely stand. "We'll be back." He led me away, or did I lead him? We stumbled into the forest, gasping for privacy before the need to connect overwhelmed us.

"So the tales are true," spoke a fading voice.

We moved swiftly, but not with sure feet. Our senses were becoming less tuned to our surroundings and more tuned to each other. We fell to the forest floor, our bodies tangled, the leaves and needles cushioning us. We stripped, not so much to satisfy erotic desires, but to increase the amount of skin to skin contact. Each supplemental square sim intensified the exchange of energies. A fine electro-magnetic mist filled the air around us. Time became irrelevant as we experienced passion in more than one medium. The signal to break apart came when the rate of energy flow diminished. Our attraction to each other couldn't continue at that intensity, but I think it had more to do with the residual energy becoming exhausted. The sparks became intermittent, a tap left open to drip. Slow but accumulative was the loss. After contact was broken I still tingled, the radiant afterglow illuminating more than my skin

When we returned to Centaur and Stick we must have looked like gods, glowing micro-suns that slowly dissipated. Some people had a certain look about them after having sex. I was confident Stick and Centaur had some understanding what had occurred, but only on the most superficial of levels. What Hornet and I experienced was more intimate. The exchange of energies were as much mental and emotional as physical. I saw everything Hornet had experienced in his life, and everything he felt. He was concerned that he may have actually murdered someone, a murder he had no memory of. If I knew that much about him, that deeply, that meant he knew that much about me. He was an angel compared to me. How could he stand to be in my prescience aware of my evil deeds and thoughts? To want to have spiritual intercourse with me again with unfathomable. But I also had seen his reply to my insecurities. He didn't care. What was in the past was in the past, even the past that was the present just seconds ago. He saw that I was a different person now. I think I would have fallen in love with him even if we didn't have that forced magnetism between us. Maybe that's why we were assigned to the same location on Limbo. The potential for us being a match was high.

The four of us didn't talk the rest of the way to Gnotting Hill. What could one say? It appeared to be more awkward for the two not involved. Was it better to speak of it or not? Which would be less rude?

Chapter 31

HALF AS TIDY

We heard Gnotting Hill before we saw it. Fiddles? The music apparently moved us, because we began to move our feet to the rhythm. I intended to enter the terran hamlet haughtily, exuding confidence. Obstacles, intentional or coincidental, weren't going to unsettle me. Dancing was joyous, not intimidating.

At the perimeter of the hamlet a score of 75 sim tall insect hybrids greeted us. In each of their six hands they held a dart. "One of them is neutrally-positive. The others, their positive attributes outweigh their negative. Let them pass." The swarm broke into two columns, through which we passed.

Gnotting Hill was a rocky knob. Pathways, often crisscrossing one another, led to numerous entries into its catacombed interior.

These INSECTS couldn't be terrans. My intuition proved true when a scattering of nervous creatures twice as tall, but half as tidy---as the insects---were spotted skittering on a hill more mound than mountain. Their mutations were minimal. The most obvious was their short stature, but their skin was also chalky gray, and their noses elongated. They wore robes. All were dirty, torn, and ill-fitting. They looked like bags with holes cut out---for their head, arms, and legs.

On a rocky perch, three stories above us, was the origin of the music. Four of the insects rubbed their arms against their legs in a manner that produced perfectly pitched tones. With their delicate wings flared out behind them they looked like they were wearing elegant gowns.

The commotion our presence caused emptied the hill. Most of the terrans kept their distance, peering at us from their holes, but a small contingent walked down switchbacks to us from the top of the hill. Following two terrans were two humans, a gent, and a drak. CLAW AND THUMBRINGER! I rushed up to them, meeting them before they reached the bottom of the hill. I wrapped my arms around each of them, tentatively. It was possible they no longer recognized me, considering how drastic my last mutations were. In the manner they reciprocated there was no doubt they were able to see past the superficial shell that concealed me. I made introductions. What a menagerie I had surrounded myself with.

The copper-scaled drak was embarrassingly enthusiastic. "The terrans are exceedingly generous. There are spiders, and flies, and roaches everywhere. It's a perpetual smorgasbord."

"Acorn will always be welcome here," spoke the terran with a pine needle necklace. "As will Claw and Thumbringer. They have offered to renovate Gnotting Hill."

"Have they?" It wasn't that I was displeased---just surprised. As I understood the term, Claw and Thumbringer were true neutrals, not intentionally harming someone, but not helping them either. Prospectors worked hard to pad their wallet, not to help others. But...Thumbringer hadn't been himself since the willow healed him.

"It was Thumbringer's idea," Claw explained. "We've been partners for so long, I don't think I could function without him. It looks like you now have new companions, so it worked out for the best. You weren't re-created to be an elem harvester---or a carpenter."

"I'll continue to travel with you," said Pulp. "If I'm not able to settle down, I can at least harness my wanderlust."

"Don't you recognize me?" asked the other terran. Was he talking to me? I didn't recognize him, but that may have been because he was as mutated as I. Hornet, Centaur, and Stick studied him closer. A glint of recognition slowly spread across their countenances.

"PEBBLE!" Stick stepped up to embrace him, but recoiled--- abruptly---after grasping the gruesome consequences of placing a metal vice around someone half your size. He patted him on his shoulder instead, duplicated by Hornet and Centaur. Pebble appeared uncomfortable with the contact, but he didn't back away.

"Terrans are bashful, which contributes to our poverty," spoke the terran with the necklace---the mayor, perhaps? "We aren't comfortable associating with dissimilar species, gnats being the one exception. We're also stubborn. We manufacture a limited variety of weapons from the metal we buy from the trogs. If we were slightly more gregarious, and catered to our clients, we would be living in mansions. Alas, we have our pride."

"It takes a brave man to own up to his shortcomings," I said. "A bold man to express them publicly."

"Terrans are brave, and I think more humble now that Pebble is here. His views have filtered through our society, inflicting us with enough openness to permit Thumbringer and Claw to assist us."

"We've come for the Sapphire Pearl," said Centaur, bluntly. "Is that what drew you here, Pebble?"

"So you were able to obtain the Emerald?" A longing lit his face, but was quickly doused.

"We have something to discuss with you---in private."

"Then it might be best if you didn't discuss it with me. Terrans acquire little. What they do they share freely, including knowledge. I've changed, Centaur. More, and less, than I ever imagined. What I am now isn't something I never thought I could be, but something I never knew existed, something inconceivable to that person I was before I mutated. Possessions no longer matter to me. I think that's why terrans don't care how they look, or how they live. But we can become selfish in our uncaring. Although we instinctively starve ourselves of necessities, I don't think it's immoral for someone else to help us, as long as we don't ask for it."

"Does hitting a target from a hundred meters no longer inspire you?" asked Stick.

"I still use a bow, but strictly for recreation. If a person seeks perfection he will find torment."

"Follow me," said the mayor. He escorted us into Gnotting Hill's core. Its chiseled interior was an architectural and artistic marvel. The tattered furniture and pieces of garbage haphazardly strewn about, weren't. The quality of the construction and absence of upkeep didn't match.

"You are artisans in more than metal," I commented. "Your city is exquisite."

"We didn't build Gnotting Hill," the mayor responded humbly.

"Who did then? The gnats?"

The mayor wasn't able to completely conceal his amused reaction to the absurd suggestion. His mouth remained taciturn, but his eyes brightened. "Gnobs."

"The same creatures who serve the gents in Cloud Home?"

"From your tone you imply gnobs are indentured servants or slaves. Gnobs serve who they wish, be it gents, or a mountain. After hollowing Gnotting Hill they sought additional endeavors. The process is more important to them than the finished product."

Our tour ended in the uppermost room. Eight apertures, evenly spaced, permitting exquisite views in every direction. A tunnel spiraled down from the center of the room.

"The sphere you seek is at the end of the tunnel," spoke the mayor. "Only one may enter at a time. All may try. The sphere is our most valuable possession, but possessions are selfish."

"Why don't we just bypass all this tediousness," said Centaur. "We will pay you a small fortune for this pearl." From the expression on the mayor's face this was the wrong tactic. Centaur modified his approach. "If you give us the pearl you would be

233

helping us, not yourselves. Carrying the pearl will encumber us. Taking some gold off our hands would remedy the situation. It would be wasteful to not exchange it for some of the necessities you are lacking."

"What is a necessity to some is enrichment to others. We give the sphere freely to one who needs it. The need is to be proven by successfully ascertaining the morality of each of the nine individuals you meet. Neutral-positive holds the sphere. One false conjecture forfeits additional attempts. Those failing will not be able to speak of what they have seen."

"Not everyone regards honor as highly as you," I commented. "Promises are broken."

"We do rate honor highly, but we are realists. Those who are unsuccessful won't tell because they will no longer have knowledge of what they have seen. However fearsome your antagonists might appear, the true battle is within."

"Anyone wish to volunteer to go first?" asked Centaur. There were no takers.

"I hesitate because I believe Hornet is best equipped," said Stick. "He found the Emerald Pearl."

"That doesn't mean I'll return with the Sapphire," he countered. He looked at me. "Someone else go." I don't think he was afraid. He just had more to live for now. The task of distinguishing moral orientations wasn't necessarily dangerous, but it could be. How might someone from the Negative Frontier react to being interrogated?

"I guess I could go," spoke Centaur without much enthusiasm. "If I can carry equines on my back I should be able to ascertain a few moral identities."

I considered making the attempt, but I didn't want to go first. I think it had to do with me wanting to be in control. If someone else was the guinea pig I had more time to analyze the situation, and possibly learn from their mistake. The mayor said the answers would come from within. Did I really want to fight my eternal demons? Hornet didn't seem to mind my emotional and moral flaws. Maybe I should go first. It Centaur failed he wouldn't be able to share his error, so what was I going to learn from him? I was motivated now. These things tended to wax and wane. A quarter later I might not feel the same way.

It was too late. Stick walked into the downwardly spiraling tunnel. It was prudent to analyze before committing, but sometimes a direct approach was more effective.

Chapter 32

MORE THAN A PEARL

A few minutes later Stick reappeared. "How did I get turned around? I was walking down this tunnel, then suddenly found myself walking out."

The mayor enlightened. "Once a morality is interpreted falsely there is no reason for the seeker to continue."

"But I never saw anyone."

"You don't remember seeing anyone."

"I'll try next," I volunteered.

Now that someone had broken-the-ice I was ready to take the plunge. But please, don't make the water too cold. A few meters into the tunnel it abruptly terminated. I turned around and walked back out.

"Those substantially mutated aren't granted access," the mayor explained. "They can too easily ascertain another's morality by comparison to their own." Why didn't he say that earlier?

It would have been gratifying for it to be me who successfully solved the puzzle. For years I have told myself I didn't wish to compete because it didn't interest me, but I think it had more to do with me not wanting to fail. Failure meant not being in control. I learned, painfully at times, that for a person to survive on Limbo they had to rely on others. Being part of a group was safer than being on your own. Having friends now, for the first time in my life, I craved their admiration, their adulation of my abilities. Well, if I couldn't navigate the moral maze maybe one of my friends could. That was another advantage of having friends, you could share in their triumphs.

Centaur was next. He was gone longer than Stick, but his perplexed expression conveyed that he too had failed.

Both Claw and Thumbringer declined when asked if they wished to make an attempt. Like Hornet, I don't think it had anything to do with them being afraid. They no longer had the desire to obtain the pearl. That reinforced my decision to move on with the new friends I made.

Well, it was do or die now. Hornet looked at me. I smiled and nodded. My attempt made his previous hesitation moot. If anyone could navigate the moral maze, it was he, the person who successfully extracted the Emerald Pearl from the arbols. Although he and I had met just hours before---officially---I considered him my...husband? Was there a minimal time two people had to be together to be considered soul-mates? Some people spend their entire lives together and never come close to sharing what we did. The longing to be with him was already beginning to build. How much longer before we had to rush off into the woods again? Would being physically apart reduce the longing, possibly stopping it all together? Or make it stronger?

Thumbringer handed Hornet his ring. "It's too valuable for me to borrow it," Hornet insisted.

"Keep it, to protect Dinga." If Thumbringer wanted me to be protected why didn't he give ME the ring? I liked the idea of someone being my protector, especially Hornet, but enough of the OLD ME remained to feel offended.

Hornet slid the ring onto his left hand, on the finger reserved for commitment. Without hesitation he moved towards the tunnel, then dropped out of sight. An hour later he reappeared. An iridescent, metallic blue sphere was held before him in his open hand. It was the most beautiful thing I've ever seen. Yes, I'm a girl. Get over it.

Hornet appeared to be on the verge of collapse. Now that the task was complete, his strength---physical, mental and emotional---was visibly draining. A chair, constructed from gnarled roots, was provided for him.

I cut him off as he attempted to speak. "Wait until you've rested."

"I must share my tale while the experience is fresh. The tunnel emptied into a cavern. A pool of water was below the ledge I was on. A large fish, about the size of a dolphin, burst from the water. Its scales looked metallic, shifting in color. Its massive mouth was directly across from me. It could have swallowed me whole, but its mouth was just a diversion. Four tentacles, two on each side of it, attempted to strike me. The initial attacks were unsuccessful. Thanks again for the ring. Eventually, one of the tentacles did make contact. The hand that it hit began to itch. Looking down at it, I saw that the skin had transformed, into a transparent, slimy membrane. Whenever the creature inadvertently splashed water onto it, it felt better---momentarily--- until it began to itch again as it dried. At first I couldn't move to draw my dagger, the fish's chaotic pattern mesmerizing me. What broke me out of my trance was the creature striking me. As I withdrew my blade, my mind now clear, I deliberated what morals this fish might have. Just because something strikes at you doesn't make it evil. It could be defending itself or trying to feed. But would something that was truly good try to change someone, attempt to transform them into a copy of themselves?"

"They might if they thought it best for them," commented Pulp.

"I wouldn't have thought of that," said Stick. "That's probably why I got it wrong."

"I almost did, but my scientific background conditioned me to analyze a situation fully before making a decision. I saw past the obvious and determined that it had to be morally positive, because it was helping me by transforming me into something superior: itself. Ascertaining the second part of its morality was easier. It obviously attempted to confuse me. That meant chaos. It was chaotically-positive."

"I sure don't remember meeting something like that," said Pulp. "And I've lived in the chaotically-positive part of the Frontier for over 20 years."

"How much of that time have you spent underwater?" asked Centaur.

"Good point."

"After I determined the creature's morality I found myself in the tunnel again, like I had never entered that cavern.

"Another cavern. Snow and ice. A biting wind. Extreme cold. I would have fled if the consequences of my flight wouldn't have been so dire. I don't know how it was possible, but the sun began bearing down at me, although I was many meters below the surface. About the time I warmed up it got dark. The cold returned, but it and the darkness were forgotten when a gent appeared. The five meter brute---no offense." Hornet looked at Pulp.

"No offense taken. Many of my siblings have been known to act brutish."

"The gent began to transfer the pile of rocks beside it to where I stood. Fortunately, they all missed. Either Thumbringer's ring saved me again, the gent was a poor shot, or he just wanted to frighten me. I believe the latter, because he began to taunt me. He asked if I was cold, then made rude comments about my mother. I was on the verge of charging him, my sword outstretched before me like a lance, when I realized he hadn't actually harmed me. But he did make fun of me and my circumstances. He had to be neutral, but did he veer towards order or chaos? He had provoked me, becoming insidious in his attempt to force an altercation. He had to be chaotically-neutral. He disappeared, leaving me alone in the dark. I found myself back in the tunnel, again.

"I walked into a third cavern a few seconds later. I had no time to analyze the situation. An avian hybrid with a four meter wingspan dived at me from an impossible height, impossible relative to the height of Gnotting Hill. Instead of attacking with its claws it had a javelin in each hand. As I futilely withdrew my sword, I prepared to be skewered. Even if I successfully embedded my weapon it would have been after I was punctured. A meter from me the bird veered, harpooning two rats beside me. It flew away. It was just after food, so it couldn't be evil. There wasn't evidence of either chaotic or ordered behavior, or positive or negative. It was probably a true neutral, but I wasn't confident. It's been said that unless you're certain your first choice is wrong you shouldn't change it. I breathed a sigh of relief when I found myself in the tunnel again."

"That must have been where I went wrong," said Centaur. "As soon as I heard you say it swooped down at you I assumed it was evil. Even if it hadn't actually struck me, it would have scared the feek out of me."

"My next...encounter...was even more frightening. A 12 meter long snake with a dozen legs discharged a lightning bolt at me. The defensive ring prevented a direct hit. The grazing wound was still severe enough to cause third degree burns. The initial acute pain turned into a throbbing. Both made it difficult to concentrate. What saved me was the creature having to recharge between lightening attacks. It flanked me, to bring more of its limbs within range to attack. Of the six legs that could attack, two had to remain planted for it to retain its balance. I was beginning to weaken, my blistering wound draining me as much as the parleying did. The creature was obviously evil. That sneak attack when I appeared prevented it from being ordered, but after the initial mischief it was consistent. It had to be neutral-negative. I returned to the tunnel, healed. Aware that my injuries were temporary permitted additional analytical consideration at the expense of personal safety.

"My fifth encounter was odd. A bipedal hippo asked me if I needed assistance. It wore no armor---no clothes at all, except for a loin cloth---but when something had skin as thick as it did such protection was redundant. It was slightly taller than me, but much bulkier. I wished to take him up on his offer, but if my success was more determined by reasoning than from brawn the thing might just get in the way. Before it offered its assistance it didn't know if I was good or evil, so it had to be neutral. If it was to be a trusted mercenary it had to be ordered. Ordered-neutral. This one wasn't too difficult. Maybe I was getting the hang of it.

"Another snake. I immediately thought evil, so I attacked it. It was blue with multi-colored wings. It was beautiful---a dynamic, sentient rainbow, just beyond my fingertips---but it could also be deadly. In fairy tales evil was ugly and good was beautiful, but the real world didn't work that way. The snake flapped its wings, creating a wind so substantial that it not only countered my attack, but pushed me back. I stumbled, then fell. An additional attack was countered by an additional gale. It only attacked with wind, and only after I had first attacked. It could have bit me while I was down. It was ordered-positive.

"The next cavern was forested, very densely. Something moved. I thought at first it was one of the trees because of how large it was, but it was too uniformly green to be vegetation. Before I could react, it belched at me, a thick nauseous plume that filled my lungs. The eruption began in my belly, but took just seconds to travel through my esophagus and burst to the surface. I felt better, initially, until the rumbling resumed. It laughed at me, the thing still partially hidden in the woods, then it struck me with its tail. So exact was the incision that I didn't bleed initially. Then it told me what it was going to do to me. Salt was going to be sprinkled on the wound, then my fingers would be broken, piecemeal. It was evil without pretense. It could only be ordered-negative.

"The second to last encounter was a formality. Definitely one I could live without. A transparent woman floated towards me. Her hair was in disarray. Her features contorted in her despair. The wail that spewed from her paralyzed me with fear. I felt my sanity slipping away. But there was an easy out. Since the creature behind the last door had to be neutrally-positive, by elimination this atrocity had to be chaotically-negative.

"The final cavern contained a single tree. Hanging from one of its branches was the Sapphire Pearl. I was surprised something from the plant kingdom was capable of having morals, but there it was."

"A willow saved Thumbringer," I stated.

"I guess on Limbo anything was possible. If we can be modified, why can't plants? Or maybe the plants were once human."

Centaur withdrew an iridescent, metallic green sphere from a pouch that was hidden within his trousers. The two sphere's were brought together to compare. About a meter apart there appeared to be resistance. As the spheres were brought closer the resistance increased. The spheres were brought back apart. At about a meter the resistance became attraction. The attraction diminished after that, becoming negligible after two meters. The spheres were then brought together again, stopping a meter apart. Centaur hesitantly released the green sphere. It didn't fall. Hornet moved the blue sphere. The green sphere followed it, retaining its distance.

"There's a slight nudge that way," Hornet indicated with his head.

A large grin plastered Stick's face. "I think we found the

next pearl."

Then it hit me. Metallic green and blue swirling around me---and red, yellow, purple, and orange. Just before I entered Limbo. The spheres were part of a transport portal.

"Whose that at the door?" asked Claw.

"Someone I promised to introduce you to."

*** This concludes Book 2 of the Limbo Chronicles. ***

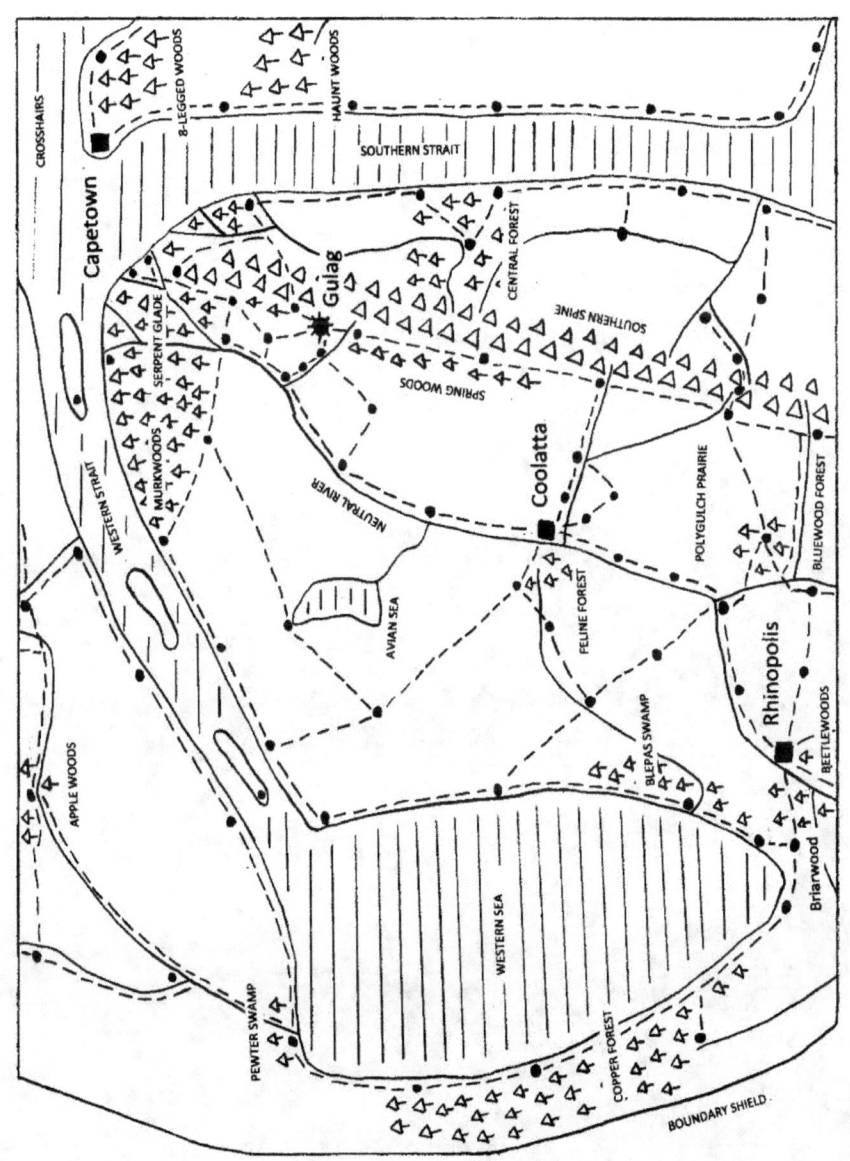

www.ingramcontent.com/pod-product-compliance
Lightning Source LLC
Chambersburg PA
CBHW071856220626
47052CB00002B/139